TRUTH OR MORE TRUTH

Books by Dana Wilkerson

Throwback RomComs
More Than Before (prequel)
More Than Pen Pals
So Much More
Truth or More Truth

KC Crew Sports Romance
Blocking the Chaos

Books by D.A. Wilkerson

Totally 80s Mysteries
A Totally Killer Wedding
Most Likely to Kill
Of Heist and Men
A Totally 80s Christmas
Desperately Seeking Suspects

Mystery Journals
Mysterious Musings
My Totally Suspect Notebook

TRUTH OR MORE TRUTH

A Throwback RomCom

DANA WILKERSON

Truth or More Truth
A Throwback RomCom – Book 3
by Dana Wilkerson

© 2025 Dana Wilkerson

Designed in the USA
Published by Dana Wilkerson, LLC
Edmond, OK
danawilkerson.com

First Edition: May 2025

Paperback ISBN: 978-1-948148-54-2
eBook ISBN: 978-1-948148-55-9

*Dedicated to everyone who loves
a good road trip*

prologue

. . .

Melissa

November 1988
Milwaukee, Wisconsin
Hamilton - O'Halloran Wedding Reception

"Where's Bobby?" my friend and fellow bridesmaid Leslie Beckett asks. "It's time for Ash to make his best-man toast, but we're not all here."

I roll my eyes as I stand from the head table at Randall and Wendy Hamilton's wedding reception and scan the tent for the man in question. "I'll find him," I assure her.

Five bucks says Bobby Jacobs is off somewhere doing who-knows-what with his date. I saw them locked in an embrace behind a large potted plant earlier. The man is at least thirty-five years old. What's he doing making out in public?

I weave through the round tables, scanning faces as I go. No Bobby in sight, but his date is chatting with Leslie's twin brother Shannon and his girlfriend, and I make a beeline for them.

"Have you seen Bobby?" I ask Bobby's date. I can't remember her name but I figure there's no point in asking, since I likely won't see her again.

"Not lately," she says. "Last I saw him, he was at the head table."

My eyes travel to Shannon and Christi, who both shake their heads and tell me they haven't seen him, either.

"Great," I mutter as I hurry off. The man can easily broker multi-million-dollar deals for professional athletes but can't manage to be where he needs to be at a wedding.

I head out of the large tent, my head swiveling side to side as I continue to search and grow more irritated by the second. As I pass the same potted plant I spied him behind earlier, a deep voice catches my attention—Bobby's voice.

"I know, baby," his low voice rumbles. "I'm sorry. We'll figure it out when I get home tomorrow night."

I stiffen and my irritation morphs into anger. The man's date is no more than fifty feet away, and he's over here talking to another woman and calling her "baby"?

"Look, I gotta go," he says. "This phone's about to run out of juice. ... Love you, too. Bye."

Bobby steps out from behind the plant with a cellular phone in his hand and nearly bowls me over. He grabs my arm with one hand while sliding the brick-like phone into his tuxedo jacket pocket, making that side hang much lower than the other.

"Whoa, there." He looks me up and down. "You okay?"

I jerk out of his grasp and shoot him a death glare. "I'm fine. It's time for the toasts. They sent me to look for you."

"Sorry," he says smoothly as he turns toward the tent. "Just needed to make a quick phone call."

"Why did you even bring that monstrosity to the wedding?" I glance down at the phone sticking halfway out of his pocket. "Can you not take a few hours off work?"

"The call wasn't for work."

I wait for him to explain further, but he doesn't.

"At least put that thing where nobody can see it," I say. "You look like a tool."

His eyebrows shoot up as we enter the tent, but he doesn't respond to my rude comment. Not that he deserves better, since he's apparently dating two women at once. I briefly wonder if I should say anything to his date, but I decide it's not my place to interfere in whatever they have going on. Maybe she knows and doesn't care.

On paper, the man is a catch—handsome, rich, and ridiculously successful. But in reality, he's ... well, he's a tool. He's gruff and frowny and often rude, and he's well known for his ruthlessness as a sports agent. He also seems to make it his mission to irritate everyone around him. At least that's the way he is with me. Why women fall at his feet is beyond my comprehension, but they can have him. I have no desire to spend one more second with Bobby Jacobs.

one

. . .

Melissa

December 29, 1988
O'Hare International Airport, Chicago

"Attention, passengers of flight 379 to Little Rock. Due to inclement weather, your flight has been cancelled. Please see the agent at the desk for re-booking. Thank you."

My head whips toward the floor-to-ceiling airport windows. The sun is shining, and the baggage handlers outside the plane at the next gate are wearing light jackets due to the unseasonably warm temperatures we're having. *What inclement weather?*

As voices rise around me, I realize I need to get to the gate agent pronto. Regardless of the reason for my flight's cancellation, I have to get to Little Rock for Leslie and Ash's wedding. The rehearsal is tomorrow night, and the wedding is the following afternoon. I grab my purse and carry-on bag and hightail it toward the airline counter.

I reach the counter at the same time as a dark-haired man in a form-fitting cashmere sweater. For a second, I'm distracted by the body beneath the material, which allows him time to step in front of me. "I have to get to Little Rock *today*," he growls to the lady at the counter. "If you can't make that happen, there's going to be a problem."

My body stills. I'd know that deep voice anywhere.

What is Bobby Jacobs doing here? I mean, I know why he's going to Little Rock—for the same reason I am—but why isn't he heading there from Los Angeles, where he lives? I mentally roll my eyes when I realize he must be here for work, even though it's the week between Christmas and New Year's, when nobody does any real work.

"And what inclement weather are you talking about?" he demands as he sweeps his hand toward the windows. "The sun is shining, if you couldn't tell."

I tap his shoulder.

He rolls his shoulder and barks over it toward me, "Not now. I'm trying to get to Little Rock for a wedding."

"So am I," I retort, hands on my hips.

He slowly turns and gives me a once-over, his perusal pausing briefly at my mouth before stopping at my eyes. "Melissa Teague."

"Bobby Jacobs."

I sneer at him, and he raises an eyebrow before turning back to the airline agent.

"Sir, ma'am," the woman says, "I'm sorry about your flight. The inclement weather is in Boston, where your plane is currently stranded."

"Then get another plane," Bobby orders as I step up beside him.

"It's not that simple, sir." I'm impressed by the woman's even tone, considering Bobby almost has smoke coming out of his ears.

"It should be." He jabs his finger into the counter.

As my dad would say, this man could drive a brass ape insane.

I elbow Bobby in the side. When he flinches, I weasel my way between him and the desk, take a quick look at the woman's name tag, and say kindly, "Please ignore him, Cheryl. He hasn't had his daily breakfast of spiders and yak blood yet."

Cheryl barks out a laugh as Bobby growls, and this time I elbow him in the gut.

I smile at Cheryl. "We understand the issue, but we really do need to get to Little Rock for this wedding. We're both in the wedding party, though I'm extremely unclear about why anyone would choose him to be a groomsman. Anyway, if you could get us on the next flight, we'd be eternally grateful."

"Maybe not eternally," Bobby mutters behind me.

Cheryl narrows her eyes at Bobby and then gives me a pitying smile, no doubt for having to put up with him. "There's a flight at the same time tomorrow morning and the next morning," she says. "But they're both full flights. You could try standby, but there's no guarantee."

"What about another airline?" Bobby barks. "Or routing through another airport?"

"We've already checked with other airlines," she says calmly, "and all their flights are fully booked for the next few days, as are ours. It's the holidays."

Strong hands land on my waist, and I'm suddenly two feet to the left. I squeak out my displeasure, but Bobby isn't focused on me.

He leans across the counter and demands, "Why did the announcement tell us to talk to you about re-booking if there are no flights to re-book?"

"That's standard protocol, sir."

"Well, you can take your standard protocol and—"

"Cheryl," I cut in, before Bobby can make a bigger spectacle of himself, "you're telling us there's no way for us to get to Little Rock today or tomorrow?"

"Not via plane."

Bobby curses, and I grab his arm and yank him away from the desk as he demands, "I'd better get my money back!"

"Don't take your frustration out on her," I say, spinning him away from the desk, which isn't as easy as one would assume. The man has some muscle on him. "None of this is her fault."

I holler back over my shoulder, "Sorry about him, Cheryl. You have a good day, now."

"It might not be her fault," Bobby grouses, "but it's her job to get us to Arkansas."

"No, it's not."

He crosses his arms over his chest, shifting my focus to how his sweater strains over his pecs, and I try not to think about how his arm muscles rippled under my hand a few seconds ago.

"Yes, it is," he declares.

I close my eyes and take a deep breath. "Bobby, whether it's her job or not, that woman cannot get us to Little Rock. You need to let this go, and we need to figure out how to get to that wedding."

"Oh, *we* do, do we?"

My finger jabs into his chest of its own accord, nearly spraining it due to the solidity of his pecs.

"I don't like this situation any better than you do, but we're both going to the same place for the same reason, so yes, *we* need to figure this out."

He peruses me before he says, "My assistant will figure it out." Then he pulls his monstrosity of a cellular phone out of his Rollaboard suitcase.

I pluck it from his hands. "What's your assistant going to be able to do about this? Nothing, that's what."

"Then what's your plan, Einstein?"

I can't believe I'm going to say this, but it's our only option. "We drive."

"To *Arkansas?*"

"No, to Antarctica. Yes, to Arkansas, you frustrating man."

Bobby holds his hands up. "Whoa, there, missy. Calm down."

"Calm down? *Calm down?* Don't you tell me to calm down, mister." I jab his chest again, but not quite so hard this time. I value the use of my finger. "You're the one who's been out of control here."

"Fine. Don't be calm." He retrieves his phone from my grasp, sticks it back into his bag, and turns away from me.

"Wait, where are you going?" I ask as he strides away.

"To rent a car," he throws over his shoulder. "I suggest you do the same."

I grab my bag and hurry after him. "I have a car."

"Well, bully for you," he says when I catch up to him.

"Why are you being such a jerk?" I ask. In all my twenty-six years, I don't think I've ever experienced a man quite so frustrating as Bobby, and considering I went to an Ivy League school and worked on Wall Street, I've encountered some real doozies in my day.

"I've been told it's my default mode," he mutters.

"Seriously?" I smack his arm with the back of my hand. "If you realize that, why don't you change it? Do you *like* being a jerk?"

He shoots me a glance and sighs. "Look, I'm sorry. It's been a long few days, I haven't gotten much sleep, and I don't want to mess up any of the wedding plans for Ash and Leslie."

Look at him, being considerate of others for once in his life. "Neither do I. Now, are you coming with me, or not?"

"Considering how well this conversation has gone, I'm thinking I need to rent my own car."

"You really think there will be any rentals available right now? Like the nice lady said, it's the holidays. Anyway, it would be dumb for us to take two cars when we're going to the same place. You're coming with me."

I highly anticipate regretting that choice many times over the course of this day and the however-many-hundred miles between here and Arkansas.

two

. . .

Bobby

"How long does it take to drive to Arkansas?" I ask Melissa as I match her shorter strides on the way to baggage claim to retrieve her luggage. "And do you know how to get there?"

"I have no idea, other than heading south-ish. Why don't you ask your assistant?" she asks in a snide tone.

I can't decide if I love or hate her attitude. I'm leaning toward love. I do enjoy a good battle, and she seems intent on fighting me every step of the way. I was tempted to continue to argue with her on the car issue, but I knew she was right. Rental cars would be few and far between right now. There's no reason to waste time trying to find a car that doesn't exist or, if it does, take it from someone who truly needs it.

"Maybe I *will* call her," I reply.

"You do that."

"Or maybe we should pick up a road atlas."

She's silent for a good twenty seconds as she marches along beside me before she admits, "There's one in my car."

Of course there is. She seems like a woman who's always prepared.

"You know who we actually should call, though?" I ask.

"Who?"

"Ash and Leslie."

Melissa stops in her tracks. "Oh. Yeah. That would be important."

I lightly place my hand on her lower back to prompt her to move again, and I tell myself to ignore the electricity that sparks up my arm at the touch, even through her several layers of clothing. Regardless of her animosity toward me, it's hard to deny my attraction to her. I don't know what I did to earn her extreme dislike, but something shifted between us at Randall and Wendy's wedding last month. Not that the two of us were friends before then, but that was the turning point when she began to actively show her disdain for me, and I have no clue why.

"I'll call them while you grab your suitcase," I say as we continue along.

"You don't have another bag?" She eyes the small carry-on suitcase I'm rolling behind me.

"No. Ash has my tux and wedding shoes, and I pack light."

"I guess so."

"Does Leslie have your bridesmaid dress, or is it in your suitcase?" I ask.

"It's in my suitcase—garment bag, actually. I really hope it's at baggage claim, like they said."

So do I. Leslie and Ash deserve to have the perfect wedding, with no mishaps like missing dresses.

Melissa adds, "Right about now, I'm wishing I'd carried it on."

"Why didn't you?" Seems to me that would've been a no-brainer.

"I didn't want to have to schlep the bag through the airport. I don't have a fancy-schmancy rolling suitcase like you. And yes, I realize that's a dumb reason, but it's the one I've got, so don't give me any grief about it."

I won't, as long as the bag shows up, but I don't say that. Instead, I take her carry-on bag from her, silently chastising myself for not doing so earlier. I may often be a jerk, but I'm usually a gentleman, as is proven by the fact that I feel bad about the way I treated the airline lady at the gate and wish I had time to go back and apologize.

Shockingly, Melissa doesn't protest my act of chivalry, and we walk the rest of the way to baggage claim in silence. When we find the right carousel, I leave her there and head to a nearby payphone. There's no reason to use up the battery and minutes on my cellular phone if it's not necessary.

I reach the phone and realize I have no idea where I'm supposed to call. I doubt it will do much good to call the hotel where the wedding party is staying. It's miles from Leslie's small hometown, and nobody will be there until later today anyway. Randall and Wendy are flying from Milwaukee, where they've been celebrating their first Christmas as a married couple with her family. Diego Sanchez—my friend, client, and Ash's boss at the Diego Sanchez Foundation—is flying from his winter home in his native Dominican Republic. I have no idea when Ash's mom and sisters will arrive there, and I hope they weren't supposed to be on the same flight from Chicago as Melissa and me. It should've occurred to me to check on that when we were at the gate.

Leslie and Ash are already in Arkansas, and they're staying at Leslie's parents' house. I decide that's where I should call, but I can't remember her dad's name. Hopefully there aren't any other Becketts in Oakville, Arkansas.

Thankfully, the operator is helpful and connects me to the number of the Ernie Beckett residence. A woman answers the phone.

"Hi," I say. "Am I speaking to Leslie Beckett's mom? This is Bobby Jacobs."

"Oh, Bobby! Hi there. Do you need to talk to Ash?"

"That would be great. Thank you, Mrs. Beckett."

"Please call me Helen. I'll get Ash for you."

When Ash comes on the line, I tell him what's happening and then ask, "Your mom and sisters weren't on our same flight, were they?"

"No, they got here yesterday."

"That's good. How long is it going to take us to drive there?"

"That's a question for Leslie. Let me get her."

Leslie informs me that with stops, it should take us twelve to thirteen hours to get to Oakville. "There are several routes you can take," she explains, "but I'd stick with one that's interstates all the way, because there's a chance of snow north of us this afternoon and evening. You might hit it in southern Illinois, but if you stick to the main roads, you should be okay. I don't want you getting stuck in the snow on some little backroad in the Ozarks." She tells me which highways to take, and I jot notes on the small notepad I keep in my pocket.

When I hang up, I'm about to make another quick call when I spot Melissa struggling toward me with a garment bag hanging off one shoulder and a larger suitcase in her other hand. I rush to help her and relieve her of everything but her purse.

"Thanks," she says. "I may have overpacked."

I chuckle. "You think?"

She glares at me, even though I was simply agreeing with her statement.

"Did you talk to them?" she asks.

As she leads the way to the parking shuttle while rolling my small suitcase, I recount my phone conversation.

She asks, "So you're telling me we might have to drive through snow?"

"Sounds like it."

Melissa gives me an assessing look. "Have you ever driven in snow?"

"I have not." I'm a Southern California boy, through and through. I travel a lot, but I rarely rent a car, opting instead for taxis and other car-hire services, so I can work while riding.

"Have you *seen* snow?" she teases.

"Only at the movin' picture show," I say with a ridiculous country twang.

When she giggles, I decide I love the sound and want to hear it again.

"Seriously?"

"No," I admit. "I go skiing several times a year."

Melissa raises an eyebrow. "You ski?"

"What? I don't look like I'm capable of skiing?"

She slowly looks me up and down as we stand in line for the shuttle, and a long-dormant fluttery feeling fires up in my belly at her perusal.

"You look like you're capable of a lot of things," she finally says.

What's that supposed to mean?

three

. . .

Melissa

Why did I say that? Why am I flirting with Bobby Jacobs? I hate him! Well, maybe I don't hate him, but I'm not exactly a fan, even if he looks even better in his dark-wash jeans and camel-colored cashmere sweater than he does in a suit. But I do hate the look he's giving me right now, informing me he knows I'm checking him out and like what I see.

I stifle a groan. "I mean, I know you live in L.A., so I guess I assumed you're not into winter sports. Where do you ski?"

"Usually Tahoe. Sometimes Vail. Do you ski?" he asks.

"My grandparents had a cabin in Vermont." Well, they called it a cabin. Most people would call it a chalet. "When I was a kid, we went there every winter to ski. My parents sold the place after my grandparents passed. I went skiing in Aspen with friends a few times during college, but that was more about partying than skiing, if I'm honest."

The shuttle arrives, and Bobby carries all our bags on and slots them onto the luggage rack before taking a seat beside me. We're silent on the ride to the long-term parking lot, and I try not to focus on the fact that his shoulder is pressed up against mine. There's nobody on his other side, so I'm not sure why he won't shift over, but I'm not about to ask him to do so. Undoubtedly he'd make a big deal out of it.

When we reach our stop, he gathers my luggage again and follows me through the lot until we reach my car.

"*This* is your car?" he asks as I unlock the trunk of my blue, two-door Honda Prelude.

I whirl toward him. "What's wrong with my car?"

Bobby's eyes widen. "Nothing. Nothing is wrong with your car."

"You got that right," I mutter as I grab for my suitcase.

"I've got it." Bobby snatches the suitcase out from under me, and before I know it, all my bags are in the trunk.

I'm braced to argue with him on who's going to drive—even though it's my car—but he rounds the car to the passenger side and waits for me to get in and unlock his door. Even more shocking, after he gets in and adjusts the seat, he puts on his seatbelt.

"I didn't take you for a seatbelt kind of guy," I state.

He angles his body toward me as much as he can in the confining space. He's not an overly large man—I'd estimate six feet and maybe 180 pounds—but my small car definitely won't be comfortable for him on this long trip. Not that I feel sorry for him.

He holds one finger up. "One, it's the law now, and I'm a law-abiding citizen. And two," another finger goes up, "you don't take me for someone who values their own life?"

I roll my eyes and reach into the backseat, grab my road atlas, and plop it on his lap. "Shut up and tell me where to go."

"Hmm." He taps a finger on his lips. "Which part of that order should I obey—the shutting up part or the talking part? It'll be hard to do both."

"Bobby Jacobs, I swear if you don't stop irritating me, I'm dropping you off at the bus station." I purse my lips. "Also, I need to know your middle name, so I can use it when I'm extra irritated."

"It's Ebenezer," he deadpans.

A laugh bursts out of me before I can stop it. "Nice one."

"Honest."

I shift the car into reverse to leave the parking spot. "Still don't believe you."

"Believe whatever you want." He pauses. "But maybe it's Sebastian."

"Robert Sebastian Jacobs?" I huff out a laugh. "I don't think so. I'm going to call you Bobby Joe."

"Why would you call me that?"

"Because it'll annoy you."

"You're right about that," he mutters.

I back out of the parking space. "Can you just be nice to me for once?"

Bobby's mouth drops open. "I'm always nice to you."

"Tell me one time you've been nice to me," I demand.

When he doesn't answer within three seconds, I say, "Exactly. Now tell me where to go, Bobby Joe, and be quick about it."

If I don't murder this man by the time we get out of the Chicago metro area, I'll deserve a medal. We're only thirty minutes in, and my hands are itching to clamp around his neck. I promise I'm not a murderer, just an overly annoyed woman.

"Stop with the commentary on my driving skills," I say through clenched teeth, "and tell me what lane I should be in."

"The right lane."

"The right lane? Bobby Joe, if you're messing with me, I'll pull this car over and make you walk to Arkansas. Fifteen seconds ago you were deciding whether I should be in the left or middle lane."

"That's before I looked at your gas gauge."

I glance down at the gauge and groan. How long has the "low gas" light been on? I flip on my blinker and ease into the right lane so I can take the next exit. A quick glance ahead informs me there's a gas station just off the interstate.

When I pull up to the pump at the self-service station, I wonder if Bobby will be a gentleman and offer to pump the gas for me.

"I need to make a phone call," he says, answering my unspoken question. "You need anything from inside? Drink? Snacks?"

"Yeah, but I'm picky about my road-trip snacks, and I don't trust you to not mess up my order. I'll get them when I go in to pay."

"I'm paying for the gas," he declares.

"No, you're not."

"It's your car we're putting a thousand-plus miles on. It's only fair that I pay for the gas."

What he says makes sense, so I agree, even though I'm annoyed about it for no good reason.

I pump the gas and then grab my purse to go inside and pick out my snacks. When I pass Bobby on the payphone outside the door, I overhear him saying, "Baby, I'm sorry I haven't been there, but I'll see you when I get home in a few days." I wonder if he's talking to the same woman he secretly called at Wendy and Randall's wedding. Knowing him, probably not.

A few minutes later, I can feel Bobby watching over my shoulder as I pay for my snacks and he waits to pay for the gas. I silently dare him to comment on my array of candy, chips, pre-packaged baked goods, and drinks. When he doesn't, I feel an odd sense of loss. Instead of waiting for him to pay, I return to the car, dig my Whitney Houston *Whitney* cassette out of the glovebox, and pop it into the tape player, because I'm one thousand percent sure Bobby is not a Whitney fan. Then I start munching my way through a bag of Cheetos.

"Cheetos?" he says as he slides into his seat. "That seems like the absolute worst choice of snack for the car."

I roll my eyes. He sounds like a dad.

"Why is that, Bobby Joe?" I ask, as I purposely swipe orange dust onto the radio knobs, ensuring he won't be changing the volume anytime soon. "They're delicious."

"That is disgusting."

I lick my fingers before shifting the car into drive. "My car, my rules."

Why am I acting like a child? I never act like this. The man brings out the worst in me. Considering our ten-year age difference, you'd think I'd try to act more mature around him, not less.

"You have rules about Cheetos?" he asks.

I glance over and catch the grin he's trying to hide.

"I do." I give him a haughty look. "I can eat them anytime, anywhere, anyhow."

"Any*how*? Is that a word? And is there more than one way to eat a Cheeto?"

"Wouldn't you like to know?" What in the world is wrong with me?

"I would, actually."

"Well, I'm not going to tell you or show you. You're just going to have to imagine all the ways I could devour Cheetos."

Melissa, shut your trap. You sound like an idiot.

"I think I will."

What's that supposed to mean? Is he trying to flirt with me?

four

. . .

Bobby

Did I just tell Melissa I'm going to imagine all the ways she can eat Cheetos? That was a bizarre thing to say. What is wrong with me?

"So, no date for the wedding?" she asks.

It takes me a second to register the abrupt change in subject. "Why would you assume that?"

"Uh, because there's nobody else here with us?"

She makes a good point, but I say, "Maybe she's flying in from somewhere else. Or maybe she's coming tomorrow or Saturday morning."

Melissa cuts a glance toward me as she pulls back onto the interstate. "Is she?"

"No," I mutter.

"Hmph." She taps her fingers on the steering wheel to the beat of the music on the radio. "So no date, then?"

"No."

"You could've just said that in the first place."

"Maybe I like to irritate you."

"Sounds about right."

"Why does that sound right?" I fold my arms over my chest.

"Have you already forgotten our conversation about you being a jerk?"

No. It was surprisingly hurtful, but I'm not going to admit that. "Yep."

"Suit yourself."

She turns up the volume on the radio, transferring Cheeto dust from the knob back to the steering wheel in the process. Then she proceeds to sing along with "Didn't We Almost Have It All" as if she's trying to win a beauty pageant.

I grab a tissue from the box on the floor behind her seat and use it to turn the radio back down.

"Didn't want my Cheeto cooties?" she asks with a smirk.

"Do *you* have a date?" I say in response, though I'm not sure why I'm asking.

"None of your business."

"I'm going to find out come Saturday, so you might as well tell me now."

"There's no one else here with us, is there?"

"Maybe he's coming from somewhere else," I say mockingly. "Maybe he's coming tomorrow or Saturday morning."

She shrugs.

"Is he?" I ask.

"You'll have to wait and find out."

I turn the music back up and stare out the window. This is going to be a long twelve hours.

When we're about an hour outside Chicago, Melissa finally turns down the music on the second time through the album and speaks again. "Why couldn't your girlfriend come to the wedding?"

"What girlfriend?"

"The one you were talking to on the phone."

My eyebrows raise at her admission she overheard part of my conversation. "Why do you think I was talking to my girlfriend?"

"I just assumed. Who else would you be dying to call from a gas station?"

I briefly hesitate before answering, "Maybe it was a work call."

"Was it?"

I sigh. "No."

"So who was it, then?"

I turn my head to study her profile. "Why are you so curious about who I was talking to?"

"Just making conversation."

"I can think of a thousand other less personal things we could make conversation about."

"Ah, I get it."

"Get what?" I'm unable to keep the frustration out of my voice.

"Trouble in paradise. What did you do to her, Bobby Joe?"

She's going to make me lose my mind, but she obviously didn't hear enough of my conversation to know who I was talking to. And she doesn't need to know. Only people I fully trust get to know about the person I was talking to, and I'm not yet sure if I fully trust Melissa Teague.

"Why are you like this?" I ask.

"Like what?"

"All …," I wave my hand around, "questiony."

"Questiony?" She snorts. "Is that a word?"

"It is now." It's also now time to change the subject. "You have more tapes in here, or will we continue to listen to Whitney on repeat all the way to Arkansas?"

"Ooo, I'm impressed you know who this is." She points at the radio, as if that's where Whitney resides.

"Everybody knows Whitney," I say. "The woman has some pipes."

"Huh. Who'da thought you'd be a closet Whitney fan?"

"Not sure I'd say I'm a fan." I'm totally lying. I'm a fan.

"Agree to disagree. Anyway, I have more tapes in the glove box and even more in a shoebox behind your seat. Help yourself. I mean, you can't go wrong with any of them, because I chose them."

I chuckle and rub my hands together before popping open the glove compartment. It's now Melissa's turn to laugh, since my knees block it from opening more than an inch. I adjust my legs so

I can get my hand into the compartment and pull out a handful of cassettes.

"Paula Abdul, Metallica, Bon Jovi, and the Pet Shop Boys," I say as I shuffle through them. "I like the variety."

I shake the Bon Jovi tape out of its case, switch it out with Whitney, and turn up the volume. The chorus of "Livin' on a Prayer" blasts out, and I decide to surprise Melissa by singing along.

She turns to me with wide eyes before giving me the biggest grin I've ever seen on her. I give her one right back and start playing air guitar. Her responding laugh is the best thing I've heard all day.

"You're really not going to tell me about your girlfriend?"

We're sitting at a Steak 'n Shake in Effingham, Illinois, eating lunch. I suggested we get the food to go and eat on the road, but Melissa insisted we'd make a mess of her car. How she thinks burgers are worse than Cheetos, I'll never know.

I also don't know why she's hung up on the girlfriend thing.

"I'm a private person," I say. "I don't talk to many people about my relationships." Not that I'm in one—at least not the type of relationship she's talking about.

"I see." She pops a handful of shoestring fries into her mouth and chews it before continuing, "You're one of those types."

"One of what types?"

She points another fry at me, and ketchup drips off the end onto the table. "The type of man who can't talk about his feelings."

I use a napkin to wipe up the ketchup. "I can talk about my feelings."

"Prove it."

The Melissa sitting across from me right now is nowhere in the ballpark of what I thought the Melissa I see in the Chicago Cubs front office was like, based on our limited interactions. There, at work, she's the epitome of professionalism and politeness. Even at the pre-wedding events for Ash and Leslie's wedding and all the events surrounding Randall and Wendy's wedding in the fall, she seemed pretty buttoned up. Here? She's nosy, snarky, and a little bit rude. I have to admit I like this Melissa better, even though I have no intention of answering her probing questions.

"Nope." I take a bite of my burger.

"Then I don't believe you."

"I don't need you to," I say with my mouth full, wondering if she'll call me out on it.

She doesn't, which leaves me a tad disappointed.

Instead, she asks, "Why were you in Chicago today instead of in L.A. *with your girlfriend?*"

Why won't she let this girlfriend thing go?

"Maybe that's none of your business."

"Here we go again. You can trust me, you know. I'm not going to go blab all your dirty secrets to anybody."

That's exactly what I'm afraid she might do, which is why I'm keeping my mouth shut about things she doesn't need to know.

"What makes you think I have dirty secrets?" I ask.

She flutters her hand toward me. "You have that whole mafia look going on."

"Mafia look? What mafia look?" I hold my hands out to my sides. "I'm wearing jeans and a sweater, and I'm not even Italian."

"You don't have to be Italian to be in the mafia, Bobby Joe. That's just insulting to the Russian mafia."

I huff. "Far be it from me to insult the Russian mafia."

"I'd like to see you try to insult them to their faces. See where that gets you."

"What is it you want from me?" I ask. "Why are you being like this?"

"All questiony?" She smirks.

"Yeah. That."

"Maybe it's simply because I enjoy irritating you."

"You're doing an excellent job of it. Gold star for you."

An hour or so later, Melissa turns down the music and asks, "Truth or dare?"

She has done nothing but sing along with the Pet Shop Boys for almost an entire album, and now she wants to play a game? "Excuse me?"

"We're playing 'Truth or Dare.'"

"Oh, no, we're not." I shake my head. First of all, it's a silly child's game. And second, although she seems to be warming toward me, I'm not ready to share my secrets, so "truth" is out. And goodness only knows what this woman would dare me to do.

"Dare, then. Let's see …" She rubs her chin as if she's thinking hard.

"We'll see nothing."

"Okay, then, I'll start. Truth or dare," she says in a comically low voice.

I bark out a laugh. "Is that supposed to be my voice?"

"Yeah, was it good?"

She gives me a goofy smile, and I can't help but laugh again.

"It was terrible. And fine. Truth or dare?"

"Dare!" she shouts gleefully.

"You're driving a car. There's not much I can dare you to do that won't put our lives in danger."

"Guess you'll have to get creative, then."

I look around the car, trying to find some inspiration. When my gaze lands on the radio, I get an idea, and I pop the tape out.

"What do you think you're doing?" Melissa asks with narrowed eyes.

"Setting up my dare." I wave the Paula Abdul tape in her face before shoving it into the tape player.

"Oooookay."

I check the album liner and get the tape cued up to where I want it before ejecting it.

"Whatcha doing there, Bobby Joe?"

"I dare you to listen to 'Straight Up' and not sing along, bob your head, tap your hand on the steering wheel, nothing. You have to stay perfectly still and mute."

Melissa's eyes go wide. "Noooooooo. I'll never make it!"

"You have to, because I double dog dare you."

She gives me a pouty face that is ridiculously adorable, but I keep my face passive.

"Not the double dog dare!" she whines.

"Watch it, or I'll triple dog dare."

"Fine. What do I get if I succeed?"

"The satisfaction of knowing you can show a little bit of restraint."

Melissa shakes her head. "There's no satisfaction in that."

I shrug. "Too bad. Those are the 'Truth or Dare' rules. I didn't make them up."

"It feels like you did, but I'll play along. I'm gonna nail this."

"I thought you said you'd never make it."

"I've changed my mind." She jabs a finger into the air. "I'll make it if it's the last thing I do."

"I hope it's not the last thing you do, because if so, we're both in trouble."

"Facts. Okay, play it." She pretends to zip her lips and throw away the key before putting both hands on the steering wheel and staring straight ahead.

I push the tape back in, and when the music starts, I begin bobbing my head to the beat while keeping my eyes on her. Her eyes dart over to me for a second, and she smiles. Even though she doesn't look at me again, her smile gets bigger as I start tapping my hand on my knee.

"No laughing either," I say right before I start singing along to the chorus with gusto.

It's all she can do to keep from laughing. Her stomach muscles are contracting so much her entire body is shaking.

"I said you can't move!" I point at her with a big grin.

Somehow she makes it until the bridge without audibly laughing or moving in any other way, but she finally lets out a giant belly laugh and then sings along to the rest of the song.

"That was amazing!" she says through giggles when the next song starts. "I can't wait to tell everybody about your singing performance."

"You're not telling *anybody* about that." I shake my head.

"That wasn't part of the deal."

"Hey, you lost the dare, so you'll be keeping your mouth shut."

"That's not how it works!"

"It is now."

"All right. If it means that much to you, Bobby Joe, I promise I won't tell anyone about your excellent singing skills or your intimate knowledge of Paula Abdul lyrics."

I honestly don't care if she tells our friends about it, but I'm beginning to think she might keep my secrets.

five

. . .

Melissa

"It's your turn now, Bobby Joe," I say. "Truth or dare?" I really hope he picks truth. I have so many questions I want to ask.

"Dare."

I should've known. "Hmmm. What can I dare you to do that will fully humiliate you?"

"Hey, why does my dare have to be humiliating?"

"Because it's more fun that way." I think for a minute. "Ah! I've got it." I do a drumroll on the steering wheel before saying, "I dare you to get a trucker to honk his horn at you."

"Seriously?" he asks.

"What? It'll be fun!"

"No self-respecting trucker is going to honk his horn for me. I'm a grown man—not a kid or a pretty lady. I'm not doing it."

"We'll just have to hope for a non-self-respecting trucker then, won't we?"

"You're going to have to dare me to do something else."

"Nope." I shake my head. "The dare has been put out into the universe, and therefore, it must be accepted. Those are the rules."

"Fine."

I move into the passing lane and speed up so we're right next to a semi truck. Then I slow down so we're driving at the same pace.

"Here we go," I say. "First chance. Go for it, big guy."

Bobby lets out a giant sigh before closing his right hand into a fist and pumping his arm up and down. I giggle at the sight.

"He didn't honk," I say. "Is he looking at you?"

He peers out the window. "Uh, yeah."

"And?"

"He's flipping me off."

I laugh so hard Bobby grabs the wheel to keep us in our lane.

"Pay attention to the road and get around him," Bobby orders. "I'm afraid of what he might do next."

Honestly, I am, too, so I do as I'm told.

"Are you really going to make me do that again?" he asks.

"Yep. A dare is a dare." I point forward. "Here's another truck up ahead. Get your arm ready, Bobby Joe."

To my surprise, Bobby stretches and flexes his right arm. I smile as I pull up next to the truck, wondering how many times we're going to have to do this before he's successful.

Bobby pumps his fist, and I jump in my seat as the truck's horn blares three times.

A few seconds later, Bobby yells, "Speed up! Speed up!"

I say, "Why? You were successful! Go, Bobby Joe!"

He turns to fully face me with wide eyes. "Melissa, if you don't move past this truck right now—"

I hit the gas before he can articulate the rest of his threat.

"What happened?" I ask as I pass a few more cars. "Why are you so wigged out?"

"Wigged out?"

"Yeah, you're totally wigged out. Explain yourself."

"Um, the driver was a woman."

I smirk. "No wonder she honked."

"Honking isn't all she did."

Now my eyes widen. "What did she do?"

"She flashed me."

I snort. "And that's a problem why? Are you not attracted to women?"

"Yes, I'm attracted to women. Just not ones thirty years my senior."

Once again, I laugh so hard he has to take control of the wheel.

We're in yet another part of nowhere Illinois when Bobby ejects Paula Abdul and fiddles with the radio to try to find a station that'll come in clearly. A light snow has begun to fall, and we need a weather update. He finally lands on a station that's not complete static.

"… receiving heavy snowfall here in southern Illinois. If it hasn't started yet where you are, get ready. It's coming fast and furious. If you don't need to be on the roads, stay where you are or get home as quickly as possible. We've gotten three inches here in Carbondale in the last two hours, and we're getting reports of towns in southern Missouri with nearly a foot of snow. Hunker down, people. And now back to your favorite country music."

Bobby turns the volume down as music begins to play, but he doesn't turn it off, likely so we can hear any further updates.

"That doesn't sound good," he states unnecessarily.

"How far are we from Carbondale?" I ask.

He unfolds the Illinois map he picked up at the gas station earlier and asks, "What was the name of the town where we stopped to get gas a bit ago? Any idea?"

"I think it was Mount … something. Sorry. I don't pay a lot of attention to road signs. I'm the pilot here. You're the navigator."

"Mount Vernon?" he asks.

"Yep, that was it. Don't remember seeing any mountains or presidential homes, though," I quip.

He ignores my joke as he peruses the map. "Carbondale isn't directly on the interstate," he says, "but I'd say we're about thirty miles northeast of it."

I sneak a glance at him. "What do we do?"

"I don't know that there's much to do other than keep going as long as we can."

I nod toward the map. "Does it seem like there will be any towns along the interstate with motels or anything?"

"I don't know. Most of these places look pretty small. But surely some of them have motels for truckers and such, right?"

My eyes widen. "We might have to stop at a trucker motel?"

He chuckles. "Don't worry. I'll be there to protect you. All my mafia training prepared me for this exact scenario."

"They get a lot of snowstorms in Italy, do they, Bobby Joe?"

"Hey, lady," he says in a terrible accent. "I'm in the Russian mafia. Lots of snow in Russia."

"Lots of truckers, too?" I tease, loving that he's joking around with me instead of being a jerk.

"You have no idea."

"What if your lady trucker friend stops at the same motel we do? Or the finger-bird guy?"

"Again," he says, "mafia training."

Within minutes, the snow starts falling more heavily, and it begins accumulating along the sides of the road.

"Seriously, Bobby, what are we going to do?"

"Well, the snow's not piling up on the road yet, so we're okay for now."

"But we won't be for long."

"No, I don't think so."

I grip the steering wheel tighter. "I don't like this."

"We can stop if you want to," he says.

"But it's only four o'clock in the afternoon. And we need to get to Arkansas." I can hear the anxiety in my voice.

"We don't have to get there today," he says soothingly. Since when is Bobby Jacobs soothing? "And this snow isn't stopping anytime soon."

As if on cue, the snowfall increases to where I can't see more than twenty feet in front of the car. I turn on my hazard lights and slow down, but I'm not sure that's what I'm supposed to do. What if the people behind me can't see me and are driving the speed limit? My heart begins to race.

"I don't know what to do. I've never really driven in snow. Not like this—only in the city, with the roads cleared."

Bobby's warm hand closes over one of mine on the steering wheel, and heat radiates up my arm at the contact. I focus on his hand for a moment before shifting my attention back to the road.

"Are you scared?" he asks.

I nod.

He squeezes my hand. "We're going to pull off at the next exit, okay? I'll guide you."

"O-okay."

"We can do this." He removes his hand from mine, and I suddenly feel cold, even with the car's heater going full blast.

"How many miles, you think?" I ask.

"Just a few more."

"Are you sure about that, or are you trying to make me feel better, since I have your life in my hands?"

"Both. We haven't passed an exit since we heard that weather report a few minutes ago, and there's an exit about every ten miles."

"What if there's not a motel at the next exit?"

"We'll cross that bridge when we come to it." He's silent for a few seconds before he asks, "How do you make a handkerchief dance?"

I snort before I can stop it. "What?"

"I'm telling you a joke to help you not be scared. How do you make a handkerchief dance?"

I shake my head, a smile on my face. "I don't know. How?"

"You put a little boogie in it."

I risk a quick glance over at him. He's giving me the biggest grin I've ever seen on him, and holy moly if that man doesn't have a dimple in his left cheek. *Where has that been hiding?* I want to poke my finger in it, but instead I burst into laughter, and he joins me.

"Got any more of those up your sleeve?" I ask.

"How do you scare a bee?"

I shrug. "Sic a wasp on him?"

"Nope. You say, "Boo, bee!'" He laughs even harder than he did before. "Get it? Boobie?"

I shake my head as I chuckle at him. "Yes, I get it, you goofball. And I also think perhaps you're a five-year-old boy deep down inside."

"Maybe I am."

"You lucky folks got here just in time." The lady at the front desk of the Elm Tree Motel doesn't stop chewing her gum as she speaks to us. Her name tag informs us her name is Wanda. "Only one room left. This storm's a doozy. Phones are already out and I can't imagine the power will last much longer."

"One room?" I squeak out, ignoring everything else she said. I'm still shaking from the last several minutes of our drive. We were in near-whiteout conditions by the time we arrived. I was surprised we were able to see the motel sign.

Bobby must notice my distress, because he gently places an arm around me, and I automatically sink against him, choosing for a moment to forget his penchant for dating multiple women at once and enjoy the feeling of a man's comforting arm around me for the first time in longer than I care to remember.

"Like I said," Wanda says, "you're lucky."

That wasn't what I was getting at. If she even tells us there's only one bed in the room …

"We've got a room with two double beds." She holds up the key and looks between me and Bobby. "Looks like you two lovebirds will only need one, though. Okay if I let the next people through the door share your room?"

"What?"

Wanda chuckles. "Just joshin' ya, ma'am. I need you to fill out this here form, and we take cash or credit card."

I dig in my purse for my wallet, but Bobby puts his hand on mine to stop me, pulls out his wallet, and hands the woman a card. "We'll put it on this card." He gives me a look that tells me not to argue with him about it.

I won't argue now, but I will later.

"Your room is out the door and all the way on the end to your right," Wanda says as she fills out the credit card slip. "Should be able to park right outside your door. Sorry about the snow in the parking lot and on the sidewalks. Ain't no use trying to keep them clear at this point."

"Is there anywhere to eat near here?" Bobby asks her as he completes the information card.

"There's a diner a few blocks down, but I wouldn't recommend trying to get there while the storm's raging. My advice is to stay right here and cozy up in your room." She winks at us. "We got a vending machine in the little alcove with the ice maker just outside."

Bobby puts the pen down and holds his hand out to the lady. "Thank you, ma'am. We appreciate it."

Wanda chuckles again and shakes his hand. "It's my pleasure. You two enjoy your stay, you hear?"

"Oh, we will." Bobby leads the way to the door. "And we'll name our firstborn after you, Wanda!"

She chuckles again as I elbow him.

"You do that," she says. "You do that."

six

. . .

Bobby

"Weren't you charming back there?" Melissa says as she eats Cheetos on her bed and watches me dig through my suitcase.

"What do you mean?"

"It was weird seeing you be nice to a woman—to anybody, actually." She licks her fingers. I wonder if she usually does that, or if she's only doing it now because she knows it drives me crazy. "I think Wanda has a crush on you."

"No, she doesn't." Does she? I'm terrible at determining if a woman is interested in me, though I'm typically an expert at reading people.

"She definitely thinks you have a crush on me, though." Melissa grins at me as she sticks another Cheeto in her mouth.

"You're a hard one to figure out, you know that?" I ask her as I pull a pair of gray sweatpants and a black T-shirt out of my suitcase.

"Why do you say that?"

"At work, you're all prim and proper in your skirt suits and will barely even look at or speak to me when I'm there. And here you are, eating Cheetos on a trucker motel bed in your Columbia University sweatshirt and happy-face socks with no makeup, teasing me like I'm your brother or something. The two don't exactly jive."

"Wow. There's a lot to unpack there, Sport."

"Sport?"

"Seemed appropriate, considering your job."

"Don't call me Sport." The nickname makes me sound like I'm six.

"Okay … Sport. You know I'm switching from Bobby Joe to that now, right?"

"See? This is what I'm talking about." I stalk to the bathroom with my clothes and close the door none too softly behind me.

"What's what you're talking about?" she calls out.

I ignore her as I quickly change my clothes. When I emerge from the bathroom, she stares at me. I stop and look down at myself. "What? What are you looking at? Is there a stain on my clothes or something?"

She shakes her head. "No. It's nothing. I was just thinking about something unrelated to the non-stains on your clothes."

She's lying, but I drop it.

"Want to watch TV?" she asks.

"Sure. Nothing else to do." I turn it on and twirl the knob and adjust the antenna on the ancient set until I land on a channel that actually comes in. It's an old western movie, and Melissa seems inordinately excited about watching it.

"Want some Cheetos?" She holds the bag across the small gap between our beds.

"No, thanks." As she would say, I don't want her Cheeto cooties. "What else do you have in your bag of snacks over there?"

She flings it over to my bed. "See for yourself. Don't go too crazy."

After John Wayne beats the bad guys, yet another western comes on. I get up to try and find another channel, to no avail.

"Want to play cards?" Melissa asks.

"You brought cards?"

"Yep. You never know when you might have an entertainment emergency and need a deck of cards."

"Have a lot of entertainment emergencies, do you?"

"More than you'd think. Hey, is it still snowing?"

I peek through the gap in the curtains. "Yep. Looks like maybe seven or eight inches out there."

"Yikes." She jumps off her bed to join me at the window. "I hope we're able to get out of here tomorrow."

She places a hand on my arm, and I stare down at it, wondering if she realizes she's touching me.

"You think they're worried about us? Leslie and Ash?" she asks. "I wish we could call them."

"They're probably not worried yet, because we weren't supposed to arrive until late tonight."

"But when we don't show up …"

"I don't think they'll be worried then, either. They'll just assume we didn't want to bother them and are all tucked up in our hotel beds."

She plops down on the edge of my bed. "Instead we'll be here, tucked up in our slightly scary trucker beds. I don't think they've updated the bedspreads in here since the 50s. At least they seem clean."

"Hopefully the storm will be over soon, and by morning the phone lines will be back up and the roads will be cleared."

Melissa cocks her head at me. "Look at you, being all Positive Polly on me. I didn't know you had it in you."

"What can I say? I'm an enigma."

I round my bed and lie down on it, and she turns to sit cross-legged facing me.

"No, you're not."

I roll onto my side and prop myself up on my elbow facing her. "Have my actions not confused you today?"

"I guess they have."

"Enigma."

"You think I'm an enigma, too."

"I do." I seriously can't figure her out. "You truly seem like two different people—one person at work and another outside of work."

"Aren't most people like that?" she asks.

I roll onto my back and clasp my hands behind my head. "I'm not."

"True. You're a jerk no matter where you are." She smiles, but her words pierce me.

I bite the inside of my cheek. "Am I really always a jerk?"

"At work? Yes. To the Hamilton brothers and their ladies? Not that I've noticed, and I can't imagine Ash and Randall would put up with you being a jerk to Leslie and Wendy. Were you a jerk today? Not really. Well, you were a little jerkish with the lady at the airport, and maybe every once in a while since then. But mostly no."

I look away from her. "I'm trying to do better." I don't know why I told her that, but it's true. And little does she know it was all instigated by my desire for her to like me, and not just in a romantic way, but as a friend. Last summer, Ash pointed out my tendency to act like a grumpy jerk—even outside of work and specifically in relation to Melissa—and I've been trying to change. It's been a slow process, though.

When she doesn't respond, I look back over at her, and her gaze has noticeably softened. She opens her mouth to say something when the room plunges into darkness.

After a few seconds of silence, Melissa says, "I guess we're not going to be playing cards."

Much to my surprise, I laugh, and she joins in.

"You have a flashlight or candles in any of your twelve bags?" I ask.

"I have some matches," she says, "but it's going to be a chore to find them."

"Why do you have matches? Are you a secret smoker?" I really hope she's not.

"Nope. I have them for … uh … well, they help remove smells … in the bathroom."

I smile into the darkness. "Ah."

"Uh-huh."

I bet if I could see her, her cheeks would be red.

"I don't think I've ever experienced complete darkness like this before," she says. Since it's now nighttime, and snow is still falling, there's not even any light filtering through the small gap in the curtains. "It's disconcerting."

"That's an understatement," I say. "Do you know which bag the matches are in and where that bag is?"

"They're in one of my toiletry bags. I think in the one that's in the bathroom. Let me see if I can make my way in there."

I move my hand over until it brushes up against her leg. "Be careful."

She grasps my hand for a second. "I will."

The bedcovers rustle as she gets up and feels her way across the room to the bathroom.

"This is so weird," she says as items rattle around in the bathroom. "Okay, got them. But now what? What do we need to do that requires light? There's only about eight matches here, and I don't want to waste them if we don't need to."

"Do you need to do anything to get ready for bed?" I ask.

"Brush my teeth and, you know, use the facilities."

"Same here. Get your toothbrush and toothpaste out and ready. I'll find mine, too, and I'll join you, and we'll light up when we think we need to."

I carefully get off my bed and move toward my suitcase.

"Maybe we won't need to."

"I'd prefer you to not spit toothpaste onto my feet."

She laughs. "Same."

I find my toothbrush and toothpaste and make my way to the bathroom.

"I need you to say something," I say, "so I know where you are. I'd rather not knock you over or grab your chest or anything."

She giggles. "I'm here, and I'm putting my hand out in front of me to try to find you. Above waist level."

I laugh and slowly move toward her voice, and soon her fingertips brush my chest, sending goosebumps over my body, which I'm glad she can't see.

seven

. . .

Melissa

Bobby's hand grasps mine in the dark, and he moves closer to me—close enough I can feel his body heat. And now his shoulder is bumped up against mine, sending a shiver through me. I'm glad he couldn't see it, but did he feel it? His scent—a heady wood and floral combination—fills the tiny room.

"Think we can get toothpaste onto our brushes in the dark?" he asks.

"I'm certain I can, but I have my doubts about you," I tease.

"Game on, Teague."

I giggle as he lets go of my hand, and I feel his arm muscles move against mine as he loads up his toothbrush. I do the same.

"I'm turning on the water now," he says, and in a few seconds the sound of running water fills the small room. "I've got my brush wet. Your turn."

I feel around until I find the stream of water and swipe my brush under it. I feel bad about leaving the water running while we brush, but not enough to turn it off. Now the sounds of tooth brushing fill the room.

"Okay," he mumbles. "I'm ready to spit and rinse. You?"

"Yup," I say around my toothbrush. I leave it dangling from my mouth as I fumble around trying to find the matches again. I pull one from the box and manage to light it on the first try. It takes a second for my eyes to adjust to the light, and when they do, I catch Bobby's eyes in the mirror. I smile at the sight of him with toothpaste foaming out of his mouth. He gives me a goofy grin before spitting it out into the sink and quickly rinsing his mouth. Then he takes the match from me while I do the same. I finish just as he's forced to shake the flame out, and I catch his smile in the mirror before darkness descends again.

"Perfect timing," he says.

"Now for the awkward part," I say.

"Yes," he says, "the using the facilities part. I can handle it on my own, but do you need me to hold a match for you? While facing the other way, obviously."

I take a deep breath. "I think I can do it in the dark. But stay there in case I decide I need light, okay? Here are the matches." I transfer the box to his hand. "Sorry you're going to hear this, but there's not much we can do about that."

Thankfully, I'm able to take care of business and wash my hands in the dark.

"Okay," I say. "You're between me and the door in this minuscule space. How are we going to do this?"

"You find me," he says. "Like before. Then we'll spin around and switch places."

I reach a hand out, and it soon hits his firm chest. Then, instead of using the knowledge of our relative positions to help us spin around, my palm flattens against his chest, and I hold it there. I hear him suck in a breath, and within seconds his hand covers mine, sending a tremor all the way to my toes. His other hand lightly touches my shoulder, and his fingers skim down my arm until they find my hip. Now I'm the one sucking in a breath.

"You ready to spin?" His voice sounds husky.

"Yes," I whisper, as I can't seem to find my voice.

He slowly turns us.

"I have no idea how far we've turned," he says.

"Me, neither." I giggle lightly, trying to break the tension.

The hand covering mine on his chest disappears. "I feel the sink over here," he says, "so we're where we need to be. Can you make your way out okay?"

I nod, but then I realize he can't see it. "Yes."

I wave my arm behind me until I find the doorjamb, and with reluctance, I remove my hand from his chest, back out of the room, close the door behind me, and climb into my bed.

When the door opens again, Bobby says into the darkness, "We're never telling anyone about that, right?"

Never. "Oh, you'd better believe that as soon as we get to Arkansas, I'm telling everyone you're a weirdo who stands in the bathroom and listens to me pee."

He groans. "Melissa."

"Bobby," I say in the same tone of voice he used.

"Is it already colder in here, or is it just me?" he asks as he makes his way around my bed to his own.

"Definitely colder." It's only going to get worse, and I'm not sure the thin blanket and bedspread on my bed will be up to the task of keeping me warm.

"I'm going to put my sweater back on," he says. "You need more clothes, or are you okay?"

My sweatshirt and flannel pants are keeping me warm enough now, but I'm not sure they will later. "I think I'm going to grab another pair of socks, and maybe another pair of pants."

"Don't get up," he says. "I'll get you my other pair of sweats and some socks."

So the man does know how to be a gentleman. Actually, he's been a gentleman for most of the day, now that I think about it.

"You know what else we need to do?" I ask.

"What?"

"Drip the faucet."

"Who the what?" he responds.

"We need to barely turn on the faucet so the water drips out," I explain. "It'll keep the water in the pipes from freezing and then exploding the pipes and flooding everything."

"But if the water is frozen, how can it flood?"

"Huh. I don't know. That's a good question. But we still need to do it."

"Okay. I'm on it."

It takes him a few minutes to make his way into the bathroom and get the faucet dripping. He stubs his toes in the process, and it's hard to keep from giggling at the string of curses he lets out.

"This dripping sound might make me want to throw things," he says.

"Close the door. That'll help."

A minute later he says, "I'm setting the clothes on the end of your bed, okay?"

"Thanks." Without fully getting out from under the covers, I pull on the socks and then slip his pants on over mine.

His bedding rustles as he gets in. Silence reigns for a few minutes before he says, "I don't know if I'm going to be able to sleep. It's barely eight o'clock, which is only six in California."

"Same. I usually don't go to sleep before eleven."

"Time to play 'Truth or Dare' again then."

I burst out laughing. "I can't believe you suggested that. What can we dare each other to do in the dark, though?"

His silence makes me think about what I just said, and my cheeks burn.

"Um," I say, "I mean ..."

"Yeah, I'm definitely telling everyone in Arkansas about that question." He chuckles.

"You wouldn't."

"You'll have to wait and see," he teases.

I smile into the darkness. "So we're playing 'Truth or More Truth,' then?"

"I'm kind of hoping for a dare now."

Warmth spreads throughout my body, and once again I'm glad he can't see me, unlike when he caught me staring at his toned arms when he came out of the bathroom earlier when the lights were on. I didn't believe his "is there a stain on my shirt" line for one second.

I say, "All right, Sport, I dare you to play 'Truth or More Truth' with me."

"Okay."

"Really?"

"Just one truth, though. And I get one veto. So think carefully about what you really want to know about me."

I want to know about the woman—women?—in his life, but I'm afraid I won't like his answer, and I don't want to ruin the burgeoning friendship between us. If he's a cheater, I don't want to know. Or do I? Can I even be friends with someone who cheats on his girlfriend? I've been on the other side of that equation, and it's a terrible place to be.

I can't help but think he's not a cheater, though. If he were, I don't think Ash and Randall would want him in their lives. But that doesn't mean he's not a player. Dating more than one person at once isn't my jam, but I'm not going to judge people who do it, as long as everyone involved is aware of the situation.

Since I have no intention of dating Bobby, regardless of how delicious he looked in his T-shirt and sweatpants or how my body responds to his touch, I determine it's not my business to ask any more questions about his romantic relationships. Instead, I need to ask him something that will help me get to know him better—help me *like* him better. Due to our intersecting jobs and mutual friends, we'll be in each other's lives for a long time.

"I can hear your brain working," he says. "It's even drowning out the dripping sound."

"I'm trying to think of something that's going to take you a long time to fully answer, since I only get one chance."

He chuckles. "Take your time."

A minute later, I say, "Tell me how you feel about your job."

"Hmm."

"Hmm, what?"

"I thought you were going to ask about my girlfriend, since you were obsessed with that topic earlier in the day."

"I wasn't obsessed!"

"You were."

I don't respond, because he's right.

He clears his throat. "So my job, huh? You definitely picked a topic that doesn't have an easy answer."

"Yeah?"

"Yeah." He almost sounds defeated.

"You don't have to tell me, you know."

"I know. But I want to. I *need* to."

eight

. . .

Bobby

"Why do you need to talk about your job?" Melissa asks me.

What is it about darkness that makes people want to spill their guts? I shouldn't be talking to her about this. I should be talking to Ash or Randall or even Diego, who's my client but also my closest friend. But here I am, about to open up to a woman I'm not sure even likes me, though I hope I might be growing on her a little.

"Because I'm not happy," I admit. I haven't said this to anyone else, so why am I admitting it to her?

"You're not?"

"No."

"Why?" she asks softly.

"Because I've discovered I hate being a jerk all the time, but I have to in order to do my job well." The word "jerk" isn't the word I'd use for myself—I'd use something a little more colorful —but since this is the word Melissa loves to use to describe me, I'll stick with it. It makes me sound not quite so awful as reality dictates.

"Are you sure you have to be a jerk?" she asks.

I think silently for awhile. "I don't know how to do it any other way. I barely know how to attempt to be nice when I'm not working."

"I disagree with that, because you've been mostly nice to me today. But anyway, can you try to do your work a different way?"

I've thought about this a lot, and I don't have a solution. "What if I do, and it backfires on me? I'll be letting my clients down. They hired me to be ruthless—to do whatever needs to be done to get them what they want. What if I can't get them what they want without that attitude?"

"Could you make small changes? Test the waters? Or just focus on not being a jerk everywhere except at the negotiation table?"

I shake my head, even though she can't see it. "I don't know. I'm afraid any kind of change toward being less ruthless will be seen as a weakness. And if there's anything that's exploited in my business, it's even the slightest hint of weakness."

"Kindness isn't a weakness, Bobby."

"I'm not sure I agree with that."

"Why do I feel like there's a story there?"

The woman is perceptive. "Maybe there is," I say, "but it's not a story for tonight."

"Okay."

I'm surprised by her willingness to drop the topic. "Okay?"

"Yeah, okay. You don't have to tell me everything. You're entitled to your privacy, and I'm sorry I pressed you earlier today. Only tell me what you're comfortable with."

I let out a long breath, thankful she's proving her trustworthiness. "Okay. Thanks for not pushing me."

"You're welcome."

We've been silent for a few minutes when she says, "Bobby?"

"Yeah?"

"I'm really cold."

The temperature in the room has dropped considerably since the power went out. This place apparently isn't insulated well, and being in the room on the end of the building isn't helping matters.

"Please take what I'm about to say at face value, nothing more." I draw in a deep breath and hope I'm not about to ruin the peace we've established between us. "I think we're going to need to share our body heat before this night is over, so if you're comfortable with it, come on over here with me."

When she doesn't respond after a few seconds, nausea settles in my belly, knowing I leaped over a line I shouldn't have gone anywhere near.

She finally says, "I want to—for the warmth, obviously—but …"

"But what?" I prompt, when she doesn't finish her thought.

"But what about your girlfriend?"

I sigh. "I don't have a girlfriend."

"Then who … you know what? I'm not going to ask that. Like I said, you're entitled to your privacy."

"I'm not ready to tell that story, either, but I'm not lying to you. I don't have a girlfriend. And for the record, I wouldn't have asked you to come over here if I did. Or at least not until our teeth were chattering and we were on the brink of hypothermia."

Then I hear rustling, and extra weight lands on me as Melissa adds her bedspread to mine, and the nauseous feeling returns as I slide over to make room for her in the double bed. Are we really going to do this? Melissa might frustrate me to no end, but she's a beautiful woman and my body doesn't discriminate. Did I truly ask her to join me in my bed? What was I thinking?

Cold air briefly hits me as the covers lift, and then Melissa's soft, warm body is snuggling into my side. I shift my arm so it's curled around her, and she lays her head on my shoulder as I settle the covers over us with my free arm.

"Thank you," she whispers.

"Anytime." I try not to think about how right it feels to be cozied up with her.

I wake to a loud scraping sound from outside. When I open one eye, I discover faint light filtering through the gap in the curtains as Melissa lifts her head off my shoulder.

"What's that horrible sound?" she says in a raspy voice.

I shake my head to try to clear it. "Snowplow, maybe?"

She drops her head back down. "Yep, that's it. And there's light outside."

"Yeah, but it's freezing in here and the lights aren't on, so no power yet."

I'm surprised Melissa didn't jerk away from me when she awoke, since she's more firmly curled around me now than when she joined me last night, but she's not taking any action to remove herself from my body.

Not that I'm complaining. I can't remember the last time I awoke to a beautiful woman in my arms. My hands itch to caress her, and my fingers twitch as I consider threading them through her soft brown hair and wonder how she'd respond. Instead, I lift the arm that's not around her to look at my watch. It's 7:15. I'm shocked we slept so long, considering how early it was when we fell asleep.

"You think they've cleared the highway yet?" she mumbles into my sweater.

"If somebody is plowing the parking lot, I'm guessing the roads are somewhat clear. I'll get up in a minute and make my way down to the office to see if Wanda is there and can give me an update."

"Don't leave me," she says, clutching me even tighter. "You're the only thing keeping me warm."

I smile. "Well, we do need to get to Arkansas. That's why we're here, if you recall."

"Stupid cancelled flight," she says.

"Isn't this road trip more fun than that flight would've been?"

"It's more something." The tone of her voice reveals she agrees with my assessment, though.

"If that flight had happened, you would've never learned how charming I can be," I tease.

"You're not charming."

I chuckle. "You told me I was last night. And you can't deny I'm warm."

She snuggles in even closer to me, if that's possible. "You are." After a few seconds, she says, "We're not telling anyone about this, right?"

"What? You don't want anyone to know we slept together? I'm offended." I keep my tone light so she'll know I'm kidding.

"We didn't sleep together!"

"I beg to differ. We're together in the same bed, with you clinging to me for dear life, and we slept. We literally slept together."

"I'm not clinging!" Ironically, she grips me tighter.

"Totally clinging."

"Okay, fine. I'm clinging. I need your body heat in this frozen tundra of a trucker hotel bed."

"Well," I say reluctantly, "you're going to have to get used to surviving without me, because I'm about to get up."

nine

. . .

Melissa

Why does it feel so right to be curled up against Bobby Jacobs? I'm not supposed to like this man, much less enjoy being held by him—in a bed, no less. But somehow I do. And I don't want him to get up and break the spell that began even before the lights went out last night. I want to stay here in this seedy motel with him. I want him to go back to sleep so I can trace his abs with my fingers like I was tempted to do before he woke up. The man might be thirty-six years old, but he has a body of steel. It was all I could do to not slip my hand up under his multiple shirts and explore his torso skin-on-skin.

What is wrong with me? Bobby's a player. I'm ninety-nine percent sure of it, though I'm now also eighty percent sure he's not a cheater. And yeah, maybe he's not as much of a jerk as I thought, but that doesn't mean I want to be his next conquest. Even so, it takes more strength than it ought to for me to scoot away from him in the bed.

As he slides out from under the covers, he says, "Stay there until I get back. No reason for you to get cold until I know what we're doing."

"Try the phone first," I say as I shift over into the warmth he left behind in the bed. "If it's working, you can call the front desk."

"Great idea." He flings the curtains open, flooding the room with blinding light, before picking up the phone from the table between the beds. "No dial tone."

He heads into the bathroom for a minute, and when he comes back out, I watch as he pulls a pair of tennis shoes out of his bag and puts them on.

"Does your suitcase double as a clown car?" I ask. "How is there so much stuff in such a tiny space?"

"When you're on the road half the time, you learn how to pack efficiently," he says.

"I guess so."

He stands and slips on his coat. "Wish me luck."

"Good luck." I smile at him.

Bobby shoots me a grin before heading out the door, sending a gust of cold air into the room as he does. I'd figured it was as cold in here as it was outside, but I was wrong.

While I wait for him to come back, I give myself a stern talking to. While it's important for me to be able to get along with Bobby, I can't let myself fall for him. Much as it pains me, I force myself to remember what it was like when I discovered my ex-fiancé in bed with another woman. Jeremy's betrayal nearly crushed me, regardless of the part I played in the whole situation. While I do believe Bobby's claim that he doesn't have a girlfriend, there's something about women he's hiding. I didn't imagine him calling someone "baby" on the phone yesterday. Maybe he's dating her but they're not exclusive and don't put a label on it? Whatever it is, I want no part in it.

Instead, I shift my thoughts to Shannon Beckett, Leslie's twin brother. Now there's a man I could date with no reservations, and fortunately for me, he and his girlfriend broke up recently. I spent a little time with him when he was in Chicago for Ash's bachelor party a few weeks ago, and we flirted shamelessly with each other. I've been looking forward to spending more time with him at the wedding and seeing where things might go. Of course, he lives in Little Rock and I live in Chicago, but if he's interested in doing more than flirting with me, I'm not going to let a little distance stop me. And surely it wouldn't take much persuading to get him to visit and potentially move to Chicago, since his sister lives there.

Within minutes, Bobby's back, snow shovel in hand.

"Wanda says the interstate has been plowed, so we're good to go."

"What's the shovel for?"

"To clear out around your car and back to where the snow-plow cleared. I'll take care of that while you get ready. I'll also start the car to get it warmed up." He grabs my keys off the top of the TV and is back outside before I can respond.

"What's our route?" I ask Bobby, with the Illinois map and road atlas both open on my lap.

He offered to drive today, and after yesterday's adventure, I gladly accepted. But that means I'm now the navigator, which is not my strongest suit.

"I-57 to I-55 to I-40," he says. "We'll hit I-55 soon after we cross into Missouri."

"Missouri?" I ask. "Didn't the guy on the radio yesterday say they got like a foot of snow, even before the storm passed? That's more than here." I estimate we got nine or ten inches. "Shouldn't we avoid Missouri if we can?"

"Wanda said we should be fine. She had a radio going in the office, so I'm guessing that's how she knew. Anyway, it should take us six or seven hours to get there if the roads continue to be as clear as they are here."

Bobby motions out the windshield, where the interstate is mostly clear of snow but not entirely. I glance at the speedometer to see he's driving a little below the speed limit.

"In an hour or so, we'll stop somewhere to see if we can find a working phone so we can update Ash and Leslie."

"I bet Leslie is frantic."

"Wendy, too," Bobby adds.

His knowledge of my two best friends is yet another reminder that the two of us need to get along. Not that we're having any trouble with that this morning.

"Hey," I say, "what about your cellular phone? Could we use that to call them?" Why didn't I think about that last night?

"I tried yesterday right after we arrived at the hotel—while you were changing clothes in the bathroom—but the call wouldn't go through. We're out in the middle of nowhere here, so the phone doesn't have service."

"Maybe the problem wasn't with our location but the storm," I say.

He shrugs. "Could be. You want to try?"

"Yeah, I want to talk to them as soon as possible. But we'll have to stop to get it out of your bag in the trunk."

"No, we won't. I put my bag in the backseat so we could get to the phone in an emergency. You should be able to reach it. The phone is just inside the zipper."

I twist around to see if I can get to it without taking off my seatbelt, which I refuse to remove with the roads the way they are. I stretch to reach the bag and am able to pull it close enough to get the phone out.

"Now what?" I say with the phone in my hands.

"You need a tutorial on how to use a phone?" Bobby asks, a smile hovering on his lips but not fully appearing.

I smack his arm. "I've never used one of these before. Give me a break."

"It's the same as a regular phone, except you type in the number first and then hit the 'send' button. There's no dial tone. You won't know if it's going to work until you hit send."

"Gotcha."

"There's one problem, though."

"What's that?" I ask.

"When I called yesterday, I had to call information to get the number, and I didn't write it down. I just had them connect me."

"I've got the number," I say, grabbing my purse from the floorboard. "Leslie gave it to me last week."

I punch in the number and then hit send. After a few seconds, it begins to ring.

"It's ringing!" I say in the same tone I'd announce a miracle, and Bobby chuckles.

"Hello?" a man's voice says. The line is staticky, but at least the call went through.

"Mr. Beckett?"

"I'm sorry. It's hard to understand you," the man says, still staticky.

"This is Melissa Teague," I say loudly.

"You don't have to yell," Bobby whispers. "That won't help."

I shoot him a glare.

"Melissa?" the man says. "Is that what you said?"

"Yes, Bobby and I got stuck in the snowstorm in Illinois. We're on the road now, and we should arrive this afternoon."

"What? Hello?"

"Hello?"

"Hello?"

"Can you hear me?" I ask.

"Hello?"

The line goes dead.

I look over at Bobby. "That didn't go well."

"Did he at least catch your name?"

"Yes."

"That should be good enough. At least they know we're alive."

"They know *I'm* alive." I jab my thumb into my chest. "You, not so much."

"Eh, I'm tough. A little snowstorm isn't enough to take me down."

I roll my eyes. "Sure."

"We'll stop soon to try to find a real phone, if you're afraid they think I'm dead in a ditch somewhere."

I scoff. "If you died in a ditch, I wouldn't leave you there. I'd at least drag you up to the side of the road."

ten

. . .

Bobby

"Who's your favorite client?" Melissa asks me, when she gets back into the car after successfully making a payphone call to Leslie.

I give her a side-eyed look from the driver's seat. "I didn't agree to play 'Truth or Dare' again. And I'm not answering that question."

"I didn't ask you to play, but now I will. Only this time, it's 'Truth or More Truth.' And I've decided I'm not asking, I'm telling." She laughs as she pokes my shoulder. "Come on. Tell me your favorite client. I promise to keep it a secret. Is it Diego?"

"Of course it's Diego. He's like a brother to me."

"Yeah?"

"Yup."

"Do you have any real brothers or sisters?" she asks.

"Is this the 'more truth' part?"

"Yep. How many siblings?"

I shift in my seat. "One." I don't elaborate.

After a few awkward seconds of silence, she says, "You're not ready to tell me that story, either, I take it."

"Nope."

"I'm going to get all your secrets out of you one day, you know," she teases.

I grunt in response. Little does she know, she doesn't want to hear some of them.

"For now, what's something you feel comfortable telling me?" she asks. "How about school? Where did you go?"

That's easy enough. "USC—for both undergrad and law school."

Melissa turns in her seat so she's facing me as much as she can with her seatbelt on. "You're a lawyer?"

"I am. A lot of agents are. It helps to understand all the legal ramifications of contracts, endorsements, and so on."

"That makes sense. I have an older cousin who went to USC. Graduated in '75. What year did you graduate?"

I give her another side eye. Does she know how old I am? This might open up a can of worms I'm not necessarily ready to open, but if I refuse to answer, she'll know something's up. "Undergrad in '71."

Again, she's quiet for a while. "So you graduated college at nineteen? How much of a genius are you?"

I laugh. "Not a genius." Technically, my IQ says I am, but I'm not about to say it. If I do, she'll never let me live it down.

"You going to tell me that story?"

I sigh and give her the *Reader's Digest* version. "Things weren't great at home. I legally emancipated myself at sixteen, my high school guidance counselor helped me apply to USC and jump through a lot of hoops, and I was accepted. I got some scholarships and a couple of jobs, and I worked my way through undergrad in three years, then law school." I clench my teeth as I pray she won't ask me to elaborate.

"Why did you decide to be a sports agent instead of another kind of lawyer?"

"I had an undergrad classmate at USC who played football. After he graduated and was drafted, a terrible agent took advantage of him. He fired that guy and asked me for legal help, so I learned all I could about athletic contracts, and I discovered I enjoyed helping athletes get the contracts and endorsements they deserve. The rest is history."

"Aww." She places her hands over her heart. "You're a softie deep down inside. I knew it!"

I roll my eyes. "I'm not."

She places her hand on my shoulder and squeezes. "You are. Instead of Sport, I'm now going to call you B.S."

My eyebrows raise. "B.S.?" Those are my first two initials, as my middle name truly is Sebastian, but I don't think that's what she's talking about.

"Big Softie."

A laugh bursts out of me as an unexpected warmth fills my chest. "You can call me B.S. as long as you never tell anyone what it really stands for."

"Deal."

We stop at a Pizza Hut somewhere in Arkansas to eat lunch. We're about an hour away from our destination, and I suggested we push on through, but Melissa was starving and claimed the Pizza Hut buffet wouldn't take long. She also explained that this way Leslie and her parents won't feel the need to feed us once we arrive, and I appreciate her thoughtfulness.

"Based on your sweatshirt last night," I say over a slice of supreme pizza, "I'm assuming you went to Columbia."

"Yep. Majored in sociology." She picks a pepperoni off her slice and pops it in her mouth.

My eyebrows raise. "Really?"

She swallows. "What's that supposed to mean?"

I shrug. "I don't know. I guess I just pegged you for a business major, considering your job in the Cubs front office."

"Yeah, but my job consists of dealing with people every day. I'm in Customer Relations."

"Oh."

Melissa gives me an incredulous look. "Did you not know what my job is?"

"I guess not." And I feel like an idiot for not knowing or even asking.

"Even though I initially met you while doing my job of checking on things in a luxury suite where you were watching a game with Ash and Leslie?"

I can feel my face turn red, which is an uncommon occurrence for me. "Uh, yeah. Sorry."

"We talked for like five minutes."

Interesting that she remembers all this. Of course, I remember it, too—well, everything but what her actual job is. "I don't know what you want me to say."

She sighs. "Nothing, I guess."

I nod. "So where did you work before this job? I'm assuming you worked somewhere else, since I only met you last spring, but I've been around the Cubs organization for a long time."

"Yeah, I did. I stayed in Manhattan after college and worked in Human Resources for a Wall Street firm."

"Wall Street, huh?"

"What? Do you have a problem with that, too?"

I raise my hands. "I haven't had a problem with anything you've said. This is all just surprising to me, which I don't want you to take offense to, as I'm not trying to offend you. I'm simply wrapping my head around it all. Especially after getting to know you this past day, Wall Street doesn't seem to fit your personality."

"I wasn't a stockbroker or anything. That's very much not my jam."

"I didn't think it would be. Anyway, what made you move back to Chicago?"

She can no longer meet my eye, and I wonder why.

"Well?" I prompt.

"I ... my dad had some major health issues, so I wanted to be close to my parents again."

"I'm so sorry," I say. "Is he okay now?"

Melissa peeks up at me through her lashes and nods, but her eyes are sad. "He was having some heart problems, and then he had a stroke last winter. He recovered well enough that most people can't tell a difference, but he didn't get fully back to normal. He never will be." Her eyes glisten with unshed tears.

"But he survived, and that's the important part. Before he got sick, I wasn't very good about calling my parents or visiting them. I won't take them for granted again."

Before I can stop it, my hand covers hers on the table. "I'm sorry. Truly."

"Thanks. It's no fun watching your parents get old."

I squeeze her hand before bringing my own back to my side of the table. As we continue to eat our pizza in silence, I consider how I've done almost nothing other than hold back personal information from her, but she freely offered the information about her her dad. I wonder if I should give her something personal in return.

"Why are you staring at me, B.S.?" she asks.

I chuckle at the nickname. "Not so much staring as thinking while looking in your direction."

"What are you thinking about, then?"

"Your honesty."

"You're not honest?"

"I am, usually to a fault. And I'm honest with what I say, but there's a lot I don't say."

"Yeah, I've picked up on that." She gives me a goofy grin.

"I'm a lot like my dad in that way," I say, deciding to open myself up to her a little more. "But I don't want to be anything like him."

Melissa searches my eyes. "He wasn't a good man?"

I shake my head. "Not in any way." I look away from her. "Like I said, I'm a lot like him."

"Bobby," she says in an intense tone, "you're a good man."

"I thought I was a jerk," I mutter.

"You can be, but that's not all you are. And you're trying to be better, right? If you weren't a good man, you wouldn't want to try. You wouldn't have told me ridiculous jokes to keep me calm when I was about to lose my mind while driving in the snow yesterday. You wouldn't have offered to help keep me warm overnight. Or maybe you would have, but you also would've tried to make a move on me. And you know how else I know you're a good man, Bobby Jacobs?"

I feel a strange pricking sensation behind my eyes as I finally look at her again. "How?"

"Because Diego Sanchez, Ash Hamilton, and Randall Hamilton are three of the best people I know, and they wouldn't let you get close enough to be like a brother or ask you to be in their wedding if you weren't a good man."

eleven

. . .

Melissa

W ho would've ever thought I'd be sitting in a Pizza Hut in Nowhere, Arkansas, trying to convince Bobby Jacobs he's a better man than he believes he is? Not me, that's for sure. A day ago, I was dreading what I thought would be an interminable twelve-hour road trip with him. Now? I'm not sure I want it to end. That's part of the reason I insisted we stop to eat instead of waiting until we arrived in Oakville.

It's not that I'm not excited to join our friends—and Shannon —in Leslie's hometown for the wedding festivities, but I've somehow become attached to the typically irritating man sitting across from me. And I continue to have mixed feelings about that.

I want to ask Bobby questions about his dad and their relationship, but I know he gave me a gift by telling me as much as he did, and I don't want to scare him off. I know he'll tell me what he wants to when he's ready. Just like I'll tell him about what happened with Jeremy when I'm ready.

"I don't know what to say," he finally says in response to my declaration about him being a good man.

"You don't have to say anything. I just want you to believe what I said. Do you believe it? *Can* you?"

He closes his eyes, and I watch his Adam's apple bob as he swallows. "I can try."

Now I reach my hand across to cover his on the table. His eyes pop back open.

"That's a great start," I say. "Now eat up so we can get back on the road."

"Hey, you're the one who wanted to stop and eat. I'm going to take my sweet time."

He takes a bite of pizza and chews it exaggeratedly slowly. I ball up my napkin and throw it at his face, resulting in a grin that makes his dimple appear again. In this moment, I decide my goal for the next few days is to see that dimple as often as possible.

"We were afraid you were dead in a ditch somewhere!" Wendy exclaims as she hugs me so tightly I'm afraid my ribs will crack.

I glance over at Bobby, who's chatting with Randall and Ash while smirking at me, which unfortunately does not bring out the dimple. "Told you so," he mouths at me, and I'm tempted to stick my tongue out at him but I give him a smile and eye roll instead.

"Let her go," Leslie orders Wendy, "before she's dead in my parents' living room from you squeezing her to death."

Wendy obliges, and Leslie gives me a long yet thankfully looser hug.

"What's that look that just passed between you and Bobby?" she whispers in my ear.

"Nothing," I mutter. It's obviously not nothing, but I have no idea what to tell my friend about what may or may not be happening between Bobby and me. Not that anything's happening. Well, except for me wanting to see his dimple and remembering how nice it felt to wake up in his arms.

"I don't believe you, and I'll be asking you again later," she murmurs. "So you'd better come up with a better answer next time." She finally lets me go.

"Where's everybody else?" I ask her. "I figured the house would be full."

"Diego's flight landed in Little Rock about an hour ago, so he should be here soon. Dad and Shannon went to pick him up."

That's not surprising in the least. Shannon couldn't believe his luck when Leslie landed his favorite baseball player as a PR client last summer. The few times the two men have been in the same place at the same time, Shannon has barely left Diego's side. Thankfully, Shannon's a fun guy, and Diego mostly doesn't mind his clinginess.

Leslie leads us into the kitchen as she says, "My mom, my sister Cynthia, my aunt Star, and Ash's mom and sisters are over at the church getting a few things ready for tomorrow. They'll be back soon. Do you want to stay here until they all arrive, or do you want to head to the hotel and get some rest and get changed for tonight?"

I look at my watch. It's almost three. "How far away is the hotel? And what time is the rehearsal?"

"Rehearsal is at six, and the hotel is a twenty-minute drive."

My eyes search out Bobby, who I can see through the archway into the living room. He's focused on me and tuned in to our conversation, although he's at least fifteen feet away. I raise my eyebrows at him, and he shrugs, letting me know he doesn't care when we go to the hotel. With a jolt, I realize we both assumed we'd go together, even though we no longer need to.

I turn my gaze back on Leslie, who's popping the top on a can of Diet Coke. "We can hang around here until four or so, and then we should probably head to the hotel to check in and get changed."

"*We?*" Wendy asks with a smirk.

"Uh, well, I just assumed Bobby and I would go together, since he doesn't have a car."

"Mmhm."

Instead of engaging any further in that conversation, I take a seat at the kitchen table, facing away from the guys, and I ask Wendy, "Is Andrea coming tonight?"

Wendy's recently discovered half-sister lives in Little Rock with her seven-year-old daughter Emily. I met both of them in the fall at Wendy's bridal shower and wedding, as Andrea was a bridesmaid and Emily was the flower girl.

"She won't be there tonight," Wendy explains as she grabs a

Sprite from a large cooler and hands me a Dr. Pepper, "but she, Emily, and her mom will be at the wedding and reception tomorrow."

"*Blades of Steel,*" an animated-sounding voice interrupts our conversation from the living room, followed by video game sounds.

I point my thumb over my shoulder toward the living room. "What's happening in there?"

"They're playing a hockey game on the Nintendo. Ash gave it to Randall for Christmas, and he insisted on bringing it with him." Wendy rolls her eyes. "The man is addicted. Ash is tired of playing it with him already, so it looks like he's now roping Bobby into it." She cups her hands around her mouth. "Hey, guys! Turn it down!"

A quick glance into the living room reveals Randall and Bobby both holding rectangular gray game controllers while their gazes are locked on the TV screen. Meanwhile Ash is reading *The Wall Street Journal.* I'm in no way surprised by any of it. Well, maybe Bobby playing a video game. He doesn't seem the type, but I've quickly learned he's not exactly the type of man I thought he was.

"Helloooo!" Wendy hollers. "Turn it down."

"Yes, dear," Randall says in a high-pitched tone, and soon the game's volume decreases.

"So, Melissa," Leslie says in her let's-get-down-to-business voice, "how was the trip?"

I take a sip of my Dr. Pepper while considering how to respond and forcing myself to not turn and look at Bobby.

"It's a simple question," Wendy says, when I take too long to reply. "Or maybe not so simple, considering the way you and Bobby have been sneaking looks at each other and having silent conversations across the room ever since you arrived."

I sigh. "It was … unexpected," I say in a voice low enough the guys can't overhear.

"Oh?" Leslie says. "In what way?"

I tilt my head. "Bobby's not what I expected. Not *who* I expected."

They both nod, as if they know exactly what I'm talking about.

Wendy says, "He's actually a good guy if you can manage to get him out of agent mode."

"But he's usually in agent mode, even when he's not working," Leslie adds. "Sounds like you might've gotten him out of it, though." She gives me a knowing look.

"It took a couple hours," I explain. "He was his typical jerkwad self at the airport. I'm impressed the airline agent didn't punch him. And then he wasn't happy about having to drive down here or to ride with me. But eventually, he chilled out, and he was even nice to me." I shake my head. "It was weird."

"Like how nice?" Wendy says. "Give us some examples."

I'm contemplating how much to tell them when a horn honks outside.

twelve

. . .

Bobby

"I'm sensing some tension between you and Melissa," Randall says in a low voice as we battle each other on the Nintendo. "And I'm talking the good kind of tension. What happened on that trip, man?"

Speaking of tension, my body is currently as tense as it can get, thanks to Randall's perceptiveness.

"Nothing," I say.

He scoffs. "Whatever. You were totally undressing her with your eyes a few minutes ago." In my peripheral vision, I see his gaze flicker toward me. "Please tell me you didn't undress her for real last night."

"Seriously? What kind of man do you think I am?" I feel like a hypocrite saying that, because at one point in my life I was exactly that kind of man.

"The kind with eyes and what I'm guessing is a healthy libido. You know I think my wife is the most gorgeous woman on the planet, but Melissa comes in a close second. And if you tell either of them I said that, I'll murder you in your sleep."

Before I can respond to his chilling declaration, the front door bursts open, and seconds later Diego enters with his arms spread wide.

"The second-best man has arrived!" he announces with a booming laugh. "The party can begin!"

Randall tosses his game controller down and leaps to his feet to hug Diego. Ash and I follow, and I greet Shannon and Mr. Beckett.

While my hand is still clasped in Leslie's dad's hand, Shannon scoots past us and wraps his arms around Melissa, who has made her way into the living room from the kitchen. My jaw clenches as he picks her up and swings her around before kissing her cheek and setting her back down on the floor. She giggles and pats his chest.

"Easy, there," Mr. Beckett says, and I release my tight grip on his hand.

I give him a sheepish look. "Sorry, sir."

"Please call me Ernie," he says. "And if you have any claim on that woman, you let my son know, and he'll back off."

"I don't." *But I might want to.* I clear my throat as I try to wipe that thought from my brain. "I thought Shannon had a girlfriend."

"Mmm. They broke things off a month or so ago." He shrugs. "It was amicable."

"Ah," I say noncommittally.

"Tell him," Ernie reiterates.

I shake my head. "It's not like that between us."

He snorts. "That's not what it looks like to me."

An hour later, I'm driving us to the hotel. Wendy and Randall came with us, as they need to change clothes before the rehearsal as well. Wendy decided there was no reason to take two cars when we could all fit in Melissa's. And somehow it's become our default for me to drive now. We didn't even discuss it. Melissa simply handed me the keys and then climbed into the backseat with Wendy.

"What kind of hotel did you stay in last night?" Wendy asks us.

I glance in the rearview mirror at Melissa, and we grin at each other.

"What's that grin for?" Wendy demands. "I'm not sure I like that you two have inside jokes that I'm not privy to."

"We stayed at a roadside trucker motel in a little town in Illinois," Melissa tells her.

"No way!"

In the mirror, I watch Wendy's eyes open comically wide.

"Yep," Melissa replies. "It was our only option. The heavy snow hit us real fast, and the only hotel at the next exit was a trucker motel. And we were lucky, because they only had one … room … left."

I can tell by the way she paused that she didn't mean to let that information slip about the room.

"Hold. The. Phone," Wendy says. "You two shared a room?"

"We kind of had to," Melissa explains. "I wasn't about to make Bobby sleep in the car during a blizzard."

"Please tell me there was only one bed," Wendy says. *"Please."*

Randall chuckles beside me. "That would make her little romance-book-loving heart so happy."

"Hey," she retorts. "I have a *big* romance-book-loving heart. Get it right."

"Sorry, dear," Randall says in a sing-song voice.

"Whatever." She reaches forward and flicks the back of his head. "Anyway, how many beds?"

"Two," Melissa says.

"Darn it."

I laugh at Wendy's response, and then I wonder if Melissa will tell them the rest of the story.

She doesn't.

After a few seconds of silence, Wendy asks, "So what did you do … in your trucker motel room … all alone … *togetherrrrr?"* She drags out the final word.

Melissa says, "Watched TV for a while. Then we were going to play cards, but the power went out, so we went to bed."

"Did you tell each other secrets in the dark?" Wendy asks. "Please tell me you did." I know without looking that her hands are clasped together under her chin.

My body tenses as I wait to see how Melissa will respond.

"Maybe we did. Maybe we didn't," Melissa replies.

"I'll get it out of you, you know," Wendy says. "Bobby, you're awfully quiet up there."

"Leave him alone, babe," Randall orders.

"Melissa's doing just fine telling you the story," I say.

Wendy harrumphs. "She's not telling me much of anything. I want all the details." When neither Melissa nor I say anything else, she says in a sly voice, "Shannon seemed to be happy to see you, Melissa."

My grip tightens on the steering wheel. I know what Wendy's trying to do, and unfortunately it's working. I shouldn't be jealous of Shannon. As I told his dad, I have no claim on Melissa. But the man looks like a swimsuit model with none of the arrogance of one. He's charm personified, but not in a creepy way. Everybody likes him, and I mean everybody—both women and men. Irrationally, that makes me want to hate him. But I can't. So instead I'll apparently just be jealous.

I glance in the mirror at Melissa, who, interestingly enough, is glaring at Wendy.

"Yes, it was good to see him again," Melissa says to Wendy in a terse tone. "Now, what did you all get up to last night? I doubt you were able to have any fun without Bobby, since he's always the life of the party."

Randall laughs as I stifle a smile at the knowledge that Melissa brought the conversation away from Shannon and back around to me. I shouldn't be as happy about that as I am. Melissa deserves better than me, with all the baggage and history I bring. She belongs with someone like Shannon—someone her age who can give her the fairytale. I'm well past being able to give that to anyone.

thirteen

. . .

Melissa

"Tell me what's up with you and Bobby and Shannon," Wendy orders from her perch on my hotel room toilet lid as I finish getting ready for the rehearsal.

"Why are you here?" I ask. "Wouldn't you rather be doing more interesting things with your new husband?"

"Oh, we took care of those interests, believe you me." She gives me a giant smile and doesn't show even a hint of a blush. Modesty is not Wendy's style. "And now I want to hear about your men and if there's any potential of you doing interesting things with either of them."

I pretend to look for something in my toiletry bag. "I don't have any men."

"Both of those guys looked like they wanted to pee a circle around you back at Leslie's parents' house. I'd say you have men."

I give her a side eye. "That's disgusting."

She shrugs. "It's the truth. It appears we have a love triangle on our hands." She rubs her hands together. "And I do enjoy a good love triangle."

"There are no triangles." I roll my eyes at her as I put on a pair of dangly silver earrings. "No squares. Not even any straight lines."

"You're lying. You shared a hotel room with Bobby. What

happened? Did you see him without his shirt on? I bet he looks gooooood without a shirt."

Based on the feel of him through all his layers, I bet he does, too. "We were both fully clothed the entire time."

"That's unfortunate."

I can't help but chuckle at her response because she's not completely wrong.

"There's something you're not telling me," Wendy says. "You might as well go ahead and spill it, because you know from experience that I'm only going to keep asking." She holds a hand up before I can even think about responding. "Understand I don't want you to tell me any secrets he might have told you, and somehow I think he did. I just want to know why there's a tiny little smile on your face every time you look at him."

My eyes widen.

"You didn't realize that, did you?" she asks.

I shake my head as I feel my face heat.

"So tell me what happened."

I turn and lean against the counter. "When the power went out, it got really cold, really fast. And ... um, well, we ..."

She pokes me in the knee. "You what?"

"We slept in the same bed," I blurt out. "But only to keep each other warm!"

Wendy cackles. "I knew it! Did he spoon you? Was he the big spoon? Was it everything you ever imagined it would be like to have those big, strong, California-tanned arms wrapped around you?"

"I have never imagined what it would be like to have his arms around me," I lie.

"I don't believe that for a second, because even *I* wondered that when I first met the man, even though I already had my sights set on Randall. But it was fantastic, wasn't it? Don't lie to me again, Melissa Teague. I have to live vicariously through you now that I'm forever attached to the love of my life."

I close my eyes and sigh. "He didn't spoon me, but he did wrap his arm around me and hold me against him all night, and it felt good. Really good. And not just because he kept me warm."

"Yesssssss." Wendy leaps up and throws her arms around me. "My baby girl is growing up and falling in love."

I try to shove her off me, but she's clinging like a monkey. "I am not. Shut up."

"Don't tell me to shut up. I'm so happy for you! And for Bobby. He's a lucky man."

"There's nothing going on between us, Wendy. Nothing."

She finally lets go of me and then follows me out into the room so I can change into my dress. "But there could be, right? You can't just be all up in his business all night and then walk away. That's rude."

"Nothing can happen there. He's got a lot of secrets, and he's a total player."

"Yes, he does have secrets, which I'm hoping he'll feel comfortable enough with you tell you about soon. But I don't think he's a player."

"Believe me," I say. "He is." But I don't tell her how I know that. "So I'm thinking I need to focus on Shannon instead."

"He is one fine-looking man, no disrespect to my handsome husband."

"Indeed." I slip on a long-sleeved pink midi dress that hugs my torso and flares out at the hips.

"And he's nice and charming and successful."

"Yup."

"But he lives in Little Rock," she states, "which is a long way from Chicago."

"Bobby lives in L.A., which is much farther."

"Oh, we're back to Bobby now, are we?" she teases.

I roll my eyes at her as I step into the heels I dyed to match my dress. "Let's go, matchmaker."

Leslie's mom has taken on the role of wedding coordinator, and the woman knows how to get things done. Within minutes of us arriving at the church, she has us all standing just so at the front of the sanctuary. We're spaced out with precision and turned at just the right angle.

It's not lost on me that due to the order we're standing in, I'll be walking out of the church with Bobby. Last I knew, I was walking with Diego, and Aunt Star would be with Bobby, but apparently Leslie is acting as matchmaker, too. I determine not to mention it to her, as that would only add fuel to the fire.

Once Mrs. Beckett is sure we all know exactly where to stand, she shoos all of us bridesmaids, plus Leslie and her dad, to the foyer so we can practice walking in. Ash's two teenage sisters go first, followed by Leslie's younger sister Cynthia, me, Aunt Star, and then Wendy, the matron of honor.

The sanctuary doors close behind Wendy, and when the pipe organ begins blasting out the *Bridal Chorus,* the doors swing back open, and tears fill my eyes at the sight of one of my best friends looking happier than I've ever seen her. I turn my head to catch Ash's reaction, and he's visibly holding back his own tears. I've never seen him cry, but something tells me I will tomorrow.

My gaze then moves past Randall and Diego and focuses on Bobby, who's looking back at me with no shame. My breath catches in my throat, and he holds my gaze for several seconds before shifting his focus to Ash and Leslie. I then catch Shannon's eye, beyond Bobby, and he winks at me. I press my lips together to keep from laughing at him. He's such a flirt.

When I slide my gaze back up the row of men, Bobby's face holds a slight frown. I wonder what that's about. He was quieter than normal on our drive from the hotel, but since Randall and Wendy are both chatterboxes, I chalked it up to him just letting them run their mouths as usual. Now I wonder if it's something else.

"So we'll do the vows and the rings, and then I'll pronounce you man and wife, and then I'll tell you to …," the preacher's voice trails off as Ash leans down to kiss Leslie.

"Well," the preacher says with a chuckle, "I guess we're practicing that part."

The rest of us clap and holler, and even though I can't see Ash's face, I'm sure it's bright red. The man has come out of his shell a bit since Leslie came into his life, but he's still very private —so much so that I'm impressed he kissed Leslie in front of us now.

They finally break off their kiss, and Leslie raises her hands and yells, "Let's parrrrrrty!"

We all whoop and shout until a wolf whistle cuts us off, and we all stop instantly.

"We'll party in due time, kids," Mrs. Beckett says, "but first, you need to walk out of here in the right order, just like you will tomorrow."

Leslie and Ash hustle down the aisle, followed by Wendy and Randall, Diego and Aunt Star, and then I loop my arm into Bobby's as he ushers me out.

"You look stunning," Bobby says under his breath.

I can feel my cheeks heat. "Thanks. You don't look so bad yourself."

He's wearing charcoal pants and a nicely fitted light blue shirt with a few buttons unbuttoned. The only thing that would make him look better is if he rolled up his sleeves. He also smells like heaven, otherwise known as Givenchy Gentleman. It's my favorite cologne, yet somehow it smells even better on him than it does on the sample papers at Marshall Field's.

"Just wait 'til you see me in my pink-and-purple paisley cummerbund and bow tie tomorrow," he quips.

I giggle as we enter the church's foyer. "I will definitely be needing a picture of that."

fourteen

. . .

Bobby

I must've angered the karmic gods in some way, because the seating arrangement at the rehearsal dinner placed Melissa smack dab between me and Shannon. Actually, I'm guessing it was Leslie I irritated in some way to make this happen. They all seem to think something happened between Melissa and me on the drive down here, but I'm guessing Leslie would prefer Melissa to be with her brother instead of me, and rightfully so. I also wonder if Melissa would prefer Shannon to me. I didn't miss the fact that while she openly stared at me during the rehearsal, she smiled at Shannon. She didn't smile at me.

Thankfully, Leslie's dad is on my other side, so I can talk to him when Melissa's chatting with Shannon. I'll admit I don't like how I feel when she laughs at something he says or touches his arm. I shouldn't feel possessive of her after our one day together, but I do.

"So, Bobby," Ernie says, "my daughter tells me you have quite the cutthroat reputation as a sports agent. I hear you always get what you want."

I tense at his words, and I nearly jolt out of my chair when Melissa's hand lands on my leg under the tablecloth. She gives my thigh a slight squeeze, as if conveying her support.

I recover quickly and respond, "Not always. And it's not about what I want, sir, but what my clients want."

"How you managed to get Houston to trade Diego to Chicago last season is beyond me."

"That was all him." I nod toward Diego at the other end of the long table.

"All?"

"Well, mostly. The man is very persuasive."

"I've heard that as well. But I'm surprised you're not taking more credit for it."

Melissa tightens her fingers on my thigh again, even though she's having a conversation with Shannon.

"It's not all about me." Which is new. I can't imagine I would've said that even two days ago, but my perspective is changing, thanks to the woman with her hand my leg. I do what I do for my clients and for my family, not for me. It hasn't always been that way, but I now realize that's changed over the years.

"That's good to hear. Who are some of your other clients?"

As Ernie and I chat about the other athletes I represent, Melissa's hand slips away. I grab for it and pull it back to my leg, leaving my hand curled over hers. I hold my breath, waiting for her to pull away again or even slap me, but she doesn't.

"Mi hermano, I haven't talked to you since Christmas Eve, which is way too long." Diego gives me a tight hug and then asks, "How's Kelli?"

I'm finally getting some one-on-one time with Diego while the guests mingle after the rehearsal dinner. The man is so much more than my favorite client—he's also my closest friend and, like I told Melissa, he's like a brother to me. Ash and Randall are also getting to that status, but I haven't known them as long as I've known Diego, who was one of my first clients. We've both had to deal with some major personal issues over the decade-plus we've been working together. I'm not sure how I'd have made it through without him.

I switch to speaking in Spanish, in case we can be overheard.

"She's not happy I wasn't around the past few days since I was in Chicago and she couldn't come with me."

Diego purses his lips in frustration. "And why were you in Chicago instead of at home with your daughter?"

"Dealing with client drama."

"Drama with a client in Chicago that's not me?" Diego lets out a belly laugh. "What's the world coming to?"

"Right? Usually you're the drama queen, but this time it was someone else."

"You're not going to tell me who? Come on, *hermano*. You can tell me."

"You know I can't. I don't tell people about your behind-the-scenes drama, so I'm not telling you about anyone else's."

"Fine. I respect that, but I know it's Jimmie Zane. That kid can't stay out of trouble. I don't know why you signed him. He creates more drama than the rest of your clients combined."

I shrug. "Apparently I'm drawn to drama. Case in point." I nod toward him with a smirk.

Diego laughs again. "Can't argue with that. Anyway, back to Kelli. She's okay other than being mad you ditched her for Jimmie?"

I pause, knowing I should tell him what's going on but not wanting to talk about this in public, even in Spanish.

"I can always tell when you're hiding something from me," he says. "Just spit it out."

My heart rate increases as I say in a rush, "I called her when I was at the hotel earlier. She sounded a little off, and I could tell something was wrong and dragged it out of her that her mom had a mild headache a couple days ago, and it hasn't gone away. In fact, it's worse today. "

He gasps and puts a hand over his heart in a way that would seem dramatic if any other man did it, but it works for him. "Oh, no. What does Nanette's doctor say?"

"She can't get in to see the doc until next week because of the holiday, so they're both pretty stressed about it."

"You, too, I bet." He claps his hand on my shoulder.

"Yeah." I'd be worried about Nanette no matter what, but

since the headaches are my fault, I feel a crushing weight on my chest that's only getting stronger.

"It's not your fault," Diego says, reading my thoughts.

"How is it not my fault?"

"You didn't drink and drive and blast through that stop sign."

I close my eyes. "Can we not talk about this now?"

"Okay, but we'll be talking about it later."

I have no intention of doing so, but I say, "We'll see," before opening my eyes again.

Diego nods. "So you're heading back to L.A. after the wedding, then?"

"I had planned to, but I don't want Melissa to have to drive back home by herself. Before I knew about Nanette, I told her I'd go back to Chicago with her the day after the wedding and then fly home from there. I should be able to catch a red-eye as soon as we get back."

"Ah." He grins at me.

"Ah, what?" I cock an eyebrow at him.

"The lovely Melissa." He shimmies his shoulders and manages to not look absolutely ridiculous in the process.

I sigh. "What about her?"

"You cannot keep your eyes off her, my friend. I like this for you."

My whole body jerks when Melissa pops up beside me and says, "Did I just hear my name? You know it's rude to talk about people in a language they don't know." She's grinning, so I know she's not that upset.

Diego says in English, "We were just talking about how lovely you look tonight, *mi encantadora*. That means 'my lovely.'"

He takes her hand and kisses the back of it, and she giggles, which I can somehow feel in my chest.

"Diego," she bats her eyelashes at him, "if I didn't know better, I'd think you were flirting with me."

"Of course I am! You see, I have no date for this wedding. And it appears you don't either." His eyes flick to me and back to Melissa. "So I can flirt all I want and not get into any trouble at all!"

Diego takes Melissa in his arms and tangoes her across the room, resulting in more giggles from her and applause from the people nearby. I feel an odd pulsing in my chest as I watch them. After a few minutes, he dances her back over to me, salutes us, and moves off to chat with Randall and Wendy.

"You having a good time?" I ask her. I stuff my hands into my pockets so I won't touch her.

"The best! Almost all of my favorite people are here in this room, other than my parents." She sweeps her hand out to encompass the room. "What's not to like?"

"I hear you. But why aren't your parents here? Or are they coming tomorrow? Didn't they go to Randall and Wendy's wedding?"

"Yes, they went to Milwaukee for that wedding, and they were invited to this one," Melissa says, "but it's tough for Dad to travel very far these days. Everybody understood why they couldn't make the trip down here. They took Ash and Leslie out to dinner to celebrate a couple weeks ago."

I smile. "That was nice of them."

"They're good people. You'd like them. In fact, you should meet them. Dad would love to talk sports with you."

My smile grows bigger. "I'd like that."

We don't share a ride with Wendy and Randall on the way back to the hotel after the rehearsal dinner. Diego also needed a ride back to the hotel, and Leslie's mom insisted he take her car, so we wouldn't all be crammed into Melissa's tiny Prelude. Randall and Wendy rode with him to navigate, and I'm driving Melissa's car yet again.

"You had fun tonight?" I ask Melissa after several minutes of companionable silence on the road.

"I did. It was good to see Leslie's family again, as well as Ash and Randall's mom and sisters. I've seen them all a lot throughout the prep for both weddings, but now I'm wondering when—or if—I'll see some of them again after tomorrow."

Hmm. It doesn't sound like she thinks she'll have contact with Shannon after the wedding. I like that idea far too much.

"Of course," she continues, "I'll probably see Shannon when he comes to visit Leslie and Ash. He comes to Chicago a lot more often than any of the rest of their family does."

I press my lips together and decide not to respond to her statement. Instead I say, "I bet Leslie's parents and aunt will visit a lot more often once she and Ash have kids."

Melissa whips her head toward me. "Do you know something?"

My forehead wrinkles in confusion. "Know what?"

"You said that as if you know there's a baby on the way."

Now my eyebrows raise. "I know no such thing. Do you?"

"No. I wonder about Wendy, though. I noticed she didn't drink any wine tonight, and that girl loves her wine."

"Could be a sign. You going to ask her about it?"

"I don't know," Melissa admits. "She wanted to start trying right away after the wedding, since she's in her thirties and they want a big family. But I'm afraid to ask in case they're trying and she's not pregnant yet. I don't want to upset her if that's the case."

"It hasn't even been two months since they got married, though," I say.

She sighs. "True. But still."

"I get it. I don't want to ask Randall, either. Something tells me he might be even more upset than Wendy if she's not pregnant yet."

Melissa laughs lightly. "I think you're right. It's cute how excited he is about wanting to be a dad."

"Do you want kids someday?" I ask before realizing I'm walking into a minefield with that question.

"Yeah. At least two. I'm an only child, and I've always wished I had siblings, especially now that my parents are getting older. My parents couldn't have more kids, so I don't blame them, but sometimes my childhood was lonely."

"I can understand that."

"Do you want kids?" she asks.

I take a few seconds to consider my answer. Do I tell her the truth? Or do I give her my typical evasive answer to this question? I mentally slap myself as I choose the easy route. "I'd like a couple."

It's the truth, though not the entire truth. I'm not ready to tell her I already have a daughter—one who's almost as close to Melissa's age as Melissa is to mine. I don't tell many people about Kelli, due to my high-profile job. I don't want the press to mess with her. But I trust Melissa now, right? She's a friend, and if the Hamilton men and their women trust her, I should, too.

I open my mouth to share my rarely told secret when she hijacks my attempt.

"I don't look forward to being the parent of a teenager, though," she says. "I adore Ash and Randall's sisters, but I can't imagine trying to keep them in line, and they're good girls." She laughs. "And thinking back on what I was like as a teenager?" In my peripheral vision, I see her nose wrinkle. "No, thank you. That sounds like no fun at all."

My heart drops, and I rethink my plan to tell her about Kelli.

She continues, "I don't know how I didn't send my mother to an early grave, especially in my junior high years." She sighs. "I was not a nice person. Just ask Ash."

My eyebrows shoot up and my head whips toward her. "What did you do to Ash?"

"You don't know that story?"

"Noooo. But now you're going to have to tell me."

fifteen

. . .

Melissa

"This isn't a very flattering story—for me, that is," I admit to Bobby.

"I don't think I'm one to throw stones," he replies.

"Touché." I take a deep breath. "You know I grew up with the Hamilton boys. We went to both school and church together, and our moms have been friends since before I was born, so we were around each other all the time and knew each other pretty well. In seventh grade, Ash and I were both at a party and we ended up in the closet together during 'Seven Minutes in Heaven.'" I bury my face in my hands and take a deep breath.

"The kissing was that, bad, huh?"

I lower my hands and shake my head. "It actually wasn't, even though it was the first kiss for both of us, though neither of us knew it at the time. Anyway, Ash wasn't the most popular kid. He was nerdy and quiet and giant and awkward. I liked him, though. But after the kiss, I didn't want to admit to anyone that I enjoyed it, so I made fun of him instead. The news that he was a terrible kisser spread around school really fast." I can feel Bobby looking at me, even though I'm looking out the side window to avoid his eyes.

"Go ahead," I say. "Tell me how terrible I am."

My body twitches when his hand lands on mine.

"Melissa," his deep voice says, "you're not terrible. Not now, at least. You were a kid, and kids do dumb things." I'm well aware of the idiotic choices thirteen-year-olds can make, since I'm the parent of one. "I did my share of them, and I'm sure Ash did, too."

"No, I don't think he did. Ash was a really good kid. He always treated everyone with kindness, even when they were terrible to him, like I was. He never would've done what I did. He didn't deserve that from me." A tear leaks out the corner of my eye.

Bobby squeezes my hand before letting it go, but he doesn't say anything else as we continue down the dark, winding road.

"I apologized to him when we reconnected this past year, and he forgave me, but that doesn't change the facts."

"Sounds like you maybe need to forgive yourself for it," Bobby says.

I finally turn to look at him, and he gives me a brief glance and a small smile before returning his attention to the road.

"Look at you being all full of wisdom," I tease.

"I'm really good at telling other people what they should do," he says.

"Let me guess," I say, "you're not that great at doing it yourself?"

"That would be correct."

I start to laugh, but it turns into a shriek as Bobby slams on the brakes, flings his right arm out in front of me, and curses while the car fishtails down the road. He moves his hand back to the steering wheel, gripping it tightly, before the car finally skids to a stop along the narrow gravel shoulder. Even though it's dark, I know if I opened my door, I'd be looking down into a deep ditch.

"What the heck, Bobby Joe?" I suck in a few lungfuls of air and press my hands over my pounding heart.

He doesn't reply. His knuckles are white on the steering wheel, and he's staring straight ahead while slightly shaking. I remove my hands from my chest and shift the car into park. Then I cover his right hand with my left, slowly prying it off the wheel. He's still not talking, which is making me nervous.

"We're okay, Bobby. Everything's fine." Well, I'm not sure he's fine, but I need to get his attention. "Bobby," I say louder, trying to bring his focus to me instead of being stuck somewhere inside his head. *"Bobby."*

He blinks a few times and then his gaze swings to me.

"What happened?" I ask. "Why'd you hit the brakes?"

He breathes deeply a few times before saying, "Deer."

Why's he calling me *dear?* Did he somehow hit his head?

"What, Bobby? What happened?" Worry bubbles up in my chest.

"Deer. Road." He's still not speaking in complete sentences, though he's finally starting to make sense.

He continues, "Deer … in the headlights. It's a … real thing."

OK, that was a complete sentence. He's coming back to me.

The car interior suddenly lights up, and it takes a second for me to register another car has come around the corner behind us and is quickly approaching. I tense, hoping it sees we're at a stop, because half of our car is still in the road. As I reach over and press the hazard light button, I briefly hope it's Diego, Randall, and Wendy coming upon us, but then I remember they left before we did. Thankfully, the vehicle slows down, but it veers around us instead of stopping, honking as it passes.

"Bobby," I say, concerned that he didn't even flinch when the car passed or honked, "we can talk about what happened later, but do you think you can drive? Can you get us to the next driveway or a turnoff or something, so we can get off the road? I don't want us to get hit."

He nods but doesn't say anything as he shifts the car back into gear and pulls onto the road. We ride in silence for a mile or two before a mailbox appears up ahead on the right. Bobby pulls into the gravel driveway, shifts into park, and kills the engine. Again, he stares straight ahead, but his hands aren't wrapped quite as tightly around the wheel.

I release both of our seatbelts, and without thinking too much about what I'm doing, I scoot on top of the emergency brake between the seats and wrap my arms around his neck. He's still tense, so I press his head onto my shoulder.

"Bobby," I whisper against his forehead. "We're OK. We're OK." I repeat the words until the tension starts to leave his body and he relaxes into me.

Then his arms slip around me, and I'm being shifted until I'm sitting sideways on his lap, my legs draped onto the passenger seat. He squeezes me so tightly I can barely breathe, though not because my lungs are crushed. It's because he's so strong and solid. I give my head a little shake. I need to focus on the man attached to the strong arms because while he might be more than OK physically, something's clearly wrong.

"Do you want to talk about it?" I ask.

He shakes his head no. I want to press him, but there'll be time to do that later.

"Do you want me to drive us the rest of the way to the hotel?"

He nods yes but doesn't loosen his grip on me.

"You're going to have to let go of me for that to happen," I explain gently.

He finally releases me, and a minute later, we're back on the road with me in the driver's seat. Since he doesn't want to talk, I turn the radio on low so we're not driving in complete silence.

When we arrive at the hotel, he holds my hand as we walk inside, and I don't ask any questions. We get to my room, which is a few doors before his, and when we stop, he turns me to face him.

It takes him a few seconds to meet my eyes, and then he takes a deep breath and asks, "Can I come in? Stay with you?" He takes another deep breath. "Not to ... you know, but ... I don't want to be alone. I can't be. I promise I'll explain, but ... not tonight. You have two beds?"

I nod as I search his eyes, hoping to find some answers to what's tormenting him, but I don't know him well enough to read him yet. "Yes, there are two beds, and yes, you can stay here. Want me to go with you to grab your stuff from your room?"

He shakes his head. "No. Thanks."

Then he shocks me by cradling my face in his hands and pressing a kiss to my forehead before turning and making his way down the hall to his room. I watch until he disappears through the doorway. Then I slump against my own door for a few moments before digging into my purse for my room key.

What in the world is happening?

sixteen

. . .

Bobby

What am I doing?
I drop onto my hotel bed and flop backward with my arms spread wide. Why did I ask Melissa if I could stay the night? I mean, I know why I don't want to be alone, but I'm alone most nights of my life—mostly because I don't want anyone to see me like this, though it hasn't happened in a long time. Why do I feel comfortable enough with Melissa to be able to ask if I can stay with her? What is it about her? And what was I thinking pulling her onto my lap and then later kissing her—even if it was just a peck on the forehead?

Instead of trying to figure it out, I get back up and change into gym shorts and a T-shirt. Then I brush my teeth, grab my room key, and head back down to Melissa's room before I can talk myself out of it. Staying with her isn't a great idea, but the thought of spending the night alone makes my heart race, and not in a good way.

I knock lightly and look up and down the hallway, hoping no other wedding guests see me. I'm confident Randall and Wendy are holed up in their room until morning, but who knows what Diego is up to, and a few of Leslie's family members that were at the rehearsal are staying here. I doubt virtual strangers would say anything to me about what I'm doing, but they might say something to Ash or Leslie, and I don't want them to know about this. The last thing they need right now is to worry about me.

Melissa opens the door, and my breath catches in my throat. She's wearing quite a bit less than she was last night, probably because it's not twenty-five degrees in this hotel. When I asked to stay with her, I pictured her in the same baggy sweatshirt and flannel pants from last night, not tiny shorts and a T-shirt.

"I …," I run my fingers through my hair, "… this isn't …," I turn to head back to my room, because this is the worst idea I've had in a long time.

Melissa stops me with a hand on my arm. "Bobby, it's fine. Come in. We did this before, and we can do it again. Please stay."

I turn to look at her, hoping I won't find pity in her gaze. Instead, I see care and compassion.

"You sure?"

She nods and sweeps her hand into the room. "I'm positive."

The room smells like her—lemon and vanilla. I'm enveloped in it as I enter, and I pause between the beds before looking at her with a raised eyebrow.

"I don't care which bed is mine. You pick," she says.

I sit on the one to my left. "I know I'm being weird—" I say.

"No," she interrupts, sitting on the edge of the other bed, facing me. "Not weird. I'm not sure what happened tonight, and I don't need to know until you're ready to tell me." She takes my hands in hers. "But I'm glad you feel comfortable enough with me to be real with me—to tell me you need to not be alone, whatever your reasons are. They don't matter. Well, they do, but what matters more right now is that you don't have to be alone. Thank you for trusting me."

I nod. "Not sure *you* should trust *me*."

"Bobby, you've given me no reason to believe you'd do anything I'm not comfortable with. I fully trust you. Okay?" She squeezes my hands and then lets them go. "I need to brush my teeth, and then I'm hitting the sack. You good?"

"Yeah." I sigh. "I'm good." At least, I hope I will be sometime in the near future.

Melissa stands and ruffles my hair before heading to the bathroom. The feel of her touch lingers as I stare after her.

While she's gone, I take off my my watch and set it on the nightstand. Then I consider whether I should leave my shirt on since Melissa will soon be in the bed next to mine, but knowing I'll sleep better without it, I take it off and get myself situated under the covers, facing away from Melissa's bed so she won't feel the need to try to talk to me. I've already encroached on her privacy. I don't want her to feel like she needs to entertain me in the process.

A few minutes later, she pads back into the room and gets into bed.

"Good night, Bobby."

"Night, Melissa. Thanks again."

"You're more than welcome."

The light between the beds flicks off, and darkness surrounds me thanks to the blackout curtains. I should've opened them a few inches to let a little light in. If I'd stayed in my own room, I could have. I should've stayed there. Why didn't I stay there?

This is the part I dread when I'm like this—the darkness. This is when I get flashbacks to that terrible night. It was so dark, just like it was tonight when that deer's eyes glowed at me and sent my heart straight up into my throat. I don't always panic when it's pitch black like this. Last night I was fine. But last night, the memories were far from me. Tonight, they came screaming back into my consciousness, thanks to not only our near accident but also learning about Nanette's recent headaches. My heart begins to race, and my breathing turns shallow as scenes from that awful night flit through my mind. *Breathe slowly,* I tell myself, with my eyes pinched shut. *Take deep breaths.*

"Bobby?"

Melissa's voice jolts me out of my stupor.

"Y-yeah?" I respond, taking gulps of air.

"Truth or dare?"

"W-what?" Did I hear her right? She wants to play a game right now?

"Dare, you say? Okay, I dare you to come sleep with me."

My eyes pop open. What is she saying?

"Like last night," she says, "except tonight it's not to keep warm, but to keep calm. Let me help. I can hear you nearly hyperventilating over there."

My body is frozen. I can't sleep with her again. I can't. My feelings for her and my need to touch her—to hold her—have exponentially increased throughout this crazy day. I don't know if I can handle being cuddled up in bed with her, knowing we can't take this any further than we already have. But I know for sure I can't handle being here in the pitch dark alone.

"Bobby?" she says again. "Please say something."

I take a deep breath and then push out, "Something."

Melissa chuckles. "Glad to know you're coherent, but if you're not coming over here, I'm coming over there."

I can't make myself move or say anything else, and I hear her covers being tossed off. Then she's sliding into my bed behind me. She fits her body up against mine, and when her arm settles along my side, I grasp her hand and pull it to to my bare chest, holding it tightly over my pounding heart.

She gasps lightly and then asks, "You okay?"

I nod, knowing she can feel the movement even if she can't see it.

"Good," she says. "Let's sleep."

It takes a while for sleep to come, but with Melissa holding me, the memories finally fade and I drift off.

I jerk upright to the sound of pounding on a door, dislodging Melissa from my body in the process. She was draped across me, sleeping as soundly as I was just seconds ago, based on the confused look in her eyes when I turn to look at her.

"Melissa!" Wendy's voice comes through the hotel room door. "Open up! We need to head to Leslie's parents' house."

"Crap," Melissa says as she scrambles off the bed. "I forgot to set the alarm." She races to the door. I can't see her from the bed, but I'm hoping she's not planning to let Wendy in. We can't let her discover me here, or we'll never hear the end of it.

"Did you just wake up?" Wendy asks Melissa. "Let's get cracking, sleepyhead."

"No, you don't need to come in," Melissa says loudly, alerting me that Wendy intends to do just that. But there's nowhere for me to hide, so there's not much I can do if she pushes her way in.

Which she does. And then she stands blinking at me from the end of the bed as her eyes open wider and wider and a smile blooms across her face.

"Well, well, well, what do we have here?" Wendy looks back and forth between me and a blushing Melissa while grinning like a maniac.

Melissa sends me a beseeching look before covering her face. "Nothing. We have nothing here."

"Except a shirtless Bobby Jacobs in your bed," Wendy states. "Possibly a completely naked Bobby Jacobs in your bed, since I can't see his bottom half."

I grab the sheet where it has pooled around my waist and cover my chest with it, which makes Wendy chuckle.

"Technically, my bed is the other one," Melissa replies.

Wendy snorts. "Whatever you want to tell yourself." She puts her hands on her hips and smirks at me. "Do you have anything to say for yourself, young man?"

I determine to play it cool. "Ask me anything you want about what happened here last night." There's no way she knows about what happened in the car, so whatever she asks will be easily answered. And since I'm mostly recovered from yesterday's events, she shouldn't be able to tell anything is wrong.

Wendy rubs her hands together and asks in a gleeful voice, "Did Melissa sleep in *her* bed or yours?"

"Neither," I reply.

Her forehead wrinkles. "What does that mean?"

"I mean, her bed is over there," I point, "and mine is down the hall." I chuckle at myself.

Wendy rolls her eyes. "Okay, funny guy, let me rephrase. Did you and Melissa sleep *in the same bed?*"

Melissa groans. "Wendy!"

"I will neither confirm nor deny," I say, "but nothing untoward happened between us. She didn't even try to feel me up. Can you believe it?" I'd never admit it to either of them, but I'm a little disappointed Melissa didn't try anything. Not that I thought she would. It was neither the time nor the place.

"Bobby!" Melissa glares at me.

"Stop yelling our names," Wendy says to her. "If you'd just tell me what happened, this can be over in a jiffy. I refuse to believe the two of you slept in the same room but not the same bed, even though both beds are messed up. As Bobby said, it's not as if he doesn't have his own bed down the hall."

"Okay, fine," Melissa says. "We slept in the same bed but, as Bobby so eloquently put it, nothing untoward happened."

"Well, why ever not?" Wendy demands. "What was stopping you?"

On my part, not much other than a panic attack, I think but don't say.

"We're friends," Melissa says, resulting in a pang in my chest region. "We were, uh, talking and then Bobby decided to sleep in here, and uh, I was cold, so we did a repeat of the night before. All we did was sleep in the same bed."

So Melissa did tell Wendy the rest of the story from the previous night. Interesting.

"Once again," Wendy says, "there's something you're not telling me. But we don't have time for me to wheedle it out of you now." She points at me and then at the door. "Out. We've got to get her dressed and out the door in two minutes. You don't need to watch." She cocks an eyebrow at me. "Unless you want to? Or maybe you're naked as a jaybird and don't want me to watch you climb out of that bed?"

I force my face to stay impassive and try not to imagine any of what she just suggested. Then I leap out of bed, snatch up my watch, shirt, and room key, and hustle out the door. "I'll see you ladies later."

When I step out into the hallway, thankfully the coast is clear of anyone I know. I give a brief nod to the curly-auburn-haired woman in the hall who grins widely at me. It's only when I'm safely back in my room that I realize I'm only wearing my shorts. No wonder the woman was smiling. I might be pushing middle age, but I do some form of exercise most days, and I've got the body to show for it.

seventeen

. . .

Melissa

"Melissa Belinda Teague, you'd better spill the beans," Wendy demands as soon as Bobby hightails it out of my room.

"My middle name is not Belinda," is all I say as I rush into the bathroom to wash my face and brush my teeth.

"That's not the point," Wendy says from the doorway, where she stands with her arms crossed. "The point is you lied to me about what happened here last night. Friends don't lie to each other."

"I'm sorry, Wendy. I wasn't completely truthful, but I can't tell you why he was here. Though I can tell you nothing romantic happened." Unless holding him until he fell asleep is romantic, which it may well be, but I can't let myself dwell on that.

"Why can't you tell me?"

I sigh as I swipe the washcloth over my face and neck. "Because it's not my story to tell, okay? There's no point in pushing me on this, because I'm not going to give in." And I also am not fully sure why Bobby was here, either, but I trust that he'll tell me when he's ready.

"Okay. But I will tell you to be careful. Bobby is … a lot."

I catch her gaze in the mirror. "What does that mean?" I ask defensively. Wait. Since when am I defensive about Bobby Jacobs?

Wendy holds her hands up. "Bobby's a good man. I know he

is. And it seems like you know that, too. But there's a lot about him and his life and his family that you don't know, and until you do know, I think you need to keep some defenses up."

"You don't think I can handle whatever it is he's hiding from me?" I ask around my toothbrush.

"I think you can. No, I know you can. And to be clear, he hides a lot of things from almost everyone. It's not just you. I only know his secrets because Randall does, and Bobby gave him his blessing to tell me if he wanted to. And the things he hides aren't things that reflect badly on him, they're just a lot."

"Hmm." I spit out my toothpaste and rinse my mouth. "So we're both hiding things about Bobby from each other, then?"

"I guess so. Because I'm not giving away his secrets, and I'm glad you're not either."

"Then why were you trying to drag it out of me?" I ask.

"Because I thought you were hiding that you two got it on. But now I know it's something personal about him, so I won't push. I'll respect his privacy."

"Um, 'getting it on' with someone *is* personal and private," I explain, "in case you're not aware."

Wendy flicks her wrist. "Yeah, but it's different. For example, I feel no violation of privacy in telling you the personal information that my husband and I got it on last night and again this morning." She doesn't even pause after that unnecessary declaration before changing the subject. "All right, you go get dressed, and I'll pack up your makeup bag to take with us. No point in putting any on yet."

I'm slipping on my shoes when Wendy comes out of the bathroom and says, "I thought it was interesting that Leslie's mom seated you between Bobby and Shannon last night."

She opens the door and motions for me to precede her through it.

"You think she did that on purpose?" I ask as we walk down the hall.

"I don't know. It was entertaining, though. Bobby's face was frownier than normal every time you talked to Shannon instead of him."

Why does her observation make my insides flutter?

Wendy says, "Be honest here. Do you like both of them? And if so, do you have a preference for one over the other? Because I have a feeling neither of them would turn you down."

I think about her question as we make our way out of the hotel. Shannon's a fun guy. He's easy to talk to, he's full of compliments, and I have no concerns about him, other than the fact that he recently got out of a relationship. Bobby, though? Red flag city. But regardless of Shannon's charm and extremely good looks, he doesn't make my insides flutter like Bobby does. His touch doesn't send sparks shooting along my skin. Shannon would be the safe choice, for sure. There's no doubt he would treat me well, and not only because Ash and Randall would kick his tail if he didn't. But is that all I'm looking for?

"You're thinking verrrry hard," Wendy says as we get in the car.

"I know. It's not an easy question to answer."

"At least give me your thoughts."

"First, tell me this: does Bobby have a girlfriend? Or even more than one girlfriend?"

Wendy turns to look at me before we take off. "You really think that man would share a bed with you two nights in a row if he has a girlfriend?"

I feel my face heating. "No." It's the truth. I've known it since yesterday, I just didn't want to admit it to myself, because that would mean he's free for me to date. And potentially dating that man scares me—in several ways.

"Good. And to be perfectly clear with my answer to your question, Bobby does not have any girlfriends at the moment. And I doubt he has ever dated more than one woman at a time— at least not seriously dated. He's not that kind of guy."

I nod. "What does it say about me that I thought he might be?"

"It says you're realistic and cautious, especially after what happened with Jeremy. Don't beat yourself up about it. Bobby's not an easy one to get to know. Now, tell me what you're thinking about both him and Shannon."

I explain my feelings about the two men while we head down the road toward Oakville.

"You deserve to be treated well," Wendy says. "But you also deserve flutters and sparks. You know Shannon doesn't provide that for you. And you don't know that Bobby wouldn't treat you well. In fact, I'm pretty sure he'd treat you like the queen you are. So I think you have your answer."

She's right.

I think we're done with the topic, but Wendy asks, "Have you told him about Jeremy?"

I sigh. "No. I had the perfect opening yesterday, but I didn't take it."

"Secret keeping seems to be the name of the game around here. You two need to do some serious talking. Today probably isn't the best time, but you'll be trapped in a car together all day tomorrow, so you'll have more than enough time to spill your guts to each other then."

As we get ready at Leslie's parents' house for the late-afternoon wedding, I try to push thoughts of Bobby from my head.

I'm not successful.

First of all, I can't get the feel of my hand on his bare chest out of my mind. Second, I really want to know what happened to him last night—what memories or trauma our near-accident brought back for him. Because that's undoubtedly what happened. There's a car accident in his past, and it was bad enough to cause a man as strong and determined as Bobby to shut down. Though I'm wondering why last night's incident sent him into panic mode but driving through a blizzard didn't.

A finger pokes into my side.

"Earth to Melissa," Leslie says in a robotic voice.

"Oh! Sorry. I was in my own little world. What did I miss?"

Leslie points to her auburn-haired cousin, who's been helping us get ready even though she's not in the wedding party. "Beckett mentioned she saw a shirtless man do the walk of shame from one hotel room to another this morning, and both rooms are on the wing we reserved for the wedding party and guests. Then Wendy tried to stifle a laugh and glanced your way." She cocks her head to the side. "What's that about? You have an overnight visitor?"

I could kill Wendy right about now. When I look at her, though, she shakes her head, letting me know she didn't say anything.

"I don't know anything about a walk of shame," I state confidently. It's not a lie. Nothing shameful happened in my hotel room last night. And even if she were right about what she thinks happened, I wouldn't find any shame in that, either.

"You sure?" Leslie asks. "Beckett's description of the man sounded a lot like a particular sports agent we all know and love. Well, we might not all love him, but we know him. And now I kinda want to see him with his shirt off." She pauses. "Don't tell my almost-husband I said that."

We all laugh.

"There's nothing to tell," I say. "Why are we talking about this anyway? This is your day! You're getting married! Wooooo!" I stand and shake my arms and hips.

The other ladies laugh and then all join in on the celebration, shouting and dancing and hip-bumping each other.

When we settle down again, Beckett asks Leslie, "What happened with Shannon and Christi? I didn't know they broke up until last night. I thought maybe Shannon had finally found the one."

"I don't know," Leslie says. "He hasn't told me what happened. He doesn't seem all that broken up about it, which I find weird, since they were together longer than he's ever dated anyone else. Granted, that was only about five months." She shrugs. "I'm worried about him, but there's nothing I can do about it if he won't talk to me."

Aunt Star clears her throat. "He talked to me about it."

"He did?" Leslie asks her aunt with a slight frown.

"Yes. I called him after your mom told me about the breakup, and I got him to open up. He felt guilty talking to me about it instead of to you, but he didn't want to bother you with your wedding coming up. And I won't break his confidence, but I will tell you not to worry. He'll be okay."

Tears glisten in Leslie's eyes. "You sure?"

"Yes." Aunt Star stands up and claps her hands together. "Now, let's dry your tears so Beckett can get your makeup finished. It's almost time!"

The wedding goes off without a hitch. Leslie looks radiant in her dress, which is fashioned after Scarlett O'Hara's "curtain dress" in *Gone With the Wind*. Our bridesmaid dresses are purple satin and of similar design, though the skirts aren't nearly as full. I'm thankful for that, as it would be difficult to dance in a skirt as full as Leslie's, and I fully intend to get my dance on at the reception.

Ash does cry when he says his vows, and he doesn't seem ashamed by it, which makes me proud of him. Bobby catches my eye a few times throughout the ceremony, and I hold his gaze for longer than would've seemed appropriate two days ago but seems normal now.

As we make our way down the aisle after the ceremony, he whispers, "Don't tell Leslie, but I much prefer the dress you wore last night."

"Your secret is safe with me," I murmur. "And I can say the same about your clothes. The pastel paisley isn't doing you any favors."

His laugh is a low rumble, and when I glance up at him, his dimple is on full display.

"I'm losing the bowtie and cummerbund the second we finish taking pictures."

"Wise move."

eighteen

. . .

Bobby

I can't keep my eyes off Melissa as she interacts with the wedding guests while they filter out of the church's sanctuary. Although her dress is borderline hideous in my opinion, she wears it well. Her brunette waves are pulled up into what Kelli would call an up-do, and my gaze keeps falling to her bare neck. For the first time in my life, I'm looking forward to a wedding reception, because it means I'll be able to get my arms back around Melissa during the wedding party dance. I don't know who I need to thank for pairing us up, but I'm grateful.

The photos take much longer than I think they should, but the photographer finally finishes up all the different poses Leslie requested, and we head down the street to the Oakville Community Center for the reception dinner and dance. Ash, Leslie, and the bridesmaids pile into cars for the five block trip, but the rest of us guys make the trek on foot, as the sun is out and it's not overly cold today.

Diego sidles up to me and asks, "You hanging in there? Have you talked to Kelli today?"

I run my fingers through my hair. "I called this morning. There's no change."

"I'm sorry, man."

"Yeah." I contemplate whether to tell him about the near accident last night.

"You going to answer my first question?" he asks.

I sigh. "I'm OK."

His eyes search my face. "You don't seem like it."

"I know. But I have to be OK. They need me to be."

"No, they don't. They may need you to be strong, but that doesn't mean you can't have feelings. You don't have to be OK."

"Yeah."

"What else?"

"What else what?" I don't look at him as we cross a street.

"There's something else you're not telling me."

My gaze cuts to him. "How do you do that?"

"I've known you a long time. I can tell when you're keeping something from me. Tell me. Is it about Melissa?"

I shake my head. "No." I pause. "Well, not directly. We almost had an accident last night." I run my fingers through my hair again. "I was driving. It was pitch black. There was a deer in the road, and I had to slam on the brakes to avoid it. I ... didn't handle it well."

Diego's hand lands on my shoulder. "What do you mean by that?"

We're almost at the community center, so I say, "I won't go into detail, but I basically shut down."

"How did Melissa respond to that?"

I don't need to think about my answer before simply saying, "Perfectly."

I decide to try to avoid Diego the rest of the night, because I don't want to talk about Kelli or Nanette or Melissa or what happened last night, and I know he won't leave any of it alone. Instead, I choose to stick by Melissa's side. I've seen a few guys eyeing her, and I don't like it. I also don't like that I'm feeling protective and possessive of someone who can never be mine, but I can't help it. After this wedding and the ride back to Chicago, I'm not sure when I'll see her again. I want to make the most of the time I have with her, even if it can't last beyond tomorrow.

And I don't feel bad keeping her from getting to know any of the single men here. None of them are from anywhere near Chicago, so there's not much of a chance she could make things work with any of them anyway. In fact, I'm doing her a service by not letting her get her hopes up. Right? Right.

Leslie chose to have a small head table at the reception, with only Randall and Wendy sitting with her and Ash. I'm happy with the setup, because that means I'm not on display to the entire room, and neither is Melissa.

She and I are assigned to a table with Wendy's half-sister Andrea along with her daughter and mom, as well as Shannon and his childhood friend Danny and Danny's wife Amelia. Somehow, I end up sitting next to seven-year-old Emily, who reminds me a lot of Kelli at that age—talkative and with a vocabulary well beyond her years.

"I know her," Emily says to me as she points at Melissa, who's sitting on my other side and chatting with Amelia. "She was in my aunt's wedding." She cocks an eyebrow at me. "You were in her wedding, too, weren't you?"

I nod. "I was."

Emily asks, "Is she your wife?" Before I can answer, she continues, "She's pretty. Is that why you married her? Uncle Randall says he married Aunt Glinda—that's what I call my aunt Wendy, because she reminds Uncle Randall of the good witch from *The Wizard of Oz*—anyway, he married her because she's pretty *and* she's smart *and* she knows how to put him in his place. I'm not sure where his place is, but that's what he says. So did you marry your wife because she's pretty or because she's smart or because she puts you in your place?"

She props her elbow on the round table and rests her chin on her hand as she waits expectantly for me to respond, and I can't help but grin at her and mimic her posture so we're facing each other.

I glance beyond her to her grandma and mom, who aren't paying any attention to us. In fact, they seem to be paying a lot of attention to Shannon, which doesn't bother me in the least, because he appears very preoccupied with Emily's pretty, red-haired mother, who looks like she could be Wendy's twin.

"Well ...?" Emily prompts, when I don't answer within two seconds.

I shake my head. "Melissa's not my wife." It shouldn't pain me to say those words, but it does.

"Hmm." Emily now taps her chin with her finger. "But she's pretty, right?"

There's no way I can stop my smile. "Indeed, she is."

"And she's smart?"

"She's that, too."

"Does she put you in your place?" Emily cocks an eyebrow at me at me again. I think it's her signature move.

I chuckle. "Sure does."

"Are you married to someone else?"

I'm not sure I can stop this line of questioning, but we're veering into dangerous territory. "Nope."

"Is *she* married to someone else?"

"She is not."

Emily pokes her finger into my chest. "Then you should marry her."

"He should marry who?" Melissa's voice interrupts our chat from behind me.

My face feels hot, and I don't turn to face her.

"You, silly!" Emily exclaims. "He thinks you're pretty." She ticks this off on one finger. "He says you're smart." She ticks another finger. "And you put him in his place!" Now she throws both arms wide. "It's a match made in heaven!"

In the silence following her declaration, I realize the entire table is watching us, and every single face holds a grin other than Melissa's, though she seems to be fighting one. I, on the other hand, feel a bit sick to my stomach.

"Honey," Emily's grandma says as she lays a hand on the little girl's shoulder, "let's take things down a notch, shall we?" To Melissa and me, she says, "Sorry about that. She's been really into weddings and people getting married ever since Wendy and Randall got engaged last summer."

"Tell me about it," Andrea mutters.

Emily's head whips around toward her mother. "What did you say, Mommy?"

Andrea's eyes go wide for a split second before she smirks at me and says, "I said, 'Tell me more about it.'"

"Oh, you mean more about why they should marry each other? Well, I don't know," Emily says. "That's all I know about Miss Melissa. Mr. Bobby, why else should you marry her?"

Thankfully the entire table erupts in laughter before Emily forces me to respond.

"You looked like a deer in the headlights," Shannon says through his laughter.

I feel like a cooler of ice water has been thrown over me as the memory of last night crashes back into my brain. Melissa's hand lands on my leg and squeezes just enough to pull me out of my head before anyone else has time to notice.

I force a smile and say, "Yeah, that's the first time I've been asked why I should marry a woman I barely even know."

Melissa's hand slips off my leg, and I immediately regret my words, although they're true. I glance at Melissa, who's looking down at her lap, and I know I need to course correct, even though I can hear my pulse in my ears and am hoping I'm not about to plunge back into panic mode.

I place my hand on the back of Melissa's chair and say, "However, over the last few days I've gotten to know her well enough to confidently say that in addition to being beautiful, smart, and assertive, Melissa is also thoughtful, caring, funny, and loyal. It'll be a lucky man who gets to watch her walk down the aisle to him someday."

Melissa's eyes shoot up to meet mine, and her cheeks flush pink. "Thank you," she says softly.

Emily claps her hands, and our focus shifts back to her beaming face. "It's gonna be you, Mr. Bobby! I just know it!"

"Okay, Emily. That's enough," Andrea says. "Why don't you tell everyone what we did for Christmas?"

As Emily chatters away about the holiday, I quietly leave the table and head toward the foyer. I need to step outside and get some fresh air to help calm my body's response to the deer-in-the-headlights comment. Okay, and also to thoughts of marrying Melissa. And to Melissa's touch and the look in her eyes after I complimented her.

As I suck in lungfuls of chilly air on the front steps of the building, the door opens behind me. I can smell Melissa before I see her.

"You okay?" Her arm slips around mine and her hand grips my bicep.

I look down at her with a small smile. "Better now."

She smiles back. "Good."

We gaze at each other for several seconds, and then she finally looks away and leans her body against mine.

"You don't have to go back in," she says. "We can go back to the hotel. Leslie and Ash will understand."

I don't miss how she said "we" instead of "you."

I shake my head. "They don't need to know what happened. I don't want them to worry about me. I'll be okay."

Melissa takes a breath as if she's going to speak, but then she doesn't.

"What?" I ask.

She tightens her hold on my arm. "You want to talk about last night? Will that help?"

I can't keep leaning on Melissa like this and not tell her what happened to make me this way. Though this isn't the ideal time or place, I need to tell her, and she's given me the opening I need. Goodness knows I won't initiate this conversation, but she deserves to have it with me. The more I'm around her, the more I want to try to make things work with her—for her. And I need to be honest with her about my family and my past if there's a chance that could happen.

"What are you two crazy kids up to?" Diego's voice booms from behind us, followed by a chuckle.

Melissa's arm drops from mine, and she spins to face him.

"Just getting some fresh air," she says as I turn to face my friend.

"Aren't you cold?" Diego asks Melissa before shooting me an

exasperated look. "Give the woman your jacket, man. What are you thinking?"

I wasn't thinking, obviously. But I quickly shrug out of my jacket and drape it around Melissa's shoulders.

nineteen

. . .

Melissa

Bobby's tuxedo jacket warms me instantly, and I grab the lapels to pull it more tightly around me, enveloping me not only in his body heat but also his delectable scent.

Diego and Bobby are having some sort of stare-down, and I look back and forth between the two of them.

"Any interest in saying out loud what you two seem to be saying with Jedi-like communication?" I ask.

Bobby's hand lands on the small of my back. "It's nothing you need to worry about," he says tersely. "Let's get back inside where it's warm."

He nudges me, and I move up the steps. Diego opens the door for us to walk through, and I glance back to catch him giving Bobby a smack on the back of the head. I raise my eyebrows at Diego, who graces me with a giant smile.

When we step back into the room, Leslie and Ash are at the cake table, ready to cut it. Bobby steers me that way so we can watch them feed each other cake, and once it's cut, he snags two plates and carries them back to the table for us. When he pulls his jacket off my shoulders and drapes it over the back of his chair, I feel a sense of loss.

Nobody else is at the table, so I ask, "You sure you're all right?"

Bobby nods. "As long as I have something else to focus on for a while, I'll get through it."

"Well, in a few minutes, you'll be able to focus on dancing." I pause. "You are going to dance, aren't you?"

"You think I don't dance?" He pops a bite of cake into his mouth.

I grin at him. "You don't really seem like a dancer."

He says around his bite of cake, "I guess you don't know everything about me, then."

I laugh. "Apparently you've never been taught not to speak with food in your mouth."

"Oh, I was taught." He swallows and smirks at me. "I just chose not to listen."

Emily's head pops between ours. "Whatcha talkin' about?"

Bobby scoots his chair away from mine a few inches and turns sideways in his seat so he can partly face Emily as she places her plate of cake on the table between us.

"Dancing and cake and societal rules," he answers.

"What's sietal rules?" Emily asks.

"Polite stuff you have to do when you're around other people," he responds. He's shockingly good at speaking with a young child.

Emily nods and forks a bite of cake into her mouth before replying, "Like not picking your nose or tooting in front of other people."

Bobby barks out a laugh before he can stop it, and I giggle.

"Yes." Bobby ruffles her hair. "Like that." He shoots a smile my way. "As well as not talking with your mouth full of food."

Emily covers her mouth with her hand. "Oops!"

"It's okay, honey," I say. Then I whisper loudly, "Mr. Bobby just did it, too."

She giggles and then says, "Mr. Bobby, will you dance with me when the dancing part starts?"

He gives Emily the sweetest smile I've ever seen on his handsome face. "Of course I will, as long as your mom says it's OK. I bet you're a good dancer."

"I'm the best! But first you have to dance with Miss Melissa." She gives us each a sly grin. "I bet she's a good dancer, too."

Bobby chuckles. "I think you're probably right about that. With your mom's approval, you'll get my second dance of the night, okay?"

Emily nods. "Yep. And then I'm going to dance with Uncle Randall and then Mr. Ash and then Mr. Shannon."

Bobby's eyebrows go up. "You have a full dance card. I'm honored to be on it."

Emily's nose scrunches up. "I don't have a dance card. Do I need a card? Where's my card?"

"It's just a saying now," Bobby says. "Though a long time ago, women did have a card they carried around where they'd write down the names of the men who wanted to dance with them."

How does he know that?

"Like as long ago as the people in *Dirty Dancing?*" Emily asks.

Bobby's eyebrows now nearly meet his hairline. "You've seen *Dirty Dancing?*"

Emily's face falls. "No. Mommy won't let me watch it." Then her face brightens. "But I love the music! We have the soundtrack."

"I love the soundtrack, too," I say. "What's your favorite song on it?"

"'Hey Baby' is my favorite." She claps in excitement. "What's yours?"

"'I've Had the Time of My Life,'" I say.

"I'm partial to 'She's Like the Wind,'" Bobby shares.

My jaw drops, but Emily nods seriously and says, "That's a good one, too."

"You're just full of surprises, aren't you?" I ask Bobby.

"I told you you don't know everything about me."

When the dance finally begins, Ash and Leslie dance to "Endless Love" to kick things off, and there are few dry eyes in the room before the song ends. The song is so perfect for the two of them.

The music then fades into REO Speedwagon's "Can't Fight This Feeling," and the DJ calls the rest of the wedding party onto the dance floor. I almost miss the wink Leslie gives me as Bobby leads me out into the open space.

Bobby pulls me against him, and my arms loop around his neck as his hands rest on my waist.

"Did Leslie wink at you?" he asks, lips twitching. I'm not sure if he's trying to suppress a frown or a smile.

"I believe she did." My heart begins to race, and I wonder if he can feel it. He has pulled me so tightly against him, he very well could. Not that I'm complaining about our close proximity.

He sweeps an escaped lock of hair behind my ear, and the imprint of his touch lingers on my skin.

"What's that about?" he asks.

I search his eyes. Does he not know? Have his friends not been trying to push him toward me as well? Is he not aware of what this song is about?

I take a deep breath and decide to go for it. It may lead to a ridiculously awkward drive home tomorrow, but I feel like I'd regret not doing this more than I'd regret doing it and getting shot down.

"Listen to the lyrics," is all I say as I look directly into his eyes.

Bobby leans his head around so his lips brush my ear, and a shiver runs all the way to my toes.

He whispers, "I know the lyrics."

My eyes close, and we sway back and forth to the music a few more seconds before I reply, "You do?"

"Yes. They played this for us, didn't they?"

Every time his lips touch my ear and his five o'clock shadow brushes against my jawline, my legs grow a little weaker as my heart speeds up past the limit of what can possibly be healthy.

"I-I think so."

My eyes open in alarm when his face moves away from mine, but when I see the heated look in his eyes, I know I'm not alone in what I'm feeling.

"Are you done fighting the feeling?" he asks.

He grips my waist even more tightly than he already was, as if he senses I can't support my own weight at the moment. It's not surprising, since I've stopped swaying.

"Are you?" I reply, and I hold my breath as I wait for his answer.

"The oars are gone, baby."

Oh. My. Word. I've always rolled my eyes when I've read about women swooning, but suddenly I can relate.

twenty

. . .

Bobby

I want to kiss Melissa so badly right now it physically pains me not to do so, but I don't want our first kiss to be in front of a few hundred people. Not all of them are paying attention to the two of us, but when I glanced around before I first pulled her into my arms, I noticed most of the rest of the wedding party's eyes were glued to us, and I knew exactly why. But right now, I only have eyes for the woman in my arms, whose body I'm currently supporting while we both consider the potential impact of what we just revealed to each other.

Deep down, I know this is a bad idea. There's a reason I don't get close to women, especially those I really like. My life is not conducive to a relationship—especially not a long-distance one— and I can't imagine how it ever will be. I don't want to hurt Melissa, but I also don't think I can stop whatever is happening between us.

"As soon as this song is over," Melissa murmurs when she regains her ability to hold herself up and begins swaying again, "we're finding ourselves a quiet corner," she pauses, "of an empty room."

I let out a belly laugh. That was not what I expected her to say, but I'm all for it. Except for one thing.

"I'm sorry to disappoint you," I say, and I don't miss the brief flicker of dismay in her eyes, "but I've already promised the next dance to another lady."

Confusion fills her gaze for a second before a smile spreads across her face. "Of course. You can't disappoint Emily." She peers over her shoulder. "You think she's watching us?"

I chuckle. "There's no doubt in my mind she hasn't taken her eyes off us, and I'll be getting an earful from her in a minute about what she thinks she's seen."

One of Melissa's hands slides up into my hair, and her fingernails lightly scratch my scalp, sending electricity down my spine. "And what do you think she thinks she's seen?" she asks flirtatiously.

"A man who has stopped fighting his feelings," I readily admit, "but who is also very much fighting his desire to kiss you right here and now."

"Thanks for fighting that," she says. "Not that I don't want you to kiss me, but I'm afraid we'd get a rousing round of applause from our friends if we did it here and now."

I glance away from Melissa for a second and then back. "Wendy looks like she's about to pull half the muscles in her face, her smile is so big."

Melissa giggles. "I believe that one hundred percent."

As the song draws to a close, I reluctantly release her waist, but then I take her hand and lead her back to our table. "Don't go too far," I whisper in her ear as I straighten and smile at Emily.

Wendy intercepts me as I take a step away from Melissa and toward the little girl.

"Where do you think you're going?" Wendy demands.

I shrug. "I promised the next dance to another lady."

"B-but—" she sputters.

I give Andrea a questioning look, and she nods her head, giving me permission to dance with her daughter. Then I hold my free hand out toward Emily who, as expected, is watching Melissa and me with wide eyes and an even wider grin. She skips over to me and takes my hand.

"You kids have fun!" Melissa says.

There's nothing I can do to stop the urge to kiss Melissa's

cheek, so I lean down and press my lips just shy of her mouth, and Emily squeals in response before dragging me out onto the dance floor as "Hey Baby" starts playing.

She stops in her tracks, turns to me with giant eyes, and says, "This is my favorite! How did they know?"

I hide my smile, not wanting her to know I talked to the DJ and requested the song just for her. "I guess it's fate!" I twirl her around and take both of her little hands in mine. "So, Miss Emily, how are we going to do this?" I ask. "Do you want to stand on my shoes, do you want me to pick you up, or do you want to dance on your own two feet?"

She holds her arms up. "Pick me up, please. It'll be easier to talk to you that way."

Of course she wants to talk.

"Your wish is my command, my lady."

Emily giggles as I lift her up, and once she's settled on my right hip with her right hand in my left, she waggles her little eyebrows at me.

"I saw you dancing with Miss Melissa. You liiiiiike her!"

"Maybe I do, maybe I don't," I hedge, trying to act nonchalant as I dance her across the floor.

She gives one firm nod. "You do. I know these things."

"Do you?"

"Yep. I'm good with love stuff."

My lips twitch. "Love stuff?"

"Uh-huh. I can tell when people are in love because they get this funny look on their face. Like this."

I do my best not to laugh when she widens her eyes multiple times and grins maniacally.

"That's what love looks like, huh?" I ask.

"It is." She pauses. "Can I tell you a secret?"

"I love secrets." Too much, especially when I'm the one keeping them.

"Promise you won't tell aaaaanybody?"

"Pinky promise." I wrap my pinky finger around hers.

Emily giggles. "You know how to pinky promise?"

"I do."

"How do you know?"

I cock my head at her. "Can *you* keep a secret?" Somehow I think she can and honestly, I'm tired of keeping Kelli a secret from people who mean something to me. I'm going to tell Melissa about her just as soon as I can get her alone. But I can't chance having Emily say anything before I do. Melissa needs to hear it from me. "You can't tell anybody, okay?"

"Yes, tell me, tell me!"

"And then you'll tell me your secret?" I ask.

"I pinky promise I'll tell you my secret!" She giggles.

"I know how to pinky promise because my little girl taught me."

She looks at me in awe. "You have a little girl?" She looks around. "Where is she? Is she here? Why wasn't she sitting with us?"

"I do have a little girl. Well, she's not so little anymore, but she was little not very long ago. And she's not here. She's with her mom in California."

Emily purses her lips as she digests this information. "Her mom isn't your wife?"

"No." I wonder how many more questions I'll get about this.

"That's okay. My mommy isn't my dad's wife, either."

I don't know much about the situation with Emily's dad—just that he's not in the picture at the moment.

"Does that make you sad?" I ask her.

"No." She shakes her head. "I haven't seen him since I was a baby, so I don't miss him. But I wish I had a daddy who wants to live with me and who loves me more than anybody in the world except my mommy. He can love her more."

My heart breaks for this little girl, and I hope she gets her wish someday soon, and I tell her as much. "I want you to have a daddy who loves you and wants to live with you, too."

Emily asks me bluntly, "Is your little girl sad that you're not married to her mom?"

"No. She lives with me part of the time and knows I love her more than anybody in the world."

She gives me a contemplative look. "But maybe someday you'll love Melissa more than her?"

I shake my head. "No. I'll never love anyone more than I love Kelli. But that doesn't mean I can't love someone else in a different way and just as much as I love Kelli. Loving your child is a different kind of love than loving someone you want to marry." I feel the need to add, "Your mom will always love you as much as or more than anyone else. You know that, right?" I don't know Andrea well, but I know enough to be sure what I'm telling her daughter is true.

"Yeah." She sighs and leans her head against my shoulder. "But I still want a daddy."

Tears prick behind my eyes as I hold Emily tightly against me. "I know," I say as I press my cheek to her soft hair.

We dance in silence for a few seconds before I say, "Hey, you never told me your secret."

Emily's head pops back off my shoulder. "Oh, yeah!" She looks around in what I assume she thinks is a stealthy manner and then whispers, "You know that love look we talked about?"

She makes the hilarious face, and I stifle my laugh yet again.

"Yeah?"

"I saw Mr. Shannon give that look to my mommy when she wasn't looking."

My eyebrows shoot up. "Oh, you did?" This kid is perceptive. I saw the same thing, though Shannon made sure Andrea didn't see it. Apparently he didn't pay as much attention to where her daughter's focus lay.

"Yep." She pops the "p" as she says it.

"Did you tell your mom?" I ask.

"Nuh-uh."

"Why not?"

"Because I don't think he wanted her to see it. When she looked at him, his face went like this."

She gives me the most serious look she can muster, and this time I do laugh.

"So you're keeping Mr. Shannon's secret?"

"I am, but he doesn't even know it."

"Do you like Mr. Shannon?"

Emily's head bobs up and down, making her red curls bounce. "I do. He's nice." She thinks for a minute before continuing, "I think I'd like it if he was my daddy someday."

"I bet he would make a great daddy." I truly mean it, and for both Emily's sake and Andrea's, I hope he doesn't keep fighting his feelings.

twenty-one

. . .

Melissa

"Spill every last one of your beans," Wendy demands as I watch Emily pull Bobby onto the dance floor.

My eyes can't leave the two of them. He's so sweet with her, I can barely stand it. Then I register what song is playing, and I feel like my heart is going to explode. He had to have asked the DJ to play "Hey Baby," because the timing is too perfect for a coincidence.

Wendy's fingers snap in front of my face, and I turn to look at her as her focus shifts back to the dancing, and the hand that was just in front of my face is now pressed over her heart. I look back at the dance floor, where Bobby has picked Emily up and is now dancing her across the floor as they have an animated discussion. I'm pretty sure I know what they're discussing.

"Look at them," Wendy says. *"Look at them!"*

"I'm looking." I move to the nearest table without taking my eyes off Bobby and Emily, and I plop down into a chair.

"That might just be the most precious thing I have ever seen in all my years," Wendy states as she drags a chair next to mine and takes a seat.

"I …," I have trouble finding the words to describe what I'm feeling. "I'm floored by the way he interacts with her. It's like he's known her forever. Until tonight, I never had one thought of

Bobby interacting with a small child, but *look* at him. He's going to make a great dad someday."

"Mmhm," is Wendy's only response.

As we watch them in rapt silence, their discussion seems to turn serious, and my eyes fill with tears when her little head lays down on his shoulder and he rests his cheek on her hair.

"I'm pretty sure every woman in the room is getting pregnant just from watching that," Wendy says, breaking my reverie.

I burst into laughter. "That's the weirdest thing I've ever heard you say. And you say some weird stuff."

"I'll take that as a compliment," Wendy says as she turns to face me. "Okay, now spill."

I shrug. "In a nutshell, we stopped fighting our feelings."

Wendy's hands shoot up to cover her mouth as she screams, and then she leans over to wrap me in a hug. "Yesssss! I knew it!"

"I don't want to move too fast, though," I say. "We both need to share the things we've been holding back from one another. I know you said I can handle whatever he's going to tell me, but you might not know everything. And what if he doesn't like what I have to tell him about what happened with Jeremy?"

Wendy places a hand on mine. "I think he'll be understanding about everything, but you won't know until you lay it all out there. And you're right, I probably don't know all the details of what he's keeping from you. But I think if you keep an open mind and remember what you know about the kind of man he is, it'll work out. There might be some bumps—who am I kidding, there *will* be some bumps—but if you think he's worth it, you can get through it."

We look back at Bobby and Emily. He has now set her on her feet, he's twirling her around, and her head is thrown back in laughter.

"I can't even take it!" Wendy says dramatically with her hand pressed to her chest again. "They are so totally adorable."

When the song ends, Bobby takes Emily's hand and escorts her to Randall, who is sitting at the table next to ours talking to Diego. I wonder how much of our conversation the two men overheard.

I don't have much time to contemplate it, though, because Bobby then comes directly to me, holds his hand out and says, "Let's go get some air."

As I stand, Wendy says with a snort, "Air. Is that what the kids are calling it these days?" Then she laughs like a hyena as we walk away, shaking our heads at her.

Bobby wordlessly leads me out into the lobby and checks out the options. An open door leads down a hallway toward the kitchen, but it's not private. Another short hallway leads to the bathrooms. Our only other option inside the building is a closed door. Bobby looks around to ensure we're alone before trying the knob. It opens, and he pulls me into the dimly lit space before shutting the door behind me.

We're in an office with a small window. I don't have time to notice anything else before Bobby turns and presses my back against the closed door. He dips his head so he can look directly into my eyes.

"Last chance to back out," he says gruffly with his lips mere inches away from mine. He moves his hands so they're braced on the door on either side of my head. Being trapped has never felt so good.

"I'm not backing anywhere," I say as I crook my index fingers into his belt loops and pull him into me. "I dare you to kiss me."

But he doesn't.

Instead, he clears his throat. "There are some things you need to know about me."

"Yes," I say as I let go of his pants and run my hands up his abs and chest until they're resting on his broad shoulders. "And there are some things you need to know about me. But there will be plenty of time to discuss all that on our drive home." I move my hands to the back of his neck and pull his head toward mine. "Dare tonight, truth tomorrow."

His lips finally meet mine, and I sigh into him. I expect intensity, but that's not what I get. He peppers tiny kisses across my top lip and then my bottom one, and my legs go limp again. One of his hands shoots down to my hip to support me, and the other wraps around the back of my neck as he continues placing small kisses along my jawline and up to my ear. I shudder in his arms, and I'm not at all embarrassed by it. In fact, I tilt my head to the side, offering him more surface area to cover with his soft, searching lips.

"Melissa," he whispers almost reverently as he kisses his way down my neck and back up. By now I'm breathing so heavily I wouldn't be surprised if anyone walking through the lobby could hear me.

"Bobby," I whimper as my fingers grasp at his short hair. "Stop torturing me."

"Doesn't feel like torture to me," he murmurs between kisses. "Feels like heaven." His tongue flicks against the spot right below my earlobe where I dab my perfume. "Tastes like it too."

I stifle a groan. "This isn't what I meant when I dared you to kiss me."

"Maybe not." His mouth moves so he can whisper in my ear. "But I'm enjoying it immensely."

Though I can't contradict him, I'm getting impatient, so I bracket his head with my hands and forcefully bring his lips to mine. A laugh rumbles through him before he kisses me the way I really want him to.

twenty-two

. . .

Bobby

I knew kissing Melissa would be amazing, but life-changing now seems a more appropriate way to describe it. I have never felt such a strong physical connection with anyone. Whether it's because of all we've been through over the past two days or because she's simply special, I don't know. But it doesn't matter.

Her hands are trailing over my chest and abs, and mine are itching to explore more of her soft curves, but I restrain myself considering our location and the fact that before I can take this any further with her, I need to tell her everything. She deserves a chance to back out before she does anything she might regret. I'm hoping she won't have any misgivings over what we're doing now.

Loud voices from the lobby bring me back to reality, and I end the kiss and pull my face far enough away from Melissa's to look her in the eye.

"You good?" I ask.

"Better than good," she replies and gives me another short kiss that I turn into a longer one. "That's my favorite game of 'Truth or Dare' ever."

"I don't recall you giving me the truth option," I say with a grin. "In fact, you refused me that option."

"Okay, fine. It was the best game of 'Dare' ever."

"Agreed." I press my mouth to hers one more time before stepping back and pulling her away from the door.

Melissa's hands go to her hair. "How's my hair? Is it a mess? Does it say, 'I just made out in a closet like a teenager'?"

I maneuver a few errant strands back into place. "It says, 'I'm the most beautiful woman here.'" I pause. "Don't tell the bride I said that."

She blushes and laughs. "I'm keeping a lot of secrets from Leslie for you. Anything else you need to add to the growing list?"

"Is it too much to ask for you to not tell her about what just happened here?"

Melissa nods. "Yep. I think it's only fair she hears about my 'Seven Minutes in Heaven' session with you. You know, to make up for the last time I played that game … with her husband." Her cheeks turn slightly pink.

"I get it. You can tell your friends about this, because goodness knows Diego will pull it out of me. But maybe don't share the details."

She places her hand on my chest and kisses my chin. "The details are just for us." She swipes her thumb over my lips. "Had a little lipstick there, B.S."

I smile, take her hand in mine, and lead her out of the room, only to be met by the triumphant faces of both Wendy and Randall. They're not even pretending they weren't waiting for us to come out.

Wendy makes a show of looking at her husband's watch. "Do you two have any idea how long you were in there?"

Melissa and I look at each other and shrug at the same time before looking back at our friends.

"Seventeen minutes!" Wendy crows.

My lips twitch. "Well, you know what they say about time flying."

Randall lets out a belly laugh. "Sure do." He puts his arm around his wife and steers her back toward the main room. "Come on, babe, let's leave them alone."

"Were we really in there for seventeen minutes?" Melissa asks me once they're gone.

"I guess so. That seems like a very specific number to make up." And it doesn't seem like nearly enough time.

As the women do the Electric Slide on the dance floor, my friends descend upon my table.

Diego speaks first. "So it's official, then?"

"Is what official?" I ask casually before sipping my drink.

"You and Melissa, doofus," Randall replies. "Don't play dumb with us."

I look at Ash, who has yet to speak, and he shrugs.

"Melissa and I are … actually, I don't know what we are." I know what I want us to be, but I have little faith that can actually happen. Once she knows the extent of my past and my family situation, she may well run, and rightfully so.

"But you want to be something with her?" Ash asks.

I nod. "Yeah, but I haven't told her about Kelli and Nanette or much about my childhood yet."

"I know you don't like to talk about any of that stuff," Randall says, "but you know you have to tell her, right? And sooner rather than later."

"I know. And I will. I tried to earlier, but she wanted to wait until the drive tomorrow so we'll have plenty of time to talk about it." I pause. "Could make for an awkward twelve hours, though, if she decides she doesn't want to deal with the craziness that is my life."

"I don't think you need to worry about that," Randall says. "She'll understand. I'm not saying I'm sure she'll want to take it all on as part of her life, too, but she won't hold it against you as a person. She won't let it be awkward."

"Melissa is good people," Diego says. "And so are you. Lay it all out there."

"I will." I look between Randall and Ash. "Not to be a downer at a wedding, but you should know Nanette is having headaches again."

"Oh, man, I'm sorry," Randall says.

Ash simply claps a hand on my shoulder and squeezes.

"I've said it before and I will say it again as many times as I need to," Diego says. "Not your fault."

"But I was driving," I say, knowing what the response will be. We've had this conversation too many times. I'm surprised he's not tired of it. Maybe he is.

"You followed the rules of the road," Randall says. "The other guy didn't. There was nothing you could've done."

"I could've been paying better attention." I drop my head into my hands. "If I had, I might've seen that he wasn't slowing down."

"I know you feel responsible," Ash says, "and that says a lot about your character. But you're wrong. Nothing about what happened that night was your fault."

"And what you've done for Nanette since then has gone waaaaay above and beyond," Randall says. "That says even more about your character. No woman worth her salt is going to think any differently—especially Melissa."

"Yeah." I sigh. "Okay." These guys always make me feel better, even if I don't fully agree with their assessment of the situation.

"They're playing another slow song," Randall says as he stands. "Let's go get our ladies."

"Hey," Diego says, "what about me? You can't leave me here all alone!"

"Andrea's mom looks a little lonely," Randall tells him with a wink. "And we know how much you love older women."

We all chuckle as we leave the table. Unsurprisingly, Diego makes a beeline for Andrea's mom. The man could charm the pants off an octopus, so the lady isn't going to know what hit her.

"How much longer do we need to stay?" I murmur in Melissa's ear an hour later as I hold her closely on the dance floor while

Lionel Richie sings "Three Times a Lady." Shannon took to the microphone to announce this dance was dedicated to Danny and Amelia, followed by whoops from several of the guests, so I'm guessing there's a story behind it. However, I'm too focused on the lady in my arms to wonder much about what that story might be.

"Dying to get your mouth on mine again?" Melissa teases.

"You'd better believe it."

Her giggle nearly takes my breath away.

"It's almost midnight," she says, "and I think Ash and Leslie are leaving right after the countdown to the new year. But since we have a long drive tomorrow, I don't think anyone would fault us for leaving soon after that. Ash hired people to clean up in the morning, so none of us will need to stay and help."

"Just so you know," I clear my throat, "I'm not spending the night in your room again."

Melissa nods. "That's probably a good idea. We need to talk before we take this any further."

My chest aches at the thought that things might not go further.

She adds, "I have some things I need to share with you, too."

"We'll have plenty of time to talk things over tomorrow. But you should also know I need to head to L.A. as soon as we get back. There's some stuff I need to take care of there. I'll be back in Chicago in a week or so, though." That timeline may be wishful thinking, depending on what's happening with Nanette, but we can also discuss that tomorrow.

"I understand," she says. "I know you're a busy man, and I also know we don't live in the same city or even time zone. That won't make things easy for us, but I don't want that to stop us from trying." She peeks at me through her lashes. "Do you?"

I run a hand up and down her back. "No. And again, we'll have plenty of time to figure out how to work things out on our drive tomorrow."

The song ends and the DJ announces, "It's almost midnight, folks. Grab your partner for one last slow dance before we count down to 1989, and then we'll send the newlyweds on their way!" Within seconds, "Always" by Atlantic Starr fills the room.

Seeing as it's New Year's Eve, most of the wedding guests have stayed until midnight, though the kids and the older crowd are both fading. A while ago I spotted Emily snoozing on her grandma's lap, and as I keep Melissa cocooned safely in my arms, I scan the room for Andrea. I'm unsurprised when I spy her slow dancing with Shannon.

Without thinking, I start singing along to the song, and Melissa laughs softly.

"You continue to surprise me, Bobby Joe."

I tilt my head and smile at her. "Yeah?"

"Yeah." She tightens her hold on my neck. "Who would've guessed you'd know the lyrics to this song?"

It's one of Kelli's favorites, but I can't tell her that—not yet.

"I like to keep you on your toes."

"I like *you*." She surprises me with a quick kiss.

"I like you, too. You want to go get ice cream with me after school?" I tease.

Melissa lets out a belly laugh. "I'm always up for ice cream."

"What flavor?"

"Butter pecan. It's the only rational choice."

"I'll have to respectfully disagree. Mint chocolate chip is the superior option."

"Hmm." She presses her lips together as she peruses me. "Agree to disagree?"

"Nope. It's objectively true that mint chocolate chip is the best ice cream flavor."

"Ah, you're bringing out the big words now, Mr. Lawyer."

"Pssh." I huff. "'Objectively' is small potatoes. Try this one: antidisestablishmentarianism."

She snorts. "You're a nut."

"I hope I'm a pecan, since you seem to enjoy those so much." My foray into flirting is surprising to me, but I have to admit, I'm enjoying it.

Melissa sifts the tips of her fingers through the hair at the nape of my neck. "You truly are a surprising man, my little pecan."

I quirk an eyebrow at her. "Little?"

She giggles. "You'd rather be a big pecan?"

"The biggest."

"All right, giant pecan, are you ready to kiss me again? Because this song is almost over, and it's less than a minute til midnight."

"You'd better believe it."

As soon as the crowd shouts, "Happy new year!" my mouth is on Melissa's. I don't want to make a scene in this crowd, but I also want this to be a memorable kiss, so I put my heart into it. By the way her mouth responds and her fingernails dig into my scalp, I'd say I accomplish my goal. After much too short a time, I pull my lips from hers. We smile at each other for several seconds before I feel a tug on my shirtsleeve. When I look down, Emily is beaming up at us.

"Happy new year, Mr. Bobby and Miss Melissa!"

We both return her greeting.

"I saw you kissing!" Emily's hands cover her mouth as she giggles.

"You sure about that?" I reach down and lightly tug on one of her curls.

She nods emphatically. "Yep! My friends think kissing is gross, but I don't. I can't wait until a boy kisses me." She clasps her little hands under her chin the same way her aunt Wendy does.

Melissa laughs.

"Oh, boy," I say, my eyes scanning for her mother. "Let's not jump into kissing too soon, short stuff. Why don't you save that until you're older?"

"Like when I'm nine?"

I shake my head at her. "Maybe when you're twenty."

Her jaw drops. "I'm not waiting until I'm *old* to kiss a boy!"

Thankfully the DJ interrupts this line of conversation. "It's time to say our goodbyes to Mr. and Mrs. Hamilton! Everyone please make your way to the lobby and the steps out front, and make sure to grab some birdseed from one of the baskets by the doors."

"Birdseed instead of rice?" I raise an eyebrow as I take Melissa's hand in one of mine and Emily's in the other as we move toward the doors. I catch Emily's grandma's eye over the crowd of people and mouth to her that I've got her granddaughter. She smiles, and I grin back when I notice Diego at her side. I wonder if he kissed her at midnight. I can't imagine he didn't kiss anyone.

"Yeah, somebody somewhere said if birds eat rice their stomachs will explode," Melissa explains, "so people have started throwing birdseed instead of rice at weddings."

"Ew, that's gross!" Emily declares as she skips along by my side, having gotten her second—or maybe third—wind.

I reply, "You'd think we'd see exploded birds littering the ground after every wedding if that's the case."

Melissa laughs as we each grab a small bundle of material that apparently hold the birdseed. "I hadn't thought about that, but you're right."

"Regardless," I say, "I'm sure it's better for birds to eat birdseed than rice, so it's not a bad idea. You think it'll catch on everywhere?"

She cocks her head at me, "You're thinking about buying stock in a birdseed company, aren't you?"

"Maybe." I don't have much time to stay on top of the stock market, but I'm going to talk to my broker about this and see what he thinks.

"What's 'buying stock'?" Emily asks.

"That's something else you can wait a while to experience."

We reach the outside steps and open our bundles of seed.

"Ooo! Here they come," Emily says. "Get ready!"

twenty-three

. . .

Melissa

After we send Ash and Leslie off on their honeymoon, it takes us longer to leave the reception than I'd anticipated. Since I've gotten to know both Ash and Leslie's extended families over the past eight months, there are a lot of people I need to say goodbye to.

Finally, Bobby growls in my ear. "We need to go. I want you alone for a bit, and then we both need a few good hours' sleep before hitting the road."

I swat his chest. "When did you turn into such a dad?" Then I grin. "Oh, wait," I say teasingly. "It's because you're so old, right?"

I can't decipher the flicker in his eyes before he gives me a pained smile and says, "Yep, that's it. Middle-aged man over here. I need at least one nap a day and eight hours of sleep every night."

"Hey," I say softly and lay my hand on his chest. "I was only teasing. I'm sorry if I offended you."

"No," he says as he places his hand over mine. "You didn't. It's been a long couple of days, and I truly am tired. Is there anyone else you absolutely need to talk to before we go?"

"There's not," I reply as I grasp his hand and pull him toward the door. "Let's go."

Bobby chuckles as he trails behind me. "Is your car here, or is it at the church?"

"It's here." I dig the keys out of my clutch. "It's been a few hours since my only glass of wine of the night, so I'm OK to drive, unless you want to." I noticed he didn't drink any alcohol tonight, and I wondered if there was a connection between that and what happened on the road last night. I purposely didn't drink much myself in case I needed to drive us back to the hotel.

"You go ahead," he says in a light tone. It's too dark to see his eyes and determine how he's truly feeling about driving. "But I'll take the first shift in the morning."

"Are we going to make out here or in one of our rooms?" I ask Bobby as I pull the car into a spot in the hotel's parking lot.

A burst of laughter escapes him. "You're not one to beat around the bush, are you?"

"No reason to. You want to kiss me. I want to kiss you. The only question is where?"

"Well, I'll start with your mouth," he says in an amused tone. "And then I might move to—"

I swat his arm. "OK, OK, let's leave a little air of mystery around what's going to happen." I grin at him. "But at which physical location would you like to do this kissing?"

"It's probably safest to do it here," he says and turns his body toward me as much as he can in my small car. "We might get caught, especially since Randall, Wendy, and Diego haven't made their way back here yet. But I don't think it's a good idea to go to either of our rooms together if we want to get any sleep tonight."

"Agreed," is my only reply.

He reaches one hand over and cups my face, stroking my lips with his thumb. I lean into his palm and close my eyes, waiting to see what he'll do next.

"Open your eyes and come over here," he says as his hand leaves my face.

My eyes flutter open, and he pats his lap.

"Come on. I'll help, but it'll be easier if you're involved in the process instead of me just hauling you over here."

I don't comment on the fact that he hauled me over the same space last night, but in the other direction. This isn't the time to bring up anything about that situation.

Turns out it's not as easy to get out from under the steering wheel in a long dress as I thought it'd be. It takes some tugging, contorting, and giggling, but I finally make my way onto his lap, with my feet extended onto the driver's seat.

"That would've been much easier if I'd just gotten out and walked around," I say.

"Yeah." He tugs a strand of my hair. "But not nearly as fun. Now, where were we?"

"Well," I say as I wrap a hand around the nape of his neck. "I think you were about to start kissing me on the mouth and then possibly moving on to—"

I can't finish my sentence because his mouth is on mine. It's on mine for a *long time.* Long enough that my rear end falls asleep from the odd angle I'm sitting on it, and I try to readjust my position.

"Stop wiggling," Bobby grits out.

"What? My butt's asleep. I need to get some feeling back into it."

"Just … don't." He briefly closes his eyes. "It's probably best for us to get out. It's a little cramped in here."

I smirk at him. "You weren't complaining about that ten seconds ago."

He chuckles. "I most certainly was not. But now that I'm thinking about it, I'm getting a little claustrophobic *and,*" he states, "that has nothing to do with the company, so don't even think it."

"Yes, sir." I giggle. "Or do I mean no, sir?"

Bobby takes a deep breath and shakes his head at me. "You're killing me. Now, lean in so when I open the door, you don't fall out."

Getting out of the car is almost as difficult and entertaining as making my way onto his lap was, since I'm facing away from the door. When we're both finally on our feet, a slow clap starts up behind us. I whirl around and am not surprised to see Wendy, Randall, and Diego's beaming faces. Diego is the one clapping.

I point back and forth between Bobby and Diego. "Don't you dare speak Spanish to each other right now."

"I'll say it in English, then," Wendy proclaims. *"Bravo!"* She claps quickly a few times and then laughs. "Oh, wait. That's Italian."

Bobby's arm slips around me, and he pulls me in front of him and loops both arms around my torso. "Show's over, folks. Some privacy would be appreciated."

"Spoilsport," Wendy says, as her husband tugs her toward the hotel lobby doors.

"Come on, Diego," Randall orders, "let's give them some privacy."

As they go, Bobby turns me so we're facing each other, and my hands land on his chest. He suggests, "Let's say goodnight out here instead of in the hallway where we could be overheard."

"I heard that!" Wendy calls.

"My point exactly!" Bobby yells back, resulting in a peal of laughter from our friend. "Get on inside, eavesdroppers!"

I peek over my shoulder to make sure they're out of sight before saying, "I had a really good time tonight. And last night. And yesterday. And the day before."

Bobby's arms tighten around me and he gives me a quick peck on the lips. "Ditto."

"All I get is a ditto and a tiny kiss?" I tease. I almost poke his chest but then remember that's not good for my finger, so I refrain.

"I had a *stupendous* time tonight. And last night. And yesterday. And the day before." He gives me a lingering kiss between each time frame he mentions.

I sigh. "That's more like it."

"I have a feeling we'll also have an excellent time tomorrow. I just wish I didn't need to head to L.A. as soon as we get back."

"Me, too. But we can talk on the phone." I tilt my head. "We should probably exchange phone numbers, huh?"

"We'll definitely do that tomorrow. Now, kiss me one more time, and then we'll head inside."

twenty-four

. . .

Bobby

The red light is blinking on my hotel room phone when I enter the room after saying goodnight to Melissa one final time outside her room. I pick it up and dial 0 to call the front desk to see what the message is. The clerk tells me my daughter called about five hours ago and I should call her back immediately at the number she left.

My fingers shake as I dial the number I don't recognize, and my heart leaps into my throat when the person on the other end answers, "UCLA Medical Center Emergency Department. How may I help you?"

"I'm returning a call from Kelli Jacobs. Is she there? Or Nanette Jacobs? I don't know what's going on, and I need to know right now!" I'm in full-on lawyer mode.

"Sir, I understand you're upset, but yelling at me isn't going to help anyone. Are you family to Ms. Jacobs?"

Which Ms. Jacobs is she talking about? "My name is Bobby *Jacobs*. I'm Kelli's dad and Nanette's ...," I don't know how I should finish that sentence. If I admit she's no longer my wife, they might not tell me anything about her. But I also don't want to lie.

"Husband?" the woman supplies. From the tone of her voice, I can tell she's guiding me to say yes, whether it's true or not.

"If that's what you want to go with," I hedge.

"Well, if you're Nanette's husband, I can tell you she's been admitted to the hospital. But if you're not, I'm really not supposed to say."

I squeeze my eyes shut. "Is Kelli there with her? Can I talk to my daughter? Please?"

The woman clears her throat. "You can probably talk to your daughter if you call Room 478."

"How about you connect me to Room 478?" It's all I can do to keep from growling at the lady, helpful though she has been. I just want to know what's happening!

"Will do, sir. You have a nice night."

There's a click in my ear, followed by a few seconds of elevator music, and then the ringtone starts. After three rings, my body finally relaxes a fraction when my daughter's voice comes on the line. "Hello?"

"Baby, it's me. Is your mom okay? What's going on? Is it her headaches?"

Kelli sniffles, and my chest squeezes. "Yeah, after I talked to you earlier, they got worse, and she said she didn't need to go to the ER, but I was scared. I couldn't get through to you on your cellular phone, and I didn't know what to do, so I finally called for an ambulance. Mom was mad, but I'm glad we came because she's not okay." She starts crying in earnest now, and I hear Nanette's voice in the background, soothing our daughter.

Then my ex-wife's voice comes on the line. "Hey, Bobby."

I let out a deep breath, as her voice sounds stronger than I feared it might. "Hey. What did the doctor say?"

She tells me about the tests that were run and explains about a procedure the doctor wants to do to relieve some pressure on her brain. "They're doing it in the morning."

"Tomorrow? On New Year's Day?"

"He doesn't want to wait, and I guess I don't either. I know you can't be here—"

My hand grips the phone tightly. "I'll be there."

"There's no way you can get here from Little Rock in time."

"Then I'll be there when you wake up," I say. "I'll be on the next flight out of here."

Nanette sighs. "If you insist. Kelli isn't allowed to stay here overnight with me, even though it's almost midnight, so Whitley's mom is coming to pick her up. She's going to bring her back in the morning and stay with her in the waiting room through the procedure. It shouldn't take long."

Whitley has been Kelli's best friend since second grade. Her mom has helped us out on more than one occasion when we needed last-minute childcare. Kelli's old enough to stay home alone for a few hours, but not overnight, and especially not when her mom is in the hospital and I'm out of town.

"All right. But I'll be there as soon as I can."

"I know you will. Thanks, Bobby. Again. For everything."

"You know I'll always be there for you—if not in person, then in spirit."

I call every airline that flies out of Little Rock and book the flight that will get me home to L.A. the quickest, which leaves in only a handful of hours. By the time I get that done, make a few other calls, and pack my bag, I realize I need to tell Melissa I can't drive home with her. However, it's 3:30 in the morning, and I don't want to wake her up. I also don't want her driving all the way to Chicago alone. While I don't want to wake her, I have no qualms about waking the man who's going to solve that problem for me.

"You realize it's the middle of the night?" Diego rubs his eyes and ushers me into his hotel room. He crawls back into bed and closes his eyes for a moment before jerking to a sitting position and fixing his eyes on me. "Why are you here? Why are you dressed? Is Kelli OK? Nanette?" He asks all these questions in rapid-fire Spanish.

I sit on the edge of Diego's bed and give him a rundown of the situation, answering a boatload of questions from him throughout.

"I'll drive to Chicago with Melissa," he declares before I can ask him to do so.

"I appreciate it. I owe you big time for this."

"You owe me nothing. This is what family does, and you are family." He holds up a finger. "Actually, maybe you could change your last name to Sanchez."

"Uh, no. But can you give this to Melissa?" I hand him a note.

A grin spreads across his face as he flips the folded paper between his fingers. "Can I read it?"

I roll my eyes. "Really? Are you twelve?"

Diego chuckles. "Times three, almost. But I'll let you have your secrets." He narrows his eyes. "Wait. Did you explain what's happening? Did you tell Melissa about Kelli and Nanette?"

"No." I close my eyes briefly. "I can't spring all that on her in a note. I just said there was an emergency back home, not to worry, and I'd call her in a few days."

"I hope you also told her how much you enjoyed the past few days."

A smile forms on my face for the first time since I got back to my hotel room tonight. "I did." My smile drops when I consider once again how complicated my life is, and how Melissa doesn't need to have to deal with any of it. She deserves a man who can always put her first—who doesn't have a host of competing priorities in his life.

"Good. I'll take good care of her for you. I even promise not to flirt with her."

I snort. "I don't think that's possible."

Diego bobs his head from side to side. "Maybe not, but for you, I will try. Now, what time do I need to take you to the airport?"

I don't deserve friends like Diego. I truly don't.

"You forget you don't have a car, and I've got a taxi coming. You get some more sleep so you'll be wide awake all day for your drive back to Chicago. We were planning to leave at 6:00, so be ready."

He reaches over to the alarm clock and sets it. "Done. Now get out of here so I can get my beauty rest. Make sure to give your girls a giant Diego hug when you see them, and keep me posted."

twenty-five

. . .

Melissa

I don't look through the peephole in my door when I swing it open in response to a light knock at 5:59 a.m., so I'm momentarily speechless when it's not Bobby standing in the hallway but a fully dressed Diego Sanchez with a giant suitcase beside him.

"Try not to look so happy to see me," he teases.

I give myself a shake. "Sorry. I wasn't expecting you. Where's Bobby?" I peer down the hallway toward his room.

"Somewhere over Oklahoma, flying through the famous wind that sweeps down the plains." Diego holds out a note. "This is from him. Let's go inside so you can read it, and then we'll hit the road."

He follows me into the room with his suitcase, and I ask while unfolding the note, "*We'll* hit the road?"

"I am driving with you to Chicago. Just read the note."

I perch on the edge of the bed and do as he says.

DEAR MELISSA,

I APOLOGIZE FOR DISAPPEARING IN THE MIDDLE OF THE NIGHT, BUT THERE'S AN EMERGENCY BACK HOME, AND I NEED TO HEAD BACK NOW TO TAKE CARE OF A FEW THINGS. THE DETAILS AREN'T SOMETHING I WANT TO

SHARE WITH YOU IN A QUICK NOTE, BUT TRY NOT TO WORRY, AND I'LL EXPLAIN EVERYTHING SOON.

I WAS REALLY LOOKING FORWARD TO OUR DRIVE TODAY, BUT HOPEFULLY DIEGO WILL BE A DECENT SUBSTITUTE. ACTUALLY, I KNOW HE WILL BE. AS I WRITE THIS, HE DOESN'T EVEN KNOW HE'LL BE GOING WITH YOU, BUT I'M CONFIDENT HE'LL DROP ANY OTHER PLANS TO DO SO, BECAUSE THAT'S THE KIND OF MAN HE IS. JUST DON'T FALL FOR HIS CHARMS. YOU KNOW HOW HE CAN BE.

THE PAST FEW DAYS WITH YOU HAVE BEEN SOME OF THE HAPPIEST OF MY LIFE. I HOPE WE CAN ADD TO THOSE DAYS IN THE NEAR FUTURE.

I'LL TALK TO YOU SOON.

BOBBY JOE (A.K.A. B.S.)

Bobby's message elicits a host of emotions I'm not sure what to do with. What happened back home? And to who? What does he need to explain? And was he serious about the past few days being some of the happiest of his life?

I look up at Diego, who's watching me carefully.

"Do you know what this emergency is?"

He nods. "I do."

"But you're not going to tell me what it is?"

"That is Bobby's story to tell. Not mine."

"He's OK, though?" I fold the note back up and stick it in my pocket. "He said not to worry, but how can I not? This has to be something really serious if he left in the middle of the night."

Diego places his hand on my shoulder. "Bobby is a strong man. He will be OK, don't you worry. But he has a lot of responsibilities, and he doesn't like letting down the people he cares about. Please just trust him, and be patient with him. It's not easy for him to let people in. He is ready to let you in, but that will have to wait a little longer."

I'm dying to know what Bobby's many responsibilities are. It don't think it's his parents, considering he emancipated himself at sixteen because his home life wasn't good. And he was cagey about any siblings when I asked. He also didn't specifically say it was a work emergency, so I don't think it's that. I really hope he wouldn't leave me in the middle of the night on New Year's Day for work. But maybe that's part of being an agent. I don't know enough about that world to take an educated guess. If it is a work thing, though, I'm not sure how I feel about that, when it comes to potentially having a long-term relationship with him. Do I want to be with a guy who has to take off unexpectedly in the middle of the night?

"OK." I nod, even though my head is spinning. "I can be patient."

"Yes, you can. Now," he claps his hands together, "the sooner we leave, the sooner we get there. Who's driving first?"

Diego is an entertaining road trip partner. His giant bag contains several cassette tapes that he brought to listen to in his Walkman, and he's introducing me to some of his favorite Spanish-language singers. Listening to him sing along is a delight. He's overly expressive, and he has excellent pitch. He occasionally takes a break from singing to translate the lyrics for me.

"What did you and Bobby do in the car on the way to Arkansas?" he asks me as he switches out one tape for another.

"Mostly listened to music. We also got to know each other a little bit. And we played 'Truth or Dare.'"

Diego rubs his hands together. "Oooo! Let's play. I'll start. Truth or dare, beautiful Melissa?"

I'm scared of what he might ask me, but I'm more afraid of what he might dare me to do, so I choose truth.

"Yes!" He pumps a fist in the air and yelps like a little girl when it hits the ceiling. Thankfully it's not his pitching hand. "What do you think of our Bobby? Does he make your heart go pitter-patter? Do you want to have his babies?"

I smack his chest with the back of my hand, making him yelp

again. "Diego! I'm not telling you any of that. It's none of your business. Plus, that was three questions. You only get one."

"It *is* my business, because Bobby is my brother from an American mother. I need to make sure you will not break his fragile little man-heart."

A laugh bursts out of me. "Nothing about Bobby is fragile."

"Ah, on this matter you're mistaken. Deep down, under all the no-nonsense agentyness, Bobby Jacobs has a sensitive soul. He feels things deeply when they are personal to him and the people he loves. You will come to see that."

I flick my gaze his way. "Yeah?"

"*Si, mi amiga.* And he is as loyal as they come, our Bobby. He is a prince among men. I wouldn't trust him with my career and my friendship and the matters of *my* fragile little man-heart if he was not. Promise me you will treat my brother with tender care."

My heart warms at how much Diego cares about Bobby. "I promise I will."

"Good. Now, answer my questions. That is the way this game works. You must answer, or you owe me one million dollars."

I laugh again. "I don't have a million dollars."

"Then you must answer!"

There's no stopping the corners of my mouth from turning up when I recall Diego's questions. I decide to answer one of them, because he already knows the answer, or he wouldn't have asked. "He does make my heart go pitter-patter." In fact, it's pitter-pattering right now, just from thinking about the way Bobby kissed me last night.

"Yes! I knew it! You know how? Because I can hear it, even now. Pitter-patter-pitter-patter." He taps his fingers on my shoulder to the beat.

I giggle. "You can't hear it."

"Maybe not, but I saw how you looked at him last night. There is *mucho* pitter-pattering in your chest."

What about Bobby's heart? Is it pitter-pattering? I want to ask Diego that, but I don't. Regardless of what happened over the past few days or what Bobby said in his note, I'm afraid I've misinterpreted everything.

"And what about babies?" Diego asks. "You want little mini-Bobby *bambinos* running around, yes? You can tell Uncle Diego." He places his hand on his chest in a dramatic manner. "I will not tell a soul."

"I'm still not answering that." I shake my head, yet I can't help but imagine little dark-haired boys running around a yard while Bobby and I watch from a cushioned porch swing.

"So you will not tell me whether you want the babies," he says slyly, "but what about the *making* of the babies?"

My face heats at the thought, and I poke my passenger in the shoulder. "You're a mess, Uncle Diego. Has anyone ever told you that?"

"Every day of my life."

twenty-six

. . .

Bobby

"Dad!" Kelli runs into my arms the second she spots me entering the hospital waiting room.

I wrap her in a tight hug. "You OK, baby? Any news yet?"

"Daa-ad, I've told you to stop calling me baby." She pulls out of my embrace but then loops her arm through mine and pulls me over to a chair.

I glance over at Whitley's mom, who holds a hand up in greeting.

"Sorry." I'm not really sorry. I've been calling Kelli "baby" since the first moment I saw her, and I can't see myself stopping anytime soon. She'll always be my baby girl. "Now tell me about your mom."

"She's gonna be OK." She sits next to me and leans her head against my shoulder. "We can go see her in a little while. They said she'll be here for a few days and then can go home, but she has to rest for a few more weeks. Will Opal come stay with us again?"

"I need to call her, but I'm sure she will."

Opal is a sixty-something retired nurse who I've hired to stay round-the-clock with Nanette before. She was with us for about nine months after the accident, while Nanette was recuperating and going through physical therapy to regain use of her legs. She also comes to stay sometimes when I'm out of town and Nanette isn't feeling her best, and she occasionally takes Kelli to and from school even when she's not staying over. I don't know what we'd have done without her these past few years since the accident. It helps that Nanette lives in the guest house on my property, but with my job taking me out of town so much, Opal has been a godsend. She always comes when we call.

Whitley's mom gives me a more detailed report about what the doctor said, and then I thank her profusely and send her back home to spend the holiday with her family.

"How was the wedding?" Kelli asks, her head back on my shoulder. "Tell me about Leslie's dress."

I chuckle. "It was white. That's about all I can tell you."

"Of course it was, you silly man. But what kind of material was it? Were there beads or lace? Was it poofy? I want to know it all."

"I guess it was poofy, as you say. The skirt part was pretty big. And I don't know one material from another, so I can't help you out there. Maybe I can ask Leslie to mail you a picture of it in a few weeks after they're home from their honeymoon and settled into their new place."

"Oooo! Where'd they go on their honeymoon?"

"Diego's resort."

Several years ago, my friend bought a run-down, struggling property near his hometown in the Dominican Republic. He fixed it up, hired and trained an entirely new staff, and ensures his workers are treated well and paid fairly. Diego is a very hands-on owner, because corruption runs rampant in his country. He's doing everything he can to battle it.

Kelli sighs. "I love that place."

"Me, too." We've been there a few times. It's a family-friendly resort, and Kelli loves all the activities they provide.

"Are you going to be home for a while now?" my daughter asks.

I kiss the top of her head. "I don't know how long for sure, but definitely until your mom is stable and we have transportation lined up for you and all your activities when I'm gone. I doubt the doctor will clear her to drive again for a while."

My chest tightens when I think about how I won't be able to go back to Chicago to see Melissa for a couple weeks, if not more. Then again, I need to just end things with her. Not that there's anything official to end. But there's no way we can make a long-distance relationship work with everything I have to deal with on a daily basis with both work and family. And it's not like I can move to Chicago, with Nanette and Kelli here. And Melissa moved back to Chicago to be closer to her parents, so I can't imagine her moving to California for me. It's a no-win situation, and I need to put an end to it before either of us get any more attached, but I'm determined to let her down gently.

"Bobby, you've done enough," Nanette says, frustration evident in her voice. "You don't need to come visit me every day, and you can't keep upending your life for me. It makes me feel like a burden."

Nanette has been in the hospital four days now, and she's ready to go home, but they want to keep her another few days. A minute ago, I sent Kelli to the hospital cafeteria to get us some drinks, so I could talk to Nanette alone.

"We've had this conversation before," I say, "and we'll keep having it if needed, but you're not a burden, and I'm never going to stop taking care of you, so it would be helpful if you'd stop arguing with me about it."

She sighs. "I'm not helpless. And the second we signed the divorce papers, you were no longer obligated to take care of me."

I cock an eyebrow at her, and she chuckles.

"OK," she says, "you were obligated to make the more-than-generous alimony and child-support payments, but that's it. You've gone above and beyond what even most spouses would do, much less a former spouse. And we've had *this* conversation before, and we'll keep having it if needed, but it would be helpful if you'd stop thinking the accident was your fault. You didn't drive drunk and blast across a cross-street without stopping. All you did was drive our daughter and me home from her soccer tournament that night."

We didn't make it home, but I'm not going to point that out. "I should've been paying better attention. It was late on a Saturday night, and I should've been on the lookout for drunk drivers, especially with Kelli in the car. If I hadn't offered to drive you—"

"No." Nanette cuts me off. "You don't get to regret doing something kind for your child and ex-wife."

"It wasn't even my weekend with her," I argue.

"Bobby Jacobs, stop it with that nonsense. We both wanted you there. We've always wanted you to spend as much time as you can with Kelli—even before I lived in your backyard."

I take her hand in mine. "It's a shame we couldn't make things work between us."

"I'll never regret getting pregnant with Kelli or marrying you to try to give her a stable home, and I couldn't ask for a better dad for her. But we were never really meant to be more than friends. You know that as well as I do."

I do know it. Nanette and I were friends who took things a little too far one night and ended up with the best thing that ever happened to me. Kelli's birth and our short-lived marriage gave me the stability and family support I didn't realize I needed. I'd been on my own for so long, I had forgotten what it was like to have people who needed and loved me, and who I needed and loved in return.

"You're right, as usual."

She gives me a soft smile and pulls her hand out of mine. "What you need is a woman to take your mind off me." My mind shoots directly to Melissa, and Nanette must see something in my expression, because her eyes widen. "Is there a woman?"

I look away from her. "No."

"You're lying. Tell me about her. Did you meet her at the wedding?"

"We're not having this conversation. And you need to rest."

She gives me a puppy-dog look. "It'll make me feel soooo much better if you tell me. You won't deny me that, will you?"

"You're the one who should've been a lawyer."

Nanette laughs. "I would've made a terrible lawyer. Teaching is much more my style."

And it's my fault she can't teach anymore. She occasionally substitute teaches at Kelli's school, but being on her feet and constantly being "on" with a group of kids all day isn't something she can currently do on a daily basis.

"No," she says firmly, "do not blame yourself for that." She knows me well—too well. "Now, tell me everything about this woman, and then I can sleep in peace."

"There's not much point in me telling you about her, because it can't go anywhere."

"Why?"

"It's complicated."

"What's complicated?" Kelli asks from the doorway, saving me from having the conversation, because I'm definitely not telling my romance-loving daughter about Melissa.

"Nothing."

My daughter narrows her eyes at me. "Which means it's *something* but you don't want me to know about it."

I hold my hands palm up. "You got me. But I'm still not talking."

"Fiiiiine." Her faces scrunches up as she hands me a cup. "Here's your Mountain Dew. I don't know how you can drink that stuff. It's so gross. Do you know what it does to your body?"

"What it does is keep me awake so I can drive my lovely daughter to all the different places she needs to be."

Kelli huffs. "Whatever. Just cut back, will you? You're already old. I don't need you dying on me."

twenty-seven

· · ·

Melissa

"He still hasn't called." I'm whining, but I don't feel bad about it. It's now the fourth of January, and I have yet to hear from Bobby. I *knew* it was all too good to be true.

"Patience, my friend," Wendy says from the other end of the phone. "He'll call."

"How do you know?" I wrap the phone cord around my finger.

"Because he's Bobby. He said he'd explain everything to you, and he always does what he says. His timeline just happens to be a little different than yours."

"Has he called Randall to get my phone number, at least?" We never did exchange numbers, since we thought we'd be spending another day together.

"No, but we're not the only people he knows who have your number."

"Well, he's not going to try to get ahold of Leslie and Ash right now, is he?" I flop onto my back on my couch in frustration.

"You make a valid point. But still, he'll call. You can count on it."

"What if I don't like what he has to say?"

"Then you don't. But you won't know whether you'll like it until you hear it."

I drape my free arm over my face. "Can't you just tell me what's going on with him?"

"I most definitely cannot. Now, we need to get your mind off all this. Why don't you come over, and we'll have dinner and watch TV. It's mostly reruns tonight, but there's a new episode of *China Beach*."

"And we'll drink wine," I add.

She hesitates before saying, "There will be wine. I'll send Randall out to get food from Pat's Diner so nobody has to cook. What do you want from there?"

Within thirty minutes, I'm knocking on the door of my friends' apartment. Wendy opens it for me and heads straight to the couch, where she plops down unceremoniously and puts her feet up. I take a seat on the other end of the couch.

"Randall's out picking up the food. Should be back soon. I'm *starving*."

Wendy pats her belly, and then she starts caressing it, which is odd. As I watch her hand and then move my focus up to her face, which has a dreamy look on it, a smile grows on my own face.

"You're pregnant!" I point at her.

Her gaze shoots to mine. "What?"

"Don't you lie to me, Wendy O'Halloran Hamilton. I never saw you drink a drop of alcohol at the wedding, and now you're rubbing your belly like it's a genie's lamp. There's a baby in there. Don't even try to deny it."

Now she's beaming. "Yeah, there's a little pea-sized baby in me." She punches the air and squeals. "We're having a baaaaaby!"

I launch myself at her, and we hug and laugh and cry like we're teenagers, not fully grown women.

When I drag myself from her and we wipe the happy tears from our faces, she says, "I have even more news."

"Bigger than having a baby?"

"Maybe not bigger, but pretty big. We're moving this month."

"This *month?*"

Wendy nods.

I grab one of her hands in both of mine. "Please tell me you're moving to Randall's mom's house earlier than planned, not that you've somehow gotten new jobs in another city and are leaving me."

"Yes, we're moving earlier because of the baby. If we waited until Sonya moves to college in August like we planned, we'd be cutting things too close with this little guy or gal." She pats her stomach. "We figured we might as well move now and get the kitchen started and set up the nursery and everything. I can't wait to start decorating!"

Randall and Ash's dad passed away unexpectedly last year, and their mom considered selling their huge estate just off the lake up in Evanston, but the four kids talked her out of it. Randall and Wendy plan to move into one wing of the house and turn it into their own "apartment," which is bigger than most people's houses. When Ash and Leslie return from their honeymoon, they'll be living in the pool house on the property. It won't be big enough for an entire family, but they're planning to wait a few years to start having kids, so it'll work for now.

"I'm so excited for you guys." I squeeze her hand.

"It'll be a little farther drive for you to get to us from Wrigleyville," she says, "but you'll never have to look for a parking spot!"

I laugh. "So true. And you'll have plenty of guest rooms if I want to stay over. Wait. You will, right? I know there's a ton of rooms in that house, but with you guys there, and Sonya and Tonya still needing rooms when they're home from college ..."

She smiles. "We will. There's plenty of space in the guest wing. Diego has already informed us he's going to give up his suite at the Drake and will be taking over a few rooms when he's in town during the season, but there will still be rooms left over."

I chuckle. "That sounds exactly like Diego. Telling—not asking."

"We don't mind. Mama Ruth loves him like he's her own child." She gives me a sly look. "He also said he's going to convince Bobby to stay there, too, when he's in town."

I groan. "I might have to avoid your house then, if things don't work out with him."

She gently pushes my shoulder. "It'll either work out romance-wise, or you'll stay friends. Stop your worrying."

Brrrring!

Wendy reaches to the side table next to her and picks up the phone. "Hello?" Her eyes shoot to me. "Hi, Bobby. How's everything going?"

I scoot closer to her to try and hear him, but she shoves me away.

"Mmhm." Wendy nods, still holding me at arms' length. She's surprisingly strong for someone so small. As she listens to whatever Bobby's saying, she responds with small noises or says vague phrases so I can't tell what he's talking about.

Finally, she says, "Thanks for letting us know. Randall's not home, but I'll fill him in. We'll be thinking about you, and please let us know if there's anything we can do." She pauses. "You're family, Bobby, and family helps out however they can. You know that better than most." Her eyes dart to me and away again as Bobby says at least several sentences I can't make out. "Yeah, I'll tell her."

Her? Who's "her"? Me? I point to my chest, but Wendy won't look directly at me.

"By the way," she says, "do you have her phone number?"

Again I point to myself, and she answers by giving Bobby my number. I sigh in relief.

"OK, bye." Wendy waves, as if Bobby can see her. "Talk to you soon."

"What did he say?" I demand the second she hangs up the phone.

"He said to tell you he's sorry he hasn't called yet, but he'll call you soon." She smirks. "I told you so."

I roll my eyes. "You did. What else did he say?"

"You know I can't tell you that."

"I had to try, though."

The door opens and Randall walks in. "The food has arrived!" He holds up the bags and kicks the door shut with his foot.

"I told her," Wendy tells him without explaining what she's talking about.

"Oh, good. Because there was no way I was going to be able to keep our big secret through an entire evening. It was hard enough at the wedding, and I've hit my limit." He's beaming even more than Wendy, which I didn't think was possible.

I push off the couch and throw my arms around him, bags and all. "I'm so happy for you guys!"

"I knew you would be. I wanted to tell you at the wedding, but this one," he jerks his head toward his wife as I let him go, "refused to let me."

"That's not true." Wendy tosses a throw pillow in his direction, but it falls short. Athletic, she is not.

"You're right. It's not." He drops the bags on the small kitchen table. "We decided ahead of time to only tell Ash and Leslie. Didn't want to overshadow their big day."

"That's very thoughtful of you." I hold out a hand to Wendy and pull her up off the couch. She's already acting like she's gained fifty pounds with this pregnancy, which is kind of cute.

"So you know our secret." Randall grabs plates out of the cabinet and sets them on the table. "Now it's time for us to hear yours."

"My secret?" I point to myself. "What secret?"

"About what you and Bobby got up to at the wedding." He grins as he pours water into glasses.

My face burns. "Um, you saw us coming out of that office."

"Yes, and coming out of your car." He chuckles. "Anything else to share?"

I sigh as I unwrap my burger and put it on my plate. "No. We each went to our own rooms when we got back to the hotel, and then when I opened my door early the next morning, it wasn't him but Diego standing there. That's the end of the story."

"It's not." Wendy dumps the entire container of French fries onto her plate. "He left you a note. And he just now told me he's going to call you. In time."

"Bobby called?" Randall tries to grab a fry off Wendy's plate, but she smacks his hand away.

"Yeah, I'll fill you in on the details later, but he told me to tell our impatient little friend here that he's sorry he hasn't called yet, but he's going to."

Wendy heaves herself out of her chair with a groan and takes the few steps to the refrigerator. After moving a few things around inside, she holds up a container of mustard like it's the holy grail. Then she empties what must be half the bottle onto the fries.

So much for me trying to steal any fries away from her. "That is disgusting."

She holds a mustard-laden fry aloft. "It's delicious. And now neither of you will try to pilfer any of my fries."

"They were supposed to be all of our fries," Randall mutters.

"What did you say, dear husband?"

"I said I hope you enjoy your fries, my gloriously beautiful Glinda."

"That's what I thought."

"So, Melissa," Randall's attention turns back to me, "are you prepared to move to L.A. if things work out with you and Bobby?"

I nearly choke on my burger. "What?"

"He lives there. You live here." He points in opposite directions. "Somebody's going to have to move if you want to be together long-term. Are you willing to move out west?"

It's not like I haven't thought about the long-distance aspect, because it's been top of mind, but I haven't thought seriously about whether I'd be willing to move to California. "I don't know."

"You just moved back here a year ago," Wendy says. "It's understandable if you don't want to move again."

I shake my head. "It's not about moving, in general. And it's not even that I'm opposed to living in California. It's that I moved back here because it's where my parents are. I don't really want to leave again, especially with my dad not in the best health."

"I get that." Randall gets up and grabs a beer out of the fridge. "But what if Bobby can't move here?"

"Randall." Wendy's tone is terse.

"What? I'm just asking."

I look back and forth between them. "What I'm reading between the lines is that Bobby isn't in a position to move here. Is that right?"

"Maybe," Randall mutters.

"Okay, fine." Wendy points a yellow fry at me. "But you can't tell Bobby we let this slip, even if we didn't technically spill any beans."

"Just tell me."

"You'll understand when you talk to him, but no, I don't think he'd be able to move here."

I groan. "The man just needs to tell me what's going on."

"We know." Randall takes a sip of his beer. "We've all told him. Multiple times."

"He's being a chicken." Wendy picks up two fries and holds them in front of her mouth in what I assume she's pretending is a beak. "Bawk-bawk!"

twenty-eight

...

Bobby

I'm being an absolute chicken, and I hate that. I'm not usually afraid of anything other than something terrible happening to my daughter, but I'm scared to tell Melissa about Kelli and Nanette. It's been a week since the wedding, and I know she deserves an explanation from me.

After what she said about not looking forward to being the parent of a teenager, I'm even more hesitant to tell her. To Melissa, that was a throwaway thought that most people have before they're parents of teenagers. Actually, it's a thought parents of teenagers have on a daily basis, if I'm honest. But what she said stuck with me. Would it even be fair of me to ask someone her age to consider being the instant parent of a thirteen-year-old? It hasn't even been a decade since she was a teen herself. Not that I think she'd be a bad parent or that Kelli wouldn't love her, but that's not the point.

I keep telling myself I need to break things off with Melissa before we really start anything, but I don't think I can make myself do it. It's been a long time since I've been interested in getting to know and spending time with a woman, and I'm hesitant to give that up. I should probably talk to one of my friends about this, but I know what they'll say—to go for it. Last night I was so desperate I almost talked to Wendy about it on the phone, but even though I trust that she wouldn't tell Melissa any details of that conversation now, I can't guarantee she wouldn't let something slip down the road, and I don't need Melissa to ever know how unsure I am about this situation.

"Ready to go see Mom?" Kelli stands in my home office doorway decked out in a New Kids on the Block T-shirt and stonewashed jeans rolled up at the hem above her bright white Keds.

I pull my wallet and keys out of my desk drawer and join my daughter at the door. She wraps her arms around me, and I squeeze her tightly, amazed by how she's less than a foot shorter than me now.

"You think the doctor will tell us she can go home tomorrow, like she thought yesterday?" Kelli asks as she leads the way through the house toward the garage.

I nod. "I hope so."

"I'm ready for her to be home. Opal's coming, right?"

"Yes." I open the passenger door to my black BMW and usher Kelli inside. "She's moving her stuff in this afternoon and will stay as long as we need her."

"Kell, why don't you go get your dad a snack from the cafeteria? He's acting bossier than usual, and I'm hoping that's just because he's hungry."

Kelli laughs at her mom's observation and waves her hand toward me in the universal "hand over the money" motion. I pull a few bills out of my wallet and slap them onto her palm.

"Thanks, Daddy." Kelli kisses my cheek and rushes out of the hospital room.

"You love it when she still calls you Daddy, don't you?" Nanette gives me a fond look.

My chest squeezes. "I do, but it rarely happens anymore—usually only when she wants something from me. I can't believe she's a teenager. When did that happen?"

"Overnight, it seems." Her face breaks out into a sly grin. "Now, before she gets back, tell me about this woman you mentioned the other day. And don't hold back. I want to know everything."

I guess Nanette is the one I'm talking to about this, and I can't say I'm upset about it. Since she doesn't know Melissa, she might be the best person to give me an unbiased opinion.

"Her name is Melissa, and she's friends with the Hamiltons. She grew up with Ash and Randall, and she's close friends with Wendy and Leslie. And she works for the Cubs, so she also has that connection to them and to Diego."

"And to you. I'm guessing she was in the wedding, then?"

"Yeah, both of the Hamilton weddings. I haven't spent much time with her ... well, I hadn't until last week. I'm sure Kelli told you my flight from Chicago to Little Rock was cancelled. Melissa was also booked on that flight." I tell her about the drive, the shared motel bed in Illinois, our conversations on the road, and even what happened at the wedding reception.

Nanette cocks her head to the side. "There's a lot to unpack there, but there's also something you're not telling me. Don't get me wrong, you've told me a lot more than I thought you would, but you're holding back. What is it?"

I groan. "How do you know me so well?"

"Might be my fifteen years of experience as your friend, wife, ex-wife, co-parent, and backyard neighbor." She crosses her arms over her chest. "But don't deflect. Tell me everything, or I won't give you my thoughts."

I look down at my hands. "After the rehearsal dinner, I was driving us back to the hotel, and a deer jumped out in front of us. I didn't handle it well."

"Oh, Bobby." Nanette's voice is full of compassion. "Panic attack?"

I nod.

"How did Melissa handle that?"

A lump forms in my throat at the memory. "Exactly the way I needed her to."

"I don't get the details on that?"

"Not on what she did or said, but ..." I close my eyes.

"But ...?"

"I didn't tell her why I reacted that way. I haven't told her about Kelli or you or the accident."

Nanette sucks in a breath. "What? Why?"

"To be fair, I was planning to tell her on our way back to Chicago, but then I came here." I hold up a hand. "I'm not blaming you. I'm just explaining. But I didn't tell her—and still haven't told her—because things happened so fast. You know I don't tell many people about my personal life and why. I do trust her, but I guess I didn't want the reality of my life to ruin what might be happening between us. She deserves a man who can give her everything, who doesn't have all these other responsibilities. She's young, being an instant step-parent of a teenager is not one of her life goals, and she moved back home to Chicago last year to be close to her parents. She can't move here, and I can't move there. It's just too much to ask of her to try to have a long-distance relationship with me when it can't go anywhere."

"But you don't know that, Bobby." Nanette holds her hand out to me, and I scoot forward on my chair so I can take it in mine. "You haven't given her the chance to decide for herself."

"She said she wants to try long-distance, but I can't imagine a scenario where she'd jump at my offer once she knows the entire truth about my life."

"You underestimate yourself. You're not everyone's cup of tea, we all know that, but since she hasn't gone running for the hills yet, it sounds like you might be her cup. And I think she's definitely *your* cup."

I chuckle. "She is, and I don't even like tea."

"That's good, because I got you a Mountain Dew." This comes from Kelli, who hands over my soda with a giant grin. "Now, tell me who this cup of tea lady is. And don't even try lying to me, Dad. You think you have a poker face, and maybe you do at work, but I can always tell when you're lying."

Now it's Nanette's turn to chuckle. "Chip off the old block."

I run my hand through my hair and then back down to cover my face. "Do I really have to do this?"

"Yes," mother and daughter demand in unison.

When I hesitate, Nanette sums up the situation for Kelli. "Your dad has a friend he drove from Chicago to Arkansas with, and it turns out he likes her a lot. I mean, *a lot.*" She smirks at me. "But she lives in Chicago, and he lives here, and he doesn't think she would move here, and therefore he's giving up and is going to die a lonely, grumpy old man."

"What?!" Kelli slams her drink down onto the small table and props her hands on her hips. "You can't give up. You never date anybody. You never *like* anybody. Scoop this woman up right now!" Her eyes dart to Nanette. "What's her name?"

"Melissa," Nanette replies in a sing-song voice.

"Oooo! Melissa and Bobby, sittin' in a—"

I slice my hand through the air. "All right, that's enough from the peanut gallery. It's not really your concern."

Kelli's jaw drops. "Not my concern? *Not my concern?* Dad, it's so totally my concern. All you do is work and take care of us. You need some fun and excitement in your life. You need to do things that don't involve me or sports. You need … you know." She waggles her eyebrows, and I almost gag at her insinuation. Not that she's wrong, but she's my *daughter.* She doesn't need to be talking about my sex life. Sheesh. This conversation has gone off the rails.

Nanette has the gall to giggle before shutting our precocious daughter down. "Kell, that's *definitely* not your concern. But you're right about one thing. Your dad needs some fun in his life, and I think Melissa is just the ticket."

My answering machine light is blinking when Kelli and I arrive back home, and when I hit the play button, Wendy's voice fills the air. "Robert Neanderthal Jacobs, if you don't call Melissa within the next twenty-four hours, I'm telling her everything myself. I don't care if that means you can't trust me ever again, because I can't take this anymore. You said you'd call her, and I know you keep your word, but it's been a week. *A week.* The statute of limitations is up tomorrow. Do I make myself clear?" She huffs. "That's what I thought." Her tone then switches from stern schoolmarm to concerned friend. "And I hope everything's going fine with Nanette. Tell her and Kelli we say hi and we're thinking about them. OK, bye." I think she's done but then she adds, "Call her," in her stern voice again.

"I guess she told you," my daughter says as she falls onto my leather couch and props her shoe-clad feet on the coffee table.

I nudge her leg with my foot.

"Feet off or shoes off. You pick."

"You want me to take my feet off?" She raises an eyebrow and gives me a look. If you've ever met a teenager, you know the one.

"You know what I mean." I sit next to her, make a show of taking off my shoes, and then put my socked feet on the coffee table.

"Don't change the subject." She pokes my side, where she knows I'm ticklish, and I swat her hand away.

"There wasn't a subject."

"There was, and her name is Melissa." Kelli kicks her shoes off and then rests her head against my shoulder. "I think you should call her right now."

"With you as an audience? I don't think so."

"I'm gonna be with you for the next twenty-four hours—and a lot more after that—so I don't think you have a choice. I haven't met Wendy, but something tells me she'll follow through on her threat."

I cup my hand around my ear. "What's that? Do I hear Whitley telling her mom she wants you to come over tonight?"

My daughter pokes me again. "Don't be silly. Be serious and call your cup of tea."

"You really think I should try to date someone who lives in Chicago?" Why am I asking a thirteen-year-old for dating advice?

"I do. You don't know that it can't work out. And yeah, you're a busy man, but I mean, aren't you old enough to retire already?" The tone of her voice tells me she's only partly joking.

When Kelli has mentioned this in the past, I've brushed it off. I'm still a few years from forty—not nearly old enough to retire, though I could financially afford to stop working today, and I'd never have to worry about having enough money for myself,

Kelli, and Nanette. My daughter's mother may be my ex-wife, but she may never be able to work full-time again, and I've vowed to myself I'll take care of her financially for the rest of her life if necessary.

"You know I'd go crazy if I weren't working," I say.

My daughter sits up straight and turns to face me. "Yeah, but you could spend soooo much more time with me. You could coach my soccer team and take me to and from school and math club and stuff." She grabs my hand. "Maybe you could work part-time. Like only have Uncle Diego as a client, and get rid of those other guys that cause you so much trouble and take you away from me. Then your work would only take you to Chicago, because Uncle Diego told me he wants to play there until he retires. And since that's where Melissa lives, that's perfect!"

Kelli makes some compelling points. I would love to spend more time with her, especially since somehow we only have five and a half more years until she goes to college. And with my workload where it currently is, I don't have much time to spend with her or any worthwhile amount to spend with Melissa. Also, what I said to Melissa about not wanting to keep working in the way I have in the past is true. I need to make a change not only in the way I work but also the amount I work, but I don't know that retirement is the answer.

However, there's at least one thing Kelli hasn't thought about. "Yeah, but that doesn't solve the problem of me needing to live here and Melissa needing to live there."

She falls back against the couch cushions. "You're right. But you need to at least try, right? Maybe you can figure something out. You won't know unless you try." She hugs my arm and bats her eyelashes at me. "Please, Daddy? Please call her. I can tell you really like her."

"Oh, yeah?"

"Yeah. You've never talked about a woman in front of me before. For all I know, you've never been on a date with anyone since you and Mom divorced a thousand years ago."

I've been on dates, but not with anyone I wanted to see more than a time or two. Melissa, though? I want to see her many, many times. And everyone is right. I can't make this decision on my own. I owe it to Melissa to let her decide what she wants once she knows everything. But there's one more thing I need to make sure of before I start anything with her.

"You really wouldn't mind me dating someone?" I'm already not able to spend as much time with Kelli as either of us would like. Dating would mean spending even less time with her.

"You care if I mind?" she asks.

I look down into her brown eyes. "Of course I mind. You're the most important person in my life, and if I date, you'd have to share me with someone else."

"I already share you with your clients," she says, not realizing how that pierces my heart.

"I'll think about cutting back on work, all right? But that's different. This is someone I might potentially love, get engaged to, and marry. She could someday be your step-mom. How do you feel about that?"

"I feel like you deserve to have somebody to love who loves you back. But …"

"But what?" I prompt when she hesitates.

"What if I don't like her?"

I cup her cheek in my palm. "I'm certain you'll like Melissa, but if you don't, then it wasn't meant to be." I kiss her forehead. "I'm not going to marry someone you don't like."

"What if …," she hesitates again and then continues in a small voice, "… what if she doesn't like me?"

Now I wrap my arms around her and squeeze her tightly. "She's going to love you. I know she is. But on the extremely small off-chance that she doesn't, again, it wasn't meant to be. Anyone who doesn't like you isn't someone I want to spend any time with, much less the rest of my life. You hear me?"

Kelli nods. "Yeah."

I loosen my grip on her and let her settle back in beside me. "So you still want me to call her?"

She bumps my shoulder with hers. "I do. But you have to tell me everything she says."

I chuckle and lean over to kiss the top of her head. "Maybe not everything, but I promise I'll call her."

"Good. And don't talk to her like you're an agent and she's your client—or worse, on the other side. Be … you know … a real person."

A laugh bursts out of me. "I'm not always a real person?"

"You're not. I've heard you on the phone for work. You're like a robot or something—like you don't have any feelings and can't possibly be wrong about anything. You're barking orders right and left and telling people exactly how it's going to be. Don't do that with Melissa."

I salute her. "Excellent advice, my little Jedi. How'd you get to be so smart?"

"I had a great teacher." She pauses dramatically. "Mom." She laughs so hard at her joke that she almost rolls onto the floor.

twenty-nine

. . .

Melissa

"Melissa?"

My heart does the Charleston in my chest when Bobby's voice rumbles over the telephone line. I'd given up on hoping he'd call, so I wasn't fully expecting to hear his voice when I answered. I press my hand over my racing heart as I sit cross-legged on my bed, where I've been reading a book.

"Hey, Bobby Joe." Instead of teasing him with his nickname, I should be reprimanding him for not calling sooner. But it appears I can't help myself when it comes to him.

"I apologize for not calling before now." He sighs. "I should've called sooner, but I ... there's a lot to tell you, and ..."

It's funny to me that this man who negotiates for a living can't figure out what to say to me.

I decide to help him out. "And you're scared?"

He lets out a rueful chuckle. "Yeah, I guess you could say that."

"Newsflash." I fling an arm out. "So am I. My last relationship didn't pan out well, so I'm a little gun-shy here, too. Why don't you just jump right in and tell me what I need to know about the secret life of Bobby Jacobs?"

I hear him suck in a deep breath before he blurts out, "I have a thirteen-year-old daughter."

Now my heart stops, but only briefly. He has thrown me for a loop with this information, but based on how he interacted with Emily, I'm not surprised. In fact, I'm surprised I didn't see the signs. How else would a grumpy, single, work-obsessed man know how to interact so easily with a little girl? This also explains how he knows the lyrics to so many current pop songs.

"Her name is Kelli," he adds, since I haven't gathered my wits about me enough to speak. "And she's amazing." I can hear the smile in his voice.

I press my hand against my chest again, where I can feel my heart beating overtime. "I'm sure she is."

I don't doubt that statement. Bobby's kid is probably awesome. The question is whether I'm prepared to potentially be a step-mom to a teenager, if things progress with Bobby. I know he's not proposing marriage here, but now that I know there's a kid involved, that drastically changes my vision of what our future might look like. It also makes things more complicated in many ways—including us needing to be sure of what we're doing and why, for the sake of his daughter if nobody else.

Bobby says, "I haven't dated anyone seriously since Kelli's mom and I divorced ten years ago. I don't know how dating as a single dad works, what you need to know, what you *want* to know. Tell me what you want to know, and I won't hold back. I just don't know the best place to start. And tell me how you feel, if you'd like to."

After taking a deep breath, I begin, "I feel a bit blindsided, to be honest. My head is spinning. But if you're worried that you having a child is going to make me run and not look back, I can put your mind at ease. It might take me a while to get used to this new information about a half-grown daughter and an ex-wife, when I had no idea you had either of those things … I mean those people … but that fact alone isn't going to run me off."

Bobby blows out a long breath. "I'm happy to hear that. I truly am sorry I didn't tell you before. I don't tell many people about them for their safety, since I have such a high-profile job and there are a lot of people who don't like me because of that job. I was going to talk to you about Kelli and her mom on the way back to Chicago, but …"

"Yeah, that didn't happen. Will you tell me why?"

"Yes, but we need to go back a ways so I can explain everything leading up to me leaving Arkansas in the middle of the night. You ready for this?"

"Bring it on, B.S." I burrow under my covers and make myself comfortable.

He laughs. "I promise there won't be any B.S. here. I met Nanette when I was in law school and she was in her last year of college to become a teacher. She was a friend of a friend, and there was a mutual attraction. We went out on one date and decided our life goals weren't compatible—she wanted to stay in L.A. and save the world through educating inner-city kids, and I wanted to fly all over the country helping athletes make as much money as possible, while also making as much money as possible myself."

I'm not sure I like "making as much money as possible" as one of Bobby's life goals. Then again, he didn't say that's still his goal —just that it was fifteen or so years ago.

He continues, "Nanette wanted kids, and I couldn't imagine myself as a parent. I also wasn't all that interested in dating anyone because I was so focused on school and work that I didn't have the time or energy. So we decided to just be friends. She and I spent a decent amount of time together with our other friends, and we engaged in harmless flirting. Well, it was harmless until one night we both had a little too much to drink and one thing led to another, and nine months later, Kelli arrived.

"When Nanette told me she was pregnant, I asked her if she wanted to get married, because that's what you did in the 70s. I didn't want her to have the stigma and struggle of being a single mom, and even though I hadn't planned on being a father, I was determined to be there for my kid—to be the supportive and loving dad I didn't have."

My heart is both swelling with pride for adult Bobby and breaking for little boy Bobby.

"Our marriage was ... OK. We got along fine, but there was something missing. I was working long hours, and when I was home, I wanted to spend time with Kelli more than with Nanette. This might sound terrible, but I realized I loved Kelli with all of my being, and while I did love—and still do love—Nanette as a person and a friend, I didn't also love *her* with all my being."

"That doesn't sound terrible," I say. "It sounds fairly normal. You didn't marry out of love, but out of a sense of responsibility to both her and Kelli. There's nothing wrong with that. Plenty of people marry for reasons other than love."

"That's true." He sighs. "But it made me feel like a failure. Like I wasn't coming through for Nanette like I should as her husband. I wanted her to have a partner who loved her with all his being, and I knew I could never be that man."

My heart squeezes again. Our mutual friends are all correct—he's a really good man.

"Nanette is the kind of woman who doesn't let people bottle up their feelings for long, and she could tell I wasn't happy, so she sat me down and we talked it out. She admitted she felt similarly—that she loved me but she wasn't 'in love' with me, either. We took some time to figure out if that was going to be OK with both of us long term, and we decided it wasn't, but we wanted the split to be amicable. We'd seen too many couples in our circle go through nasty, contentious divorces, and we didn't want that for us or for Kelli. Even though she was only three, she would've felt the stress. So we divorced as quickly and pain-lessly as possible, and we agreed to shared custody. By that time, I had a full roster of clients and was traveling a lot. We'd agreed that Nanette would get our house, and I initially bought a condo nearby. Then once Kelli was in kindergarten, I built a house near her school. Whenever I was in town, Kelli was with me most of the time, and she was with Nanette the rest of the time."

He's saying all this in the past tense, which makes me wonder if that isn't still the way things work for them.

"One weekend when Kelli was ten, she had a soccer tourna-ment. It wasn't technically my weekend with her, even though we didn't usually follow the court guidelines on that. But whenever I'm in town, I go to all of her games, so we all went together. It didn't get over until late, and I was driving us home. We were driving on an unlit section of road when a drunk driver went right through a stop sign and T-boned us on the passenger side—Nanette's side."

My hand shoots up to cover my mouth, and I think I might be sick. Is he about to tell me his ex-wife died in that accident? Is that why he had a panic attack after our near-miss with the deer?

He continues, "Kelli was sitting behind me, and we both had our seatbelts on. We were a little banged up but relatively okay. Nanette was in bad shape. I …," Bobby gets a little choked up, "I thought she was dead."

I heave a sigh of relief at the way he said that. He wouldn't say he *thought* she was dead if she really was dead, right? "But she wasn't?"

"No. Her right leg was broken in multiple places, as well as her right arm and a few of her ribs. She also had internal injuries to some of her organs along with a traumatic brain injury."

My hand goes to my throat and tears fill my eyes. "Oh, Bobby."

"It was bad, Melissa. We weren't sure she was going to make it. It was touch and go for several weeks. And it took nearly a year for her to recover from all the injuries. She still walks with a limp —she always will—and lives with random pain flare-ups."

"And her brain?"

"It healed over time, but she occasionally gets bad headaches. They had dissipated over the past six months or so, but then when I talked to Kelli before the wedding rehearsal, she told me her mom was having headaches again. I was worried, but not enough so anybody could tell other than Diego. Then when I got back to my room after the wedding, I had a message that they'd gone to the ER. When I got in touch with them, I found out Nanette needed a procedure to drain fluid from her brain, and they were doing it the next day. I packed my bag, hopped on the next flight out, and made it back here soon after the procedure was over."

Bobby's story is not even in the same universe as what I thought might've happened that sent him flying out of Arkansas in the middle of the night.

"I'm so glad you got there," I say. "Is she doing all right?"

"Yeah, the procedure went fine, and it has a fairly quick

recovery time. She's progressing as expected and should be released from the hospital tomorrow."

"So are you staying with her and Kelli while she recovers?"

"After the accident, we sold both of our houses, and I bought a home with a decent-sized guest house on the property. Nanette lives in the guest house, and Kelli comes and goes as she pleases between the two homes. I'll be keeping a close eye on Nanette over the next weeks and months, and I also hired a retired nurse to stay at the house with her as long as needed, which should hopefully only be a month or so. Opal stayed with us most of that year after the accident, and she comes to help out and drive Kelli places when I'm out of town and Nanette isn't feeling well."

"There's a lot to think about from everything you've just told me." And it has completely changed my view of who Bobby is—in a positive way.

"I know it's a lot. This is why I haven't dated. I have too many responsibilities. I don't have a lot of time or energy left over after work and family. And for the record, Nanette is family. She always will be, regardless of whether either of us marry again. She's like a sister now." He sighs. "I like you, Melissa, a lot. Those days with you were amazing and refreshing and … fantastic. But I don't see how we can make things work between us. I can't leave California, and you just moved to Chicago to be close to your parents. Long-distance relationships are hard, and I don't want to start a relationship that I know can't potentially end in marriage. I don't have the time or mental energy for anything else, as strange as that may sound.

"So it's up to you. If you think moving to California to be with me isn't possible in the future, we need to just stay friends. I don't want you to get hurt, and I don't want Kelli to get hurt. Because if she meets you, she's going to fall in love with you, and I refuse to put my little girl's heart on the line for a relationship that's destined to fail."

The way Bobby loves his daughter is arguably the sexiest thing about him, and there's a lot of competition for that status.

He continues, "But if you think this could go somewhere, if you're not scared off by my family situation and you're willing and able to potentially move someday, I'd like to give this a shot. I don't expect an answer right now. You probably need to think about it and talk it over with your friends or your mom or whoever you talk to. Leslie and Wendy both know all of this, so you won't be breaking any confidences if you tell them anything I told you. I also don't mind you telling your parents, if you want to."

"Okay, thanks. I do need to think about it and talk through it. Thanks for giving me that chance. And thank you for telling me all of this. I know it wasn't easy, but I'm glad you trusted me with it all. That means a lot."

thirty

. . .

Bobby

I still don't see how I can make things work with Melissa, but I'm relieved she knows everything now. Well, she knows about Kelli and Nanette, but not about my childhood. That can wait. I've given her enough to think about for today.

"Since you've shared your story," Melissa says, "I think it's time for me to tell you mine."

My expectation was that we'd be ending the call after my revelation, but if she's ready to talk, I'm not going to stop her. "Is it as dramatic as my story?"

She laughs. "No, but it's not great."

"OK, then. Hit me with it." I lean back in my chair and kick my feet up on the desk in my home office. I came in here because there's the least chance Kelli will overhear me from here. I wouldn't be surprised if she's hovering outside the door, though.

"I told you I moved back to Chicago to be closer to my parents after my dad's health issues, and that's true. But it's not the only reason I wanted to leave New York. My story is actually eerily similar to what happened with Randall and Colleen last year, except I was engaged. Jeremy and I were together for three years and engaged for two months when I caught him in our bed with one of our friends."

Anger blasts through and my fists clench. "Are you kidding me?"

"Unfortunately, no. But that's not the whole story. While it gutted me that he did that, I'd been thinking about calling off the engagement anyway. I had a … well, there was this guy at work. I didn't cheat with him, I promise you that, but we had a really strong connection. He wanted to pursue it, and I refused to do anything with him because I was engaged to Jeremy. But the fact is I wanted to. Not cheat—I didn't want to cheat. But I was attracted to the other guy, both physically and emotionally, more than I was to my fiancé. That wasn't fair to Jeremy, and I was trying to figure out how to tell him and break things off when I caught him with Traci. I honestly can't blame him for what he did. I'm sure I'd been distant and he was reacting to that."

"No," I say forcefully. "His cheating was *not* your fault. He chose to sleep with another woman."

"Yeah, but I wasn't exactly faithful."

"Did you do anything with that other guy? Did you go on a date with him? Did you kiss him or sleep with him? Did you have intimate conversations with him?"

"No."

"Then you weren't unfaithful. End of story."

Melissa sighs. "Maybe."

"No maybe about it." I'll keep telling her that until she believes it. "So after you dumped Jeremy, what happened? Did you end up dating that other guy?"

"The first thing I did was move out of our apartment. Jeremy's name was the only one on the lease, so I had no choice. I crashed on a friend's couch, but that wasn't a long-term solution, obviously. And I didn't date the other guy. Turned out he didn't want a long-term relationship, and I was already considering leaving New York and didn't want to jump immediately back into dating anyway. Coupled with the stuff with my dad, I decided the best thing I could do was move back home to Chicago. I haven't regretted one minute of it. I reconnected with the Hamilton boys, became friends with Leslie and Wendy, and can't imagine my life without any of them in it."

Can she imagine her life without me in it? Probably. I've only been in it as more than an acquaintance for a little over a week.

"I love my life here, Bobby. But I also really like you. I was willing to try long-distance before, but knowing about Kelli, I'm now not sure. Not because I don't want to date someone with a teenage kid, but because I don't want her to get hurt, either. Does she know about me—about whatever this might be between us?"

I sigh. "She does, which makes it more complicated. She overheard me talking to her mother about you, and then she heard the voicemail Wendy left, ordering me to call you tonight."

Melissa chuckles. "Wendy's a keeper."

"She is. But yes, since Kelli knows, there's no keeping you and me under the radar until we figure things out. And for the record, she wants this to work out. She's already invested, and sneaking around isn't an option, because she'll ferret everything out of me. Well, maybe not *everything*, but the basics at least. And I won't lie to her."

"I wouldn't want you to. While I'd love to keep talking, I'm going to let you go. I have a lot to think about, and I feel like you do, too. Let's talk again in a few days, okay? And if you change your mind and decide trying to date me long-distance isn't worth it, promise you'll let me know?"

My chest clenches. "You're worth it."

"You think that now, but you might change your mind. And if so, that's fine. I get it."

"Okay, we'll talk again in a few days. I'll let you initiate the call, whenever you're ready. Let me give you my number."

After we hang up, I stay in my chair. I'm exhausted, both physically and emotionally. I'm also relieved that Melissa didn't tell me to go take a hike. I'm not any closer to knowing how this can work out than I was before. Semi-retiring could definitely help, but that doesn't solve the problem of us living two thousand miles apart.

Part of me wonders why I'm even considering this, but the other part knows Melissa is special. I've never felt this comfortable with a woman, apart from Nanette. But the feelings I have for Melissa are different than any I ever had for my ex-wife. There's this ache deep down inside me because it's been a week since I was with her, and I just want to see her gorgeous face and give her a tight hug. And yeah, I want to kiss her and do other things I can't tell my daughter about. Then I want to fall asleep with us tangled up in each other. *Every night.* That's the kicker right there. Usually one night is all I want with a woman. I know that might make me seem like a jerk, but the women always know the deal going in.

Melissa is not a one-night woman. Not for me.

Knock, knock.

"Dad? It's quiet in there. Are you off the phone?"

I can't help but smile while I sigh. "You can come in, kitten."

The door swings open, revealing my daughter with a fist on her hip and the other hand gesturing wildly. "Kitten? Really? You think that's better than 'baby'?"

I throw my hands wide. "Then what should I call you?"

"Uh, my name?" She throws her own hands out and rolls her eyes. "It's Kelli, in case you've forgotten."

"I had forgotten. Thanks for the reminder," I say dryly.

"Whatever." She curls up in the oversized green chair she made me put in here for her soon after we moved in. I don't meet with clients at my house—other than Diego, but he actually stays here with me when he's in town—so I didn't initially have another chair in here. However, that didn't work for my daughter. She wanted pink, but I put my foot down on that, so we settled on kelly green, because she claimed that would remind me of her every time I looked at it. She wasn't wrong.

"What do you need, cupcake?" I tease her.

She slices her hand through the air. "*No.* No cupcakes or muffins or kittens or bunnies or other desserts or adorable animals. And I need to know what Melissa said."

I fold my hands in front of me on my desk. "I'm not sure that's any of your business."

Kelli sighs dramatically. "Dad, we've already discussed this. It's totally my business. Now tell me."

"She's thinking about it." That's really all she needs to know. I'm for sure not telling her about Melissa's jerkwad of an ex-fiancé.

"See? She didn't send you packing. What did I tell you?"

"Yeah, but she didn't say yes."

"But you're giving her the chance to decide for herself, and I think she appreciates that. I haven't met her, obviously, but I don't think you'd be interested in dating a woman who would let you make decisions for her. You appreciate independence."

That's pretty insightful for a thirteen-year-old. "You're right. About Melissa and in general." I hadn't ever thought about it that way, but my daughter is right.

"Of course I am. You and Mom are raising me to be an independent woman, so it only makes sense that's the type of woman you'd want to be with."

I point at her. "You're not an independent woman yet. Don't go getting any ideas."

Kelli rolls her eyes. "I know. But I will be. And you don't make all my decisions for me. You let me make some of them even if you don't agree with them, as long as they're not something that'll get me killed. And then when I screw up, you don't get mad. Well, maybe you do for a minute or two … or ten, but then you hug me and help me see what I could've done better."

I lean back in my chair and cross my arms. "When did you grow up and figure all that out?"

She shrugs and smirks at me from her chair. "When I turned thirteen."

"Hmm." She might also spend too much time around adults—the curse of the only child.

"It's what you do with your clients, too. I hear you on the phone with them sometimes. You try to talk them out of doing some of the dumb stuff they want to do, but in the end, you let them make their decisions and then help them clean up their mess when it all falls apart. And then you show them how they could've made better choices. You're like their dad."

I'm not like *my* dad, that's for sure. I'm like the dad I wish I'd had. I try to do the opposite of what my dad would've done, which has worked out pretty well for us.

"You're really good at your job," she continues. "I know a lot of people think you're a jerk, and believe me, you can be at times. Like to Mrs. Canby."

She raises an eyebrow at me, and I shrug. The headmistress at Kelli's private school is … well, she's a jerk.

Kelli continues, "And you can be a jerk when you're trying to get a deal for your clients. But you're not a jerk *to* your clients, at least not that I've overheard. I mean, Uncle Diego loves you like a brother. And Jimmie Zane is an idiot, but he trusts you with his life. You really do treat him like he's your kid. You ran off to Chicago to straighten him out two days after Christmas when you could've just let him continue to screw up his career and leave all the mess to his PR people to clean up. I repeat, it's like he's your kid and you're trying to get him on the right path. Of course, you're old enough he could be your kid," she teases.

"Haha. You're so funny. But no agent is going to let their client run wild without trying to rein them in." Plus, Leslie is his PR rep and there was no way I was letting her deal with Jimmie drama the week before her wedding.

"Maybe so. But I don't think other agents do it like you do. I know that horrible Wayne McCormack doesn't." She shivers dramatically, and I laugh. My nemesis truly is a terrible person. "You really care about those guys, even if you don't say it. You show it by the way you treat them and help them be better people."

Maybe she's right, but what she didn't point out is I left town to go be a pseudo-father to a grown man when I should've been right here with my actual teenage daughter a couple weeks ago. I got an earful about it at the time, but she seems to have moved on. I'm not sure I want her to move on from something like that, though.

"Ba—" I catch myself before fully calling her baby again. "I'm sorry I left you to go clean up Jimmie's mess. I should've left him to deal with it on his own."

"I know you're sorry. You've said it twenty times. But you can't help it. You want to help those idiots. But it would be nice if you were here more to help this idiot." She points her thumb at herself.

"You're not an idiot."

"I know. I was just making a point."

"It was well made. Sounds like I might need to be saving up money for law school."

"I'd kick some butt in a courtroom," she declares.

"You would indeed."

thirty-one

. . .

Melissa

"Told you he's a good guy." Wendy smirks at me and then takes a giant bite of her disgusting-looking ice cream float —chocolate ice cream with orange soda and strawberry syrup.

She and Randall are sitting across a booth from me in Pat's Diner. I wanted to talk to Wendy last night after I talked to Bobby, but it was 10:00, and I decided not to bother her. When I called her this morning, she said she could meet me for lunch after church. I didn't think about the fact that would also include Randall, but I really don't mind. He knows Bobby better than Wendy does, so it'll likely be helpful for me talk to him anyway.

"Lunch" for Wendy apparently means her nasty float and mustard-covered fries. Randall is downing a double bacon cheeseburger like he hasn't eaten in a week. I'm only picking at my club sandwich and chips. I don't really feel like eating.

"Yes," I tap a chip on my plate, "I already knew he was a good guy, but thanks for reiterating."

Wendy narrows her eyes. "There's no need to get snippy with me."

"She's not being snippy," Randall chides. "She's confused. Give her a break. Imagine if I sprang a thirteen-year-old daughter and a backyard ex-wife on you after knowing you for eight months."

"All right. I get your point." Wendy then eyes me as she

shovels in more of her float and I almost gag. "How do you feel about all of this?"

"I think I'm more attracted to him now than I was before. Who knew I was into single dads? But there's a lot at stake, most notably when it comes to Kelli. What if she gets attached to me, and then we break up? And then there's his ex. He says there's nothing between them anymore, but how do I know that? How can I trust what he says? The last man I trusted betrayed me in the worst way."

"I've seen them together," Randall says, "when I was in L.A. for my bachelor party. Nanette and Kelli joined us for lunch, and I'll admit I was watching her carefully to see if what Bobby had said was true—that they're just friends, because I was skeptical—and I saw nothing to make me think otherwise. They interacted like ...," he tapped his chin as he thought, "well, to compare them to people we know, like me and Leslie. We're completely ourselves with each other, and we love each other, but as friends and now siblings, not anything else."

"That's reassuring," I say, a bit relieved by his assessment of that situation, though not completely. "But that aside, with his life being centered in California, and mine being here, it's difficult to see how we could be together long-term."

"You're set on staying in Chicago, then?" Wendy asks.

I shrug. "I don't know. I mean, I was. If you'd asked me ten days ago if I'd move across the country for a man, I'd have given you a resounding no. It's still a half-resounding no. I can't make that kind of decision after spending a handful of days with someone. Ultimately, I guess I'm open to moving if I'm in love and can imagine myself marrying the guy, but I'm not at that point with Bobby. And I'm not going to rush into anything, especially considering my last relationship."

"He's not Jeremy," Wendy states. "I can't see Bobby being a cheater—not with Nanette or anyone else. And you knew Jeremy for a long time, anyway, so that argument doesn't hold much water."

"I know, but that situation has made me a bit wary when it comes to men."

"Men can be total pigs." This comes from the man at the table just before he takes a giant bite of his burger and a dollop of ketchup drops onto his light-blue oxford shirt.

Wendy and I both burst into laughter.

"What?" Randall says after he swallows. "It's true. We all have the ability. Some of us have just learned to mostly bury that tendency."

"But not always?" I tease as his wife tries to wipe the ketchup off his shirt but makes more of a mess of it.

Wendy rolls her eyes. "Definitely not always. But back to you and Bobby. If Kelli already knows about you, and you decide *not* to date her dad, she might think she's the reason why. So that's not great for her, either."

I groan. "Thanks for pointing out that no matter what I do, I'm going to hurt his kid."

"That's not what I meant," Wendy protests and then tilts her head, "though you make a good point. But *my* point is that while it's great you're thinking about her feelings, she's going to have feelings no matter what you choose. And you can't control or predict her feelings. Honestly, you can never control anyone's feelings, but especially not a teenage girl's. But you can control what you decide to do, and ultimately, you need to do what you think is best for *you*. Is seeing where things could go with Bobby what's best for you?"

I really want to try and see if it can work. It's odd that even though Bobby and I are so different, he seems to get me—the real me that's silly and fun, not the professional work version of me. Jeremy never truly understood me, so I hid that part of myself, which obviously wasn't a great move. And I think I get Bobby, too, even though I've only known the full version of him for about fourteen hours. I also miss him more than I thought it was possible to miss anyone.

"You're thinking hard over there." Randall pops a fry into his mouth. He was smart enough to order his own fries today.

"I think it is what's best for me."

Wendy waves a fry in the air, flinging mustard onto Randall's hair in the process. "Yessss! Go home and call him now."

I chuckle at her enthusiasm. "Maybe I'll finish lunch first."

She flicks her hand at my plate. "You're not eating it anyway. Get a doggie bag and take it home with you. And then call him!"

"Hello?"

I'm briefly startled to hear a girl's voice come through the phone line, but it should've occurred to me that Kelli might answer the phone at Bobby's house.

"Hi, is this Kelli?"

"Yeeees. Is this Melissa?" Her voice is full of glee and maybe a little mischief.

"It sure is. Is your dad there?"

"No, he went to go pick up my mom from the hospital. He said it would be a lot of sitting around and waiting, so I decided to stay here and sit around and watch *Can't Buy Me Love* while I wait."

How did I forget Nanette was coming home today? I should've waited a few days to call, like Bobby had suggested.

"I'm so glad she's coming home and that she'll be OK."

I'm not sure what else to say. I don't feel right having a conversation with Bobby's daughter before I talk to him. Does he want me to talk to her and get to know her yet? I don't know how to navigate this.

"Thanks. Are you going to date my dad?"

Laughter bursts out of me at her question. "I love that you just came out and asked that, but I think maybe I need to tell him the answer to that question first." It occurs to me that if I spend any more time talking to her now, she'll guess my answer, and I truly do need to talk to Bobby first. "Could you ask him to call me when he has time? It doesn't need to be today. I know you'll all be busy getting your mom settled."

"Oh, he'll have time for *you*," she says meaningfully. I can hear the grin in her voice.

I stifle another laugh. "All right. Tell him I'll be out for a few hours this evening but should be home by 8:30 my time."

"I'll let him know."

"Thanks. It's been nice talking to you, Kelli."

"You, too. And I look forward to talking to you again … and again … and again."

I allow myself to chuckle at her. "We'll see. Bye, Kelli."

"Hey, I hope it's not too late to call," Bobby's voice comes through the line.

A smile blooms on my face as I lie in my bed staring at the ceiling. "Not at all. I'm a night owl." I may be in bed, but I've been reading the latest Anne Rice vampire book for the last hour.

"Good to know."

"Is it?" I twist the phone cord around my finger.

"You tell me. Will that knowledge be useful in my future?"

I close my eyes and imagine Bobby in the bed next to me. "It will." I shiver involuntarily.

He lets out a breath loud enough I can hear it. *Very* good to know."

"Is it?" I tease.

"Indeed it is. Did Kelli tell you anything inappropriate about me when you talked to her earlier?"

I giggle. "Wouldn't you like to know?"

"I truly would, but if you girls need to keep your secrets, I get it."

"You do?"

"Teenage daughter, remember?"

"Hard to forget that. She was very nice to me on the phone, by the way. And she didn't say much other than she was sure you'd make time to call me today. She also asked if I was going to date you."

Bobby laughs, and my heart stutters. I wish I was with him in person, feeling his laugh rumbling through me as he held me tight.

"Of course she did," he says. "She doesn't beat around the

bush, much like another woman I know. But just to clarify, you do want to date me?"

"I do." I bite my lip. "I want to try to make this work."

"Me, too."

"I'm not sure what that means, though. Do we talk on the phone every day? Or is that too much? How do we deal with the time zone difference? When's a good time of day for you to talk? And how often do we visit each other? Do you have a work trip planned to come here? At what point would you want me to meet Kelli and her mom?"

"Whoa, there, Trigger. That's a lot of questions I don't have the answers to."

"I'm not sure if I find it endearing or insulting that you're comparing me to Roy Rogers' horse."

"Well, you kind of look like—"

A horse? "Hey, now! No need to—"

He cuts in loudly, "I was going to say Dale Evans with dark hair."

That shuts me up for a few seconds while I think about it. "Really?"

"Yeah."

"I don't see it, but whatever floats your boat."

"You float my boat."

My face heats and I fan it with my free hand. "And when is your boat going to be floating this way?"

"I hope to come later this week, but I want to make sure Nanette is settled and doing well with Opal before I make any firm plans. As for you coming here, let's hold off on that for now. I'd like us to spend more time getting to know each other before getting Kelli any more involved than she already is."

"I get that. She was downright ecstatic on the phone earlier. Speaking of, how often do you want to talk? Is every day too much, with everything going on in your life?"

"Not if it's OK for me to call you late like this. With work and family stuff, I'm usually on the go without much of a break all day, but once Kelli's tucked away in her room for the night, I should have time most nights unless I have a client emergency or am in the air. What about you?"

"I'm home most nights these days, especially with my two closest friends now being married." I wonder if he knows about the baby yet. "I hope I can still spend an evening or two with one or both of them each week, but we'll see how well that plan works out once Leslie and Ash are home from their honeymoon."

"And once Randall and Wendy move and then add another little person into the mix."

I smile at the thought of my friends as soon-to-be parents. "They told you?"

"They did, and they said you knew, so I knew it was OK to mention it. I'm happy for them."

"Me, too."

I must sound a little wistful, because Bobby says, "I know we briefly discussed whether we each want future kids when we were in Arkansas, but can we do it again now that you know about Kelli? Does that change anything for you, if marriage could be in our future?"

"No. I'd still like a couple kids." My mind flashes back to the image in my head when Diego mentioned me having Bobby's babies, and I smile. "And based on my own experience as an only child, I'm thinking Kelli might not mind being a big sister."

"She would love being a big sister more than anything other than maybe her mom being perfectly healthy and me being home every night. And I'm open to having more kids, though I'd prefer for it to happen in the next five years or so. I can't imagine dealing with all the sleepless nights and diaper blowouts and chasing after a toddler and everything else that comes with parenting little people when I'm much older than that."

"That makes sense." I don't mention it's good to know he plans on being an involved parent if he has more kids. My dad wasn't really part of my day-to-day life, which was common for men of his generation, but I'd like a more balanced parenting approach in my own marriage.

"Not that parenting is easy when you have a teenager," he

says with a chuckle. "In some ways it's harder, but it's not as physically taxing."

thirty-two

· · ·

Bobby

I'm still amazed by how much I want to talk to Melissa. I'm not a big talker when I'm not working. And even for work, I only have the conversations I'm required to have. Diego is the only exception when it comes to people I interact with for work. And I guess indirectly Ash and Leslie as well, since they both also work for Diego in one way or another. But wanting to talk to a woman like this? A woman I'm interested in? It honestly hasn't ever happened before. I do enjoy talking to Nanette, and I consider her one of my best friends, but I never had an overwhelming desire to constantly talk to her or be with her like I do with Melissa.

"So what've you been up to since you got back home from Arkansas?" I ask.

"You don't want to hear about the trip home with Diego?" she teases. "Make sure he didn't try to steal me away from you?"

"I have no doubt he'd have tried his best to flirt with you and maybe try to seduce you if the circumstances were different," I admit, "but I already talked to him and he said he kept his hands to himself and was the perfect gentleman."

"Well, I don't know about perfect, but he was respectful for the most part."

My eyebrows draw together. "But not for the whole part?" I practically growl. I might be needing to have a conversation with the man.

"Calm down, Bobby Joe. He just asked me some very personal questions when we played 'Truth or Dare,' but I shut him down."

"How personal are we talking?" I demand, sitting up straight in my office chair.

"More personal than I wanted to get with him, but he did respect my choice to not respond."

"Well, that's good at least." I'd still be having a chat with him about it, though.

"But enough about Diego. The trip was fine. Actually, it was fun, because how could it not be, considering the company? Since then I've mostly been working. I've seen Wendy and Randall a couple times, and tonight I went to my parents' house for dinner. I go over there every Sunday evening. Once a month the Hamilton crew joins us, or we go over to Ruth's. Well, I guess it's not going to be just Ruth's anymore, is it? That's so weird they'll all be practically living together. Good weird, mind you, but still weird."

My chest tightens. "It's also weird that my ex-wife lives in my backyard. Is *that* a good weird?" I'm honestly more worried about this being an issue for her than me having a teenager.

She hesitates the briefest of seconds, and my heart stops.

"Definitely good weird. It shows you're a compassionate man, and it also tells me you want to be as close to your daughter as possible, even when she's not living in your house."

I blow out a long breath. "I appreciate you saying that."

"I'm not just saying it. I mean it."

"Thanks."

"Anyway," she says, "I'm not sure I'd want to be a newlywed and living with my in-laws, but to each their own, I guess."

"It's a giant house and large property, and I think it'll work out OK for all of them."

"I hope so," she replies. "Now, tell me about your house. I want to be able to picture you there when I talk to you. Where are you sitting right now?"

"I'm sitting at my desk in my home office."

"That doesn't sound very comfortable."

"It's not bad. I have a fancy chair. It's padded and I can swivel it and move it up and down." I swivel back and forth a few times for no good reason other than thinking about that option. "I've even fallen asleep in it a time or two."

"Ooo, that is a fancy office chair. Mine makes my back hurt."

"Maybe I need to have a chat with your employer about getting better chairs for the office." The team management respects me because of Diego, so they'd likely make it happen without question.

"You don't need to do that."

"I can do it, though. It wouldn't be just for you but for all employees, if you're worried about being singled out."

"All right then, I won't complain if you get them to spring for comfy chairs in the office."

A smile spreads across my face. "Consider it done."

"Pretty confident in your abilities there, aren't you, Bobby Joe?"

I chuckle. "Always, when it comes to convincing baseball execs to do something they might not do otherwise."

"Or you could have Diego ask, and there will be absolutely zero chance they'll say no."

Though I should be slightly offended by that, a full-blown belly laugh bursts out of me. "True. And if they do say no, he'll just buy the chairs himself." It occurs to me I could do the same thing. However, the Cubs wouldn't find it as odd for Diego to ask for or buy new office chairs for everyone as it would be for me to do so. Plus, Leslie could potentially use it as positive PR for our mutual client.

"Either way," I say, "we're getting you and your co-workers new chairs."

Melissa cheers, and my heart soars.

"So tell me about the rest of your office," she demands. "Is it dark and brooding, with imposing mahogany furniture and a plush rug?"

I smile again. "It's nice to know you think I live like the mafia don you believe me to be."

"I bet there's also a portrait of a horse and you have an illegal gambling den in the basement."

"You nailed it."

She pauses. "Really?"

Another belly laugh bursts free. What is it about this woman that makes me laugh so much?

"No, none of that is true. Well, I do have a plush rug, but that's about it. My house is Mediterranean style, so the floors are terracotta tiles, the ceilings have exposed beams, and the walls are white. Well, except for Kelli's room, which is bright pink." It's like a Barbie box exploded in there, although she claims she's too old to play with the dolls anymore. "My office is on the second floor, with a balcony overlooking the backyard."

"There's a pool in that backyard, isn't there?"

"Yes, and a hot tub."

"Oh, man, I could use a hot tub right about now."

I try not to picture her in my hot tub with me, and I fail miserably. But then I realize since we're dating, there's nothing wrong with picturing us together in a hot tub, which makes me smile yet again.

"What's Nanette's house like?" she asks. "I'm guessing it's the same style?"

I swivel my chair so I can look outside, where the guest house is faintly glowing from the security lights I had installed. "Yes, but smaller and only one story, so she doesn't have to deal with stairs. We weren't sure she'd be able to climb them when I bought the place."

"Makes sense. Kelli told me you were off to pick her up from the hospital when I called earlier. So she's doing all right?"

"Yes, she was in the hospital a few days longer than they expected, but she's holding her own. She's glad to be home in her own bed, though, without nurses waking her up every few hours."

"Why do they do that in the hospital?" she asks. "It's never made any sense to me, at least not for most patients."

"I guess they want to be thorough." I tap my fingers on my desk. "And maybe avoid malpractice lawsuits."

"Spoken like a lawyer."

I grin. "Did you expect anything less?"

"Can't say I did."

"Now, tell me how you ended up working for the team."

"The short story is my dad has long-time connections with the team through both the Wrigley family and the Tribune. He was able to get me an interview, and I really hope I got the job because I'm qualified and not because of my dad."

I shake my head. "I'm thinking your job history of working in HR on Wall Street more than qualifies you for the job, along with your Ivy League education. And you're great at interacting with people of all kinds. They'd have been crazy not to hire you."

"I appreciate you saying that."

"I'm not just saying that," I tease, echoing her words from earlier. "I mean it."

"Thanks. And while I would love to talk to you all night long, it's getting late here, and I need my beauty sleep."

I take a second to weigh my words before saying, "You don't need beauty sleep. You're already stunning." That sounds like a line, but I mean it with all my being.

She huffs out a laugh. "Wow, B.S., that was smooth."

"Maybe so, but it's true. It's also true that you need sleep, though, so I'll let you go."

"Call me tomorrow night? I don't have any plans after work, so I'll be around all night, whenever you have time to call."

"Sounds perfect."

"How was your chat with Melissa last night?" Kelli asks as we're driving to school Monday morning.

I cut my eyes to her for a moment. "How do you know I talked to her?" I'm surprised she didn't ask me about Melissa the second she walked into the kitchen for breakfast.

She shrugs and smirks. "Because you liiiiiike her! Why would you wait?"

"OK, fine. I called her." I don't give her more details yet, because I know that will drive her crazy.

"Aaaaaaaaaaand?" She sweeps an arm out as she says it.

"I guess we're dating now."

My daughter squeals and does a cute little shimmy in her seat. "Yesssss! When do I get to meet her?"

I sigh. "Not anytime soon. She lives halfway across the country, remember? And the two of us need to get to know each other better before I spring you on her." I shoot her a grin. "I'm afraid once she meets you, she might keep dating me just because you're such a great kid and not because she likes me."

Her cheeks turn pink at the compliment. "You're pretty likable, too." She raises an eyebrow at me. "Except when you're being a jerk."

I clap a hand over my heart. "Ouch."

"If the shoe fits, grumpy pants."

I reach over and give her a playful shove on the shoulder. "I love you, kiddo."

"Love you, too. But I'd love you more if you let me meet your girlfriend soon." She barks out a laugh. "Dude, it's weird you have a girlfriend."

"Dude? Did you just call me 'dude'?"

"Sure did. Would you rather me call you 'old man'?"

"Uh, no." I pull up in front of her school. "Have a good day at school, pumpkin."

Kelli shakes a finger in my face. "No. No pumpkin."

"All right, dude."

She laughs again and flings her arms around my neck. "You're the silliest grumpy old man I know. Now, go home and call Melissa and tell her you're going to fly her out here to meet me this weekend."

"Not gonna happen." I do want to see her, but hopefully I'll be able to fly to Chicago for a couple days later this week. "See you after school." Whitley's mom offered to bring Kelli home after school every day this week, which is a great help. By next week, Opal should feel comfortable leaving Nanette long enough to make the twenty-minute round trip to go pick her up.

Kelli slams the door, waves at me through the window, and then dashes toward a group of girls a few dozen yards away.

I really don't know how I managed to raise such a great kid. Actually, most of the credit goes to Nanette, but I'm pretty sure I haven't done much to mess Kelli up, other than being out of town a lot. Oh, and let's not forget getting into a car accident that nearly cost her mom her life. As I pull out of the school drive, I shake my head at myself. If I'm going to continue to move forward with my life, I need to start believing what everyone keeps telling me—the accident was in no way my fault.

When I get back home, I'm going to need to jump right back into work mode. Since some of my clients play for teams in the Eastern time zone, I'm typically up by five a.m. If I don't have any urgent messages waiting for me, I'll spend some time in my home gym before starting the work day. Today was not one of those days. Jimmie Zane is still acting like a child, which is why I'll likely be heading back to Chicago this week. Not that I'm complaining much. I don't really want to leave Kelli and Nanette again so soon after the hospital stay, but I want to make sure my client doesn't do anything else to damage his budding career and, of course, I want to see Melissa.

My *girlfriend* Melissa. It's as weird for me to think that as it was for Kelli to say it. I've never had a girlfriend, which is bizarre for a man who has been married, but Nanette and I went straight from friendship to marriage. I didn't date during my brief stint in high school, and even in college and law school, I never went on more than a handful of dates with any one woman. It didn't help that I was a few years younger than my classmates, but I also was so busy working and studying that I didn't have much time for anything else.

Granted, I haven't even gone on one typical date with Melissa, and now I'm calling her my girlfriend. But I figure spending all that one-on-one time together and then choosing to date long-distance qualifies her for the position. Maybe I should ask her, though, before I introduce her to someone as my girlfriend and I find out she doesn't feel we're at that stage yet.

I wasn't lying when I said I don't know how to do this. Not only do I not know how to date as a single dad, I don't really know how to date in general. Everything I know I learned this past year from watching Ash and Randall navigate their own relationships. Neither of them did things the conventional way either, though. But maybe that's always the case. Life and relationships don't usually play out like movies and books suggest they will.

thirty-three

. . .

Melissa

"I'm taking the red-eye tonight to Chicago," Bobby tells me over the phone Wednesday evening. "I'll be in meetings all day tomorrow through dinner. But I want to see you after that, if it's not too late for you. I'll be heading back home early Friday morning so I'll be back by the time Kelli gets home from school, and I want Opal to be able to take the night off. She says she doesn't mind the around-the-clock work since it's hopefully only for a few weeks this time, but I don't want her to burn out. She hasn't left the house since Nanette came home Sunday other than to get some snacks Kelli was craving. The woman is a total pushover for that kid."

My heart tumbles around in my chest, both at knowing I'll be seeing Bobby in about twenty-four hours and from his dedication to his family and employee.

"I'll be free whenever you are. I don't care where or when." Maybe I shouldn't sound so eager or available, but I don't want to play games with this man. He deserves to know where I stand and how I feel.

"Excellent."

I wonder if his dimple is showing, and the mental image of his smiling face puts a grin on my own.

"I'll be at the Drake," he tells me. "Since I'm not going to be there even one full night, I'm camping out with Diego in his suite.

He came back from the Dominican today and will be in the city for a couple weeks while he does some stuff with his foundation. Would it be too much trouble for you to meet me at the hotel? Or would you rather I come to you?"

"I'm happy to go downtown."

"Great. How about you plan to get there by eight? You can hang out with your buddy Diego if I end up taking longer than expected at dinner."

"Sounds great."

"And if our little pal ends up being too much of a third wheel, we can head down to the hotel bar to get away from him."

I chuckle. "I have a feeling we'll be hitting that bar." I hesitate only a second before adding, "I can't wait to see you."

"I can't wait to kiss you."

I burst out laughing. "Yeah, that, too."

"How's my favorite road trip buddy?" Diego wraps me in a bear hug the moment I step through the door into his hotel suite. Then he grabs me by the shoulders, holds me away from him, and looks me in the eye. "You good?" He waggles his eyebrows. "Ready to see your lover?"

I wriggle out of his grasp and swat him on the chest. "Don't use that word. It squicks me out." I move past him into the living area, which is exactly as ostentatious as I expected Diego's home to be. The man likes to make a statement, and the statement here is "I miss the Caribbean, so I'm channeling that aesthetic, taking everything up a notch, and creating my own fancy tropical oasis in the middle of the Upper Midwest." I wonder if Ruth Hamilton realizes what this man will do to her home if she allows him to move in.

He follows me in. "Squicks?" His forehead wrinkles. "I don't know this word."

"That's because I made it up," I explain, plopping onto a plush orange-and-turquoise couch. I wonder if the hotel sprang for this decor for him, or if he paid for it. "It means . . ." Instead of using words, I screw up my face into a grimace, clench my fists, and make my entire body shudder.

Diego points a finger at me. "Got it. I wouldn't want you to squick again, so I'll refrain from calling Bobby your lover in the future."

I shudder again, and he laughs before holding a hand out to me.

"Up, woman. Do you not smell the deliciousness coming from the dishes on the table? Our dinner has already arrived."

No more than five minutes after I hung up with Bobby last night, Diego called, inviting me to eat dinner with him tonight while I wait to see Bobby. I accepted the invitation after ensuring he wasn't the one who would be cooking. I've heard stories of his kitchen disasters.

"You look lovely, by the way," Diego says as he leads me to the dining table, which is loaded with multiple covered dishes.

"Why thank you," I say with a curtsy as I glance down at my burgundy wrap dress. "I wore it especially for you." I considered choosing something more casual, but since I anticipated heading to the hotel bar with Bobby, I didn't want to be underdressed.

Diego laughs. "You're a liar, but a *muy bonita* one." He pulls my chair out and then takes the seat across the teak table from me.

"What are you feeding me?"

He whips the lids off two of the dishes with a flourish. "*Pollo guisado, mofongo,* and a few other Dominican dishes. I made the chef here learn to cook some of my favorites from back home." He bobs his head from side to side. "He does a decent job of it."

"OK, I know *pollo* is chicken, but what's *mofongo?*"

"Fried plantains with yummy spices."

"Sounds—and smells—wonderful."

We hear a key jiggling the lock, and Diego jumps off the couch, where we've been hanging out and chatting since finishing the delicious dinner.

"As much as I'd love to watch how this goes down, I'll leave you two to greet each other in private," he says as he jogs toward his room.

The bedroom door snicks shut as the entry door opens. I stand as Bobby appears, his eyes scanning the room until his gaze lands on me. His handsome face lights up, and my hands are suddenly clammy, so I wipe them on my thighs.

He scans me up and down and then stalks toward me. I'm only able to take a few tentative steps toward him. Bobby comes to a stop in front of me and takes my hands in his.

"Hey, are you OK?" he asks.

I nod. "Just nervous," I admit.

His dimple pops. "Me, too. Even so, I'm going to kiss you."

"You'd better. And don't tease me this time."

Bobby chuckles as his hands cup my face and his gaze slides from my eyes down to my mouth. "I'll save the teasing for later." Then one warm hand slides to the nape of my neck and he brings my lips to his.

My hands fist in his shirt as he takes the kiss from tender to heated after what seems like only a few seconds but could be minutes for all I know. One of his hands glides down to the small of my back, and he pulls me flush against him. Then he backs me toward the couch as a muffled voice calls out from the other room.

"Are you done with the kissy-kissy, or should I stay in here a little longer?" Diego asks.

Bobby and I both laugh as we pull our mouths apart.

He rests his forehead against mine. "I don't know why I thought I didn't need my own hotel room."

"It's fine," I say. "Being alone in a hotel room might've put some pressure on us that we don't need quite yet."

Bobby angles his head back and searches my eyes. "That's exactly why I did this. Not that I don't want to take things to the bedroom with you someday, but I don't think today should be that day. We should probably go on a date first."

"Might be a good idea."

"Helloooooo," comes from the other room.

Bobby sits on the couch and pulls me down onto his lap. When

I give him a questioning look, he quirks an eyebrow. "Don't you want to see how he'll respond to this?"

With a nod and a grin, I reply, "I sure do."

"It's safe to come out," Bobby calls out.

Diego is out of his room in a flash, a smile splitting his face as he takes us in. He clasps his hands under his chin like a little kid in a donut shop. "I cannot tell you how happy this makes me. All of my American friends are marrying each other!"

"Hold your horses, Uncle Diego." I hold a hand up. "We haven't even gone on a date yet."

He waves a hand in the air. "Pedantics."

Bobby shakes his head. "Pretty sure that doesn't mean what you think it means."

"Whatever." Diego perches on the coffee table in front of us. "Now, what are we going to discuss first? How about where you'll live when you get married?"

"We," I point between Bobby and myself, "are going to head downstairs to the bar and discuss various topics amongst ourselves." I point to him. "You are going to stay here and *not* start planning our wedding."

Diego sticks his lip out in a pout. "Fine. But I'm calling Kelli and finding out what she thinks about all this." He points a finger at us and moves it in a circle.

Bobby huffs. "I don't love that idea, but I'll never try to stop you from calling your favorite teenager. I actually can't believe you haven't called her to talk about us already."

"I've been busy. And calls to the US are *expensive* when I'm back home."

"I think you can afford it." Bobby nudges me up and then stands and takes my hand. "If you'll excuse us, we're going to head downstairs for a while, and then I'll take Melissa home. Don't wait up."

"Oh, I'm waiting up." Diego lets out a vaguely evil-sounding chuckle before wrapping me in one of his signature hugs. "But I guess I won't be seeing you again tonight, my beautiful Melissa. We'll get together again before I leave town, though, yes?"

"I'd love to."

"Good. Then you'll get a chance to thank me for the new, very expensive and extremely comfortable chairs that will automatically appear at your office over the weekend." He points at Bobby. "Take good care of both of my ladies tonight."

My eyebrow goes up. "Both?"

Bobby sighs. "He's talking about you, of course, and his Lamborghini, which he named Luna."

"You're going to drive me home in a Lamborghini?"

Diego bows. "Only the best for you, *señorita*. I usually make it a rule to not let anyone else drive my Luna, but your Bobby is the exception to many, many rules."

I give Bobby a soft smile. "I'm beginning to learn that about him."

"He is one in a billion." Diego claps his hand over his heart. "Treat him well."

"I will. I promise."

thirty-four

. . .

Bobby

As soon as the elevator doors close behind us and Diego is out of sight from his vantage point down the hall, I pull Melissa into my arms and kiss her again. Knowing the doors could open at any moment, I keep it short though not quite sweet.

"I missed you, Bobby Joe."

My hold on her tightens with the words that hit me right in the heart. "I missed you, too." I cock my head to the side. "I need a nickname for you. What'll it be?"

"Pookie." She nods as if to affirm her choice.

A laugh flies out of me. "Pookie? Really?"

Melissa smiles. "No."

The elevator doors open and I place my hand on the small of her back to guide her out into the lobby and toward the bar. "Too late. You'll forever be my Pookie."

My heart stutters when I realize I just said the word "forever." I hope that doesn't scare her off. Then again, if she were going to be scared off, that probably would've happened long before now.

"Welcome back, Mr. Jacobs," the hostess greets us as we approach. "Would you like a table, or would you and your guest prefer to sit at the bar?"

"A table would be great, Brandi. As private as possible, please. And we'll need a drink menu and dessert menu."

Brandi nods and grabs the menus. "Follow me."

Melissa smiles at me. "Mr. Jacobs," she whispers with a snicker. "That's what I'm calling you the rest of the night."

Why do I like the thought of that so much? "You can call me whatever you want," I murmur back as we follow Brandi to an intimate round corner booth.

Once we're settled and have ordered our drinks and a piece of strawberry cheesecake to share, I brush Melissa's hair off her shoulder and then let my hand rest on her neck while my thumb sweeps back and forth along her jawline.

"What are you doing, Mr. Jacobs?" Melissa asks with a flirty smile.

"It seems I can't keep my hands off you, Pookie." My thumb stills. "Is that OK?"

"The nickname? No. The touching? Definitely. I'm glad we're in this round booth where we don't have to sit across from each other."

I press a soft kiss to her lips. "Me, too."

"Well, isn't this interesting?"

I close my eyes at the sound of my client's voice—the client I left in this very bar twenty minutes ago and who I ordered to go home and not get into any more trouble. Seems he didn't listen.

"Jimmie," I say in a warning tone as I open my eyes and turn to face him.

The giant of a man-child rubs his hands together gleefully. "You work fast, old man." He jerks his chin toward Melissa. "Who's tonight's catch?"

I'm on my feet in less than a second with Jimmie's shirt clenched in my fist. I don't care that he's fifteen years my junior and almost twice my size. "Her name is Melissa, and she's my girlfriend," I nearly hiss out. "And you will apologize to her right now for your rudeness and disrespect."

Jimmie's eyes go wide, and he holds his hands up in surrender. "Sorry, dude. I didn't know."

"Apologize to her, not me," I order, without letting go of him.

When he flashes his trademark grin at Melissa, I growl.

"What?" he snaps. "You told me to apologize."

"Without flirting!"

"Sorry. What's crawled up your—"

I tighten my hold on his shirt. "Apologize to the lady right now," I say through clenched teeth, "or you'll be finding yourself a new agent."

"After all the sh—" his eyes dart to Melissa and back to me, "I mean *crap* I've pulled, *this* is what's gonna tip you over the edge?"

"You wanna try me?"

"Uh, no. Let go of me, man, and I'll apologize."

"Everything all right over here?" The bartender, Jorge, has left his post behind the bar and is eyeing the two of us with a look that says, "I don't care who you are, you'll settle down in my bar or you're not welcome here again."

I let go of Jimmie's shirt, and he smooths it down with his hand.

"We're good." I narrow my eyes at Jimmie. "Right?"

"Yes. Right. Sorry, dude." He aims that at Jorge, but he'd better be saying he's sorry to Melissa within ten seconds.

"That's what I thought." Jorge gives us another stern look before sauntering back over to the bar.

"You were saying?" I prompt Jimmie.

"Ma'am … I mean, well, you're not really old enough to be a ma'am, are you?" His eyes widen. "Did I just make this worse?"

"Spit it out, Zane," I say through clenched teeth.

He lets out a deep breath and dons a halfway repentant look when he addresses Melissa. "I'm sorry for everything I said. I didn't mean any disrespect to either of you." He glances at me and shrugs. "I didn't know she was your girlfriend, man. I didn't even know you *had* a girlfriend."

"Whether she's my girlfriend or not, you should treat any woman with respect. Got it?"

"Got it."

"Now go home."

He salutes me with a grin. "Yes, sir." Then he spins and swaggers out of the bar.

I drop back into my seat with a sigh. "I'm sorry about that."

Melissa's hand lands on my arm. "Oh, I'm not. It was quite

entertaining. And who knew your growly, protective side would be such a turn-on, Mr. Jacobs?"

My hand finds its way back to her leg. "Yeah?"

"Mmmhm. Now, if you'd hit him, that would be a different story, unless he was going after me physically. Violence is not attractive in the least. But a well-placed non-violent threat to a punk kid who doesn't understand how to treat women? Yes, please."

I tip my head toward hers, but before I can kiss her again, the waitress brings our drinks and kills the moment.

"Here you go," she says. "Your cheesecake will be out in a few minutes."

"No rush," I say without taking my eyes off Melissa.

The waitress chuckles and moves off to another table.

"So that was Jimmie Zane." Melissa shakes her head. "I've heard about him from Leslie, but I hadn't met him yet, obviously. You've got your hands full with that one."

"That kid just might be the death of me." I take a sip of my old fashioned. "He's the reason I was here before the wedding and the reason I'm here today. Well, one of the reasons I'm here today." I squeeze her thigh and lean over to give her a quick kiss. "Seeing you definitely made this trip worthwhile."

"When do you think you'll be back again? Do you have anything scheduled?"

"I'm not sure. I've got quite a bit of travel ahead. Next weekend I'll be in Miami for the Super—"

Melissa's eyes go wide as she interrupts. "Wait! Are you serious?"

I nod.

"Do you have some football clients that are playing in the game? Is that why you're going?"

"No, I don't have any football clients these days. I tried doing all the sports early in my career, but that got too hectic with the timing of all the various seasons. Now I'm mostly baseball with a little bit of hockey." Though Jimmie is making me rethink the hockey decision. "But I still take some of my clients to the game each year. It motivates them to want to be the best in their own sports."

I love going to the big game every year, but going this year means I can't be with Melissa. Soon after that, Diego and my other baseball guys will be heading to spring training, so I'll be back in Florida and also in Arizona at some point in the next month or so, which will also keep me away from Chicago and the woman next to me. Could I ask her to join me in one of those places, or would she think I'm moving too fast?

"I would *kill* to go to the game," she says.

"Really? Even though Chicago lost last weekend?"

"Yeah, that was a heartbreaker, but what sports fan wouldn't want to go, no matter who's playing?" Her voice is wistful, and I know she's not angling for me to take her with me, but I'm going to shoot my shot and ask her anyway.

"You wanna go with me?"

Melissa points her thumb at her chest as her jaw drops. "Me?"

"No, my other girlfriend sitting next to you," I tease, wondering if she'll comment on me calling her my girlfriend both now and earlier with Jimmie.

She playfully swats my arm. "You'd better not have any other girlfriends."

I slip my arm around her and press a kiss to her temple. "Only you, Pookie."

She rolls her eyes. "But the game is like ten days away. How will you get me a ticket?"

"I have my ways."

"Ah, there's the ol' Bobby Joe confidence rearing its head again."

"I notice you haven't answered my question." I give her a little squeeze.

Her eyebrows draw together. "What . . . oh, yes, I want to go with you!" She grabs my face between her hands and kisses me soundly. "Thank you, thank you, thank you!"

I chuckle. "If I'd known this was the way to get you to kiss me, I'd have offered you a ticket a long time ago."

She cocks her head to the side. "Like how long ago?"

I swallow. "Uh, well, since I first met you."

"And when was that, again?" she teases.

"Back in May at Diego's first game in Chicago, in the suite at Wrigley."

"When you had no idea what my job was?"

I grimace. "Yes."

"Why did you think I was there?"

I shrug. "I was so overwhelmed by your beauty that I couldn't think about anything else."

Melissa laughs. "Liar."

"It's true." I take another sip of my drink to hide my smile.

"Hmm." She taps her finger on her lips. "I guess I'll let that slide. I'll get on the phone first thing in the morning to get a plane ticket. I hope they're not already sold out."

"I've got you covered on that."

She raises an eyebrow. "Oh, yeah? You gonna fly me in your private jet you've been keeping secret from me?"

"Nope." I flick the tip of her nose with my finger. "My friend's private jet."

"If it just now occurred to you to invite me, how do you know you have a friend going to Miami from Chicago on their private jet and they'll have room to take me along?"

"Because the friend is Diego."

Her head tilts back as she laughs. "Of course. I should've known. But I didn't know he has a private jet."

"He doesn't own one. He just charters one sometimes for longer flights when there's a group going with him, and I can guarantee he'll let you tag along."

Melissa gives me an assessing look. "Jimmie Zane won't be in the group of people on that plane, will he?"

A snort flies out of me before I can stop it. "No. Diego is a generous man, but he can't stand Jimmie. He's taking a few people from his foundation along as a thank you for getting everything up and running these past few months. Unfortunately, Jimmie will be in the suite with us at the game, though. If that makes you change your mind about going, I get it."

"I can handle Jimmie Zane."

Now I don't hide my smile. "I have no doubt about that."

"Is Ash going to the game?"

Our friend runs the Diego Sanchez Foundation, so it's a valid question. "No," I say, "not since he just took a couple weeks off for the wedding and honeymoon."

Melissa nods. "I should've guessed that. Hey, since you met with Jimmie today, does that mean you saw Leslie?"

Ash and Leslie got home from their honeymoon two days ago, and she had to jump right back into the deep end at work thanks to Jimmie's antics.

"I did. She somehow looked both rested and exhausted at the same time. Have you seen her and Ash yet?"

"No. I wanted to give them time to get settled before bothering them."

I take her chin between my thumb and forefinger and search her eyes. "You wouldn't be a bother. Your friends love you like family. I hope you know that."

She removes my hand from her face and threads our fingers together. "I do. But I'm sure it's been hectic for them the last couple days. I'm planning to call Leslie after work tomorrow and hopefully get together with her and Wendy this weekend."

"Good. I'm glad you have them in your life."

"Me, too."

"Of course I'll take your Melissa with me on the plane. I'd do anything for you, *hermano,* and for my new best bud. Now she and I can be sky-trip buddies."

Diego was waiting for me when I returned to the suite after driving Melissa home in his car, as I figured he would be. It's well past midnight, but he's wide awake and ready to talk.

I clap my hand against my chest. "I thought I was your best bud!"

He guffaws. "Nobody can replace you, *Roberto,* but I like your lady a lot, too."

I feel the smile spread across my face, and there's nothing I can do to stop it. "So do I."

"I can tell. You know what you need to do?"

When most people ask me a question like that, I usually know what they're about to suggest. Not with Diego. Goodness only knows what's going to come out of his mouth. "No. Tell me."

"Drop that Jimmie Zane on his scrawny little—"

"He's a professional hockey player, my friend. Nothing about him is scrawny."

Diego rolls his eyes. "Whatever. You know what I'm talking about. Anyway, drop Jimmie. In fact, drop every one of your clients other than me. Then you can be here all the time and act as my personal servant when you're not making sweet, sweet love to your lady."

He laughs at that last part, and I roll my eyes. But the first part of what he said? I've been thinking about it ever since Kelli mentioned cutting back on my work during our chat last weekend. In fact, I haven't thought about much else other than how to make more time for both Melissa and Kelli in my life. The workaholic side of me has been fighting against taking a step back, because it goes against my nature to work less instead of more. But the rest of me wants a break, wants to spend more time with my daughter while she's still at home, wants to take a real shot at this budding relationship with the first woman I've ever missed.

Diego adds, "I'll even redo my contract with you to give you an extra percent to sweeten the deal. That'll make up for almost everyone else's fees combined."

For Diego, that extra percent is a sacrifice. Not because he's greedy, but because he's generous. He wants to make as much money as possible so he can use it to do as much good as possible. So for him to offer to give that money up is a huge deal.

The lump forming in my throat keeps me from immediately replying to his offer, so he continues. "I want you to be happy. Melissa makes you happy. Kelli makes you happy. Jimmie does not. Your other clients do not." He dramatically sweeps his hands around himself. "I do. So keep me, and let everyone else go. Spend more time with Melissa and with Kelli. Be home more so you won't be as worried about Nanette and Kelli when you're away. Do this for them, but also do it for yourself. You've worked your tail off for the past two decades to get to where you are—which is richer and more successful than almost everyone else on Earth. You deserve to spend as much time as possible with the people who make you happy."

I shoot him a wry grin. "You sure you haven't been talking to my daughter this week?"

"Positive. Has she been telling you the same thing?"

"Yes."

He spreads his arms wide. "What can I say? I knew she was a smart biscuit. And since your two favorite people have declared it, then it shall be. You'll drop all clients but me, and we'll ride off together into the sunset like in one of those western movies." He grins when I shoot him a glare. "Or maybe you'll ride off with Melissa and Kelli."

I nod. "That's better."

"It's settled, then?"

He looks so hopeful, another lump forms in my throat. What did I do to deserve a friend like him?

"I'll think about it. But I'm not taking more money from you, and that's final."

"Good enough," he pauses, "for now."

thirty-five

. . .

Melissa

"You *have* to go to Diego's resort." Leslie grins at me from across the booth. "Maybe Bobby will take you someday."

I shake my head but smile back as I cut a piece off my waffle with my fork. "Let's not get ahead of ourselves."

Wendy takes a long drag of her shake and doesn't fully swallow it before saying, "I heard Diego's already planning your wedding." She wipes ice cream off her chin with her sweatshirt sleeve.

It's Saturday morning, and once again, we're at Pat's Diner, because apparently Wendy craves it every day. I'm not sure what she'll do once she and Randall move up to Evanston in a few weeks. And even though it's nine in the morning, she's drinking a shake with a questionable combination of ice cream flavors.

"That man ... actually," I tilt my head, "since you know about that and I'm assuming it's via your husband, I should say *those men* are bigger gossipers than any women I know."

"Not Ash." Leslie smiles smugly. "He knows how to keep a secret."

"Like about how often you two did—or did *not*—leave your room at the resort last week?" Now Wendy's the one looking smug.

Leslie's eyes widen. *"He did not!"* She huffs. "He's in for it when I get home tonight."

I snort. "Yeah, I'm sure he's gonna be real scared."

"Plus, I was kidding." Wendy wiggles her shoulders. "You're the one who just let that cat out of the bag, you little minx."

Leslie groans before allowing a smile to take over her face. "It was pretty great, though."

"I bet it was." Wendy sighs and stares dreamily off into the distance. "If he's anything like—"

I hold up both hands to cut her off. "Stop! I don't need the details about what the Hamilton boys get up to with their wives behind closed doors."

Wendy giggles. "Who says we close our door?"

I laugh loudly enough to draw stares while Leslie says, "Pretty soon you're going to need to both close and lock your door. Don't want to accidentally scar Sonya for life."

"Or your mother-in-law. You sure you want to move?" I tease.

"I'm actually looking forward to it, if you can believe that." Wendy slurps up the last of her shake and sets her empty glass down. "If you'd told me one year ago that right now I'd be married to Randall, pregnant, and about to move into a wing of my mother-in-law's gigantic house that's bigger than my child-hood home—which was not tiny, mind you—I'd have told you to just say no to drugs."

Leslie shoots her a wry grin. "You probably also wouldn't believe you'd be sitting in a diner wearing a stained sweatsuit while drinking a nasty-looking shake."

Wendy glares at her but knows she's right. Our friend is nothing if not fashionable at almost all times. Pregnancy is affecting her in unexpected ways.

"All while catching up with the two best friends a girl could ever ask for." I hold my hands up for them to both give me a high five. Leslie immediately slaps my hand. Wendy wipes some mustard off her hand before slapping the other one. I'm not even sure where the mustard came from, as she hasn't ordered any fries yet. I'm sure that'll happen before we leave, though, despite it still being breakfast hours.

"Back to the most exciting topic at hand." Wendy glances at Leslie. "No offense. It's not that your honeymoon isn't exciting, or that this little peanut isn't exciting," she rubs her belly, "but ... Melissa and Bobby are dating!" She wiggles her fingers and squeals like a little girl who's just been told she's getting a pony.

I try to temper my smile but fail miserably. "I honestly can't believe it."

Wendy props her chin on her palm. "What's your favorite thing about Bobby?"

That's a great question, and I'm not sure how to answer. Is it the way he takes care of the people he loves, and even the ones he doesn't love but who he works for? Is it the way he makes me feel? Is it that he doesn't have any idea what an amazing human he is?

"It's that dimple, isn't it?" Leslie smirks at me. "Don't you just want to poke your finger in there on the rare occasions it makes an appearance?"

Wendy raises an eyebrow. "I can think of something else—"

I make a chopping motion with my hand. "Yes, I love the dimples! But I also love how much he loves his daughter ... and his ex-wife, as weird as that sounds. I like that he cares about his clients and goes above and beyond to help them be better people. I love that *he* wants to be a better man than he is, which is already pretty dang good."

"And he's verrrry easy on the eyes," Wendy adds with a decisive nod.

My entire body heats at the thought. "That he is."

"And he's a great kisser?" Leslie asks.

"Indeed." My face warms even more and I hide it behind my hands.

Wendy reaches across the table and yanks my hands away. "Nothing to be ashamed of. Own it, girl. You've got yourself a hunk of a man." She points her thumb back and forth between herself and Leslie. "Welcome to the club!"

"Thanks ... I guess. Anyway, have either of you met Kelli? Has he ever brought her out here? Or did you take a trip to L.A. and not tell me because I wasn't supposed to know about Bobby's family?"

Leslie shakes her head. "We haven't met her, but the guys did when they flew out to L.A. for Randall's bachelor party in November. In fact, they stayed at Bobby's house. Ash didn't say much about it, which is no surprise to anyone, but Randall still won't shut up about how much he loves the style of Bobby's home." She bobs her head back and forth. "Again, not out of character."

Wendy adds, "We have some photos of the guys that were taken at the house if you want to see them. None with Kelli or her mom, though."

I think about it for a second. "No, I'd rather wait and see Bobby's house when he's ready to show me."

"That makes sense," Leslie says. "I've seen a photo of Kelli, but not from Bobby. Diego is a ridiculously proud honorary uncle, and it drives him a little bit crazy that he doesn't get to show her off to many people. Once he found out I knew about Kelli, he showed me the picture of her he keeps in his wallet."

My hand presses over my heart. "That's so sweet." Then I feel my mouth pull into a frown. "But why didn't he show me? Or why didn't Bobby show me a picture? There's no doubt he's proud of his daughter."

Leslie shrugs. "Bobby probably didn't think about it. He's not used to people knowing about Kelli, much less wanting to see her picture. And maybe Diego thought it wasn't his place to show you."

That makes me feel a little better. "OK, we'll go with that."

Wendy laughs. "Girl, Bobby was thinking about how gorgeous you are and how much he wanted to get his hands and mouth on you. Showing you a picture of his daughter wasn't anywhere near his radar."

Leslie rubs her hands together. "Now let's talk about your upcoming Miami trip. How many hotel rooms will there be?"

The grin on Wendy's face could be seen for miles. "We all know you two aren't opposed to sharing a hotel room—or a bed."

"What?!" Leslie's gaze bounces back and forth between Wendy and me. "*Who* knows this? I don't know this!"

I tell her about our hotel experiences on the trip to her wedding, minus the part about Bobby having a panic attack. I know these two are aware of the accident that nearly killed Nanette, but I doubt they know about his panic attacks. They're not going to hear about them from me.

"Even though we've shared a bed before," I say, "sharing a bed now is a whole different animal. I told him I'm open to staying together, but I'm trusting him to make the decision he thinks is best for him. There's no doubt he's all in on this relationship, but he's being cautious because of Kelli. I get it. He has more at stake than I do if this all goes south."

"Mom, Dad . . ." I take a deep breath. "I'm dating someone."

My mother jumps up and rounds the table to hug me, while my dad gives me a lopsided smile and reaches across the corner of the dining room table with his good arm to pat my hand.

"Who is it?" my mom asks as she retakes her seat. "Is it someone at work?" Her eyes grow wide. "It's not a baseball player, is it?"

I chuckle at her obvious dismay at that thought. "What? You don't want me to be a baseball wife?"

"Honey, you know I want you to be happy and married and giving me grandbabies, and if that's with a professional athlete, then so be it." She points her steak knife at me. "But I'd prefer if it were with someone who lives in Chicago and has no fear of being traded to another team far away from here at any moment."

My heart sinks. "Well, the good news is he's not a baseball player. But he doesn't live here. He lives in L.A."

"Los Angeles!" My mother nearly leaps out of her chair again, but for a different reason than before. "You can't move that far away! We just got you back last spring."

"Settle down, my dear," Dad says softly. "If she loves this man, she needs to feel like she has the freedom to move to wherever the two of them need to be. We can't hold her back from her happiness."

Tears fill my eyes. "Thank you, Dad. I don't know if I love him yet. And I don't want to move. I need you to know that. But he has a daughter, and their life is in California. Moving here isn't really an option for them."

"A daughter?" Mom's eyebrows raise as she sets down her wine glass. "How old is she? Are you prepared to be a step-mother? Has he been married before? Is his ex-wife still in the picture?"

Dad settles his hand on her arm and speaks to me. "How about we start with his name and how you met him, Lissa, and we'll go from there?"

I nod, my heart squeezing at Dad's use of his childhood nick-name for me. "His name is Bobby Jacobs. He's Diego Sanchez's agent, and he was a groomsman in both of the Hamilton weddings."

Dad nods. "Yes, I remember him being one of Randall's groomsmen. And more than that, I know of him by reputation. He's a bit older than you, isn't he?"

"Yes, he's ten years older, which is closer in age to me than you two are to each other." My parents have a thirteen-year age differ-ence. "And don't let his professional reputation turn you off. He's a really good man outside the office." I tilt my head to the side. "Actually, I think he's a good man inside the office, too. He's just determined to always get the best deal possible for his clients."

"I didn't mean anything negative by mentioning his reputa-tion," Dad says. "As a businessman, I know public perception isn't always equal to reality. I'll reserve any judgment until I hear what you have to say about him and I meet the man myself."

I give my parents the CliffsNotes version of Bobby's past. I don't gloss over his previous marriage and divorce, but I also don't divulge all the details of his relationship with Nanette.

"Nanette is still a big part of his life," I say, "and Kelli's, obvi-ously. That's another reason why he needs to stay in California. If he moved here, he'd have to not only uproot his daughter but also move Nanette here, too."

"It says a lot about the man that he's taking care of a woman he's not legally or even morally obligated to," Dad says.

I shrug. "He loves her." I hold my hand up to my mom when she starts to speak. "As a friend, not as anything more. He has no intention of ever having a romantic relationship with her in the future. He's not Jeremy, Mom. He says he thinks of Nanette as a sister, and I believe him." The jury is still out on whether Nanette thinks of Bobby as a brother, though. I need to verify that for myself. "If you don't trust my judgment, then trust Diego's and Randall's and Ash's. They all speak incredibly highly of him."

"I trust you," Mom says. "You're sure about this? That this is what you want—to date this man who lives across the country and has a teenage daughter and an ex-wife who may always be around?"

"Yes, I'm absolutely certain this is what I want. I'm serious about this relationship and seeing if it could lead to marriage. If I weren't, I wouldn't be willing to put in the effort it's going to take."

thirty-six

. . .

Bobby

I t's early Saturday afternoon, and I'm waiting in the lounge at the private Miami airport where Diego's chartered plane should be landing any minute now. Actually, I'm pacing. I never pace. But I want this weekend to be perfect, and I'm nervous I won't succeed in making it so. What do I know about entertaining a woman for a weekend? Nothing. That's what. Thankfully Kelli and Nanette gave me a few pointers, as did Randall and Diego. I haven't heard from Ash since he got home from his honeymoon, but that's not surprising. He's not much of a phone talker, and I wasn't in Chicago long enough last week to meet up with him.

Even though Melissa said she'd be willing to share my hotel room, I didn't want to put her in a position she can't back out of if she changes her mind and wants her own space. There were no vacancies at my hotel, nor were there two rooms available at any other decent hotel in the Miami area, so I arranged for us to stay in a former client's vacation condo in Miami Beach. He's not in town, and Melissa and I will each have our own bedroom if we decide to go that route. It'll also be nice to have a living area where we can relax this evening and tomorrow before we head to the stadium in the afternoon.

I arrived yesterday so I could meet with a few clients who were coming in early. I wanted to get all my meetings out of the way before Melissa got here. Not that I think she can't handle being on her own for a few hours, but why would I want to waste even one moment of time we could be spending together—as long as she wants to spend every minute with me, that is?

The door bursts open, and Diego enters with his arms flung into the air in a V.

"We have arrived! The party may begin!"

I accept the tight hug he forces upon me as I say, "Why didn't you let the ladies come in first, you caveman?"

He lets go of me with a laugh. "Oops! Will you believe I was so excited to see you that I couldn't help myself?"

I shake my head as I keep my eyes trained on the door. "No. You saw me a week ago."

Diego claps me on the back. "I wish I could see you every day, *hermano*. And I could, if you'd just …"

I don't hear anything else he says because my girlfriend has entered the room. My smile is immediate, and she beelines directly to me and wraps her arms around me with no hesitation. I squeeze her tightly and drink in her lemon-and-vanilla scent. She searches my eyes for a moment, silently asking whether I'm OK with kissing in front of people we know. I answer by pressing my mouth to hers in a short but meaningful kiss.

Diego whistles and claps, making Melissa's cheeks burn. I shoot him a glare, which only serves to spur him on to cheer some more. Then he flings his arms around us and kisses us both on the cheek. I playfully shove him away, but it warms my heart to see how much he wants this to work out for me.

"OK, Foundation Family," Diego says to the rest of the group, "let's leave the lovebirds to do their own thing." To Melissa and me he says, "Have fun. I'd better not see nor hear from either of you in the next …," he checks his watch, "twenty-six hours or so."

Melissa hugs him again and thanks him for the ride.

"Anything for you, my road-trip and sky-trip buddy!"

"Truth or dare?" Melissa asks as I take a seat catty-corner from her at the white cast-iron table on the outdoor patio of the Cuban restaurant where we're eating lunch.

"Hmmm." I twist my mouth to the side. "I think I want to see what you're going to dare me to do that won't get us kicked out of this restaurant."

Her grin is a little devilish when she says, "I dare you to tell our waitress she's the most beautiful woman you've ever seen. And say it in Spanish, so she'll think I don't know what you're saying. I want to see how she'll respond." She nods and looks past me. "Here she comes. You're up."

"I can't lie to this woman," I say in a low voice. *"You're* the most beautiful woman I've ever seen."

"It's your dare," Melissa whispers as her cheeks pink at my compliment. "You have to do it."

"Hola, I'm Estella. May I get you some drinks? A mojito, perhaps?"

I finally look away from Melissa to the sprite-like Cuban woman standing next to our table, who's seventy-five if she's a day. She also sports a large, hairy mole above her upper lip. Melissa tries to suppress a giggle as I struggle to keep my facial expression neutral.

"I'd love a mojito," my troublesome date says. "Bobby, what would you like, dearest?"

My eyebrows ascend at her term of endearment, and I shoot her a look that asks: "You really expect me to do this?" She nods in assent, wide grin in place.

"Um, just ice water for me, thanks." I clear my throat and I feel my face heat as I then say in Spanish, "I also must say you're a beautiful woman." I simply can't tell anyone other than Melissa that they're the most beautiful woman I've ever seen.

Estella lets a surprisingly deep laugh fly, and she swats my shoulder with her order pad as she replies in Spanish, "You're a liar, but a handsome one." She look at Melissa and switches to English. "Keep your eye on this one. He's a charmer."

As Estella walks away, Melissa asks, "What did she say to you?"

A grin forms on my face. "She said I'm a handsome liar."

Now Melissa swats my shoulder. "She did not!"

"Indeed, she did. Now it's your turn. Truth or more truth?"

"Oh, that's what we're playing now, huh? No dares for me?"

I shake my head. "Not now. Maybe later." I give her a heated look, and she blushes again. "Anyway, I want to know how you're feeling about this weekend. I don't regret asking you to join me, but I realize it's very soon into our relationship, and it was an offer you would've had a hard time refusing. I just want to make sure you're OK with this—with spending all this time with me and then with a bunch of people you don't know tomorrow. I'll be in work mode at the game, and you'll have to meet my clients whether you want to or not, and—"

When she cuts me off with a hand over my mouth, I realize I've been rambling, which I never do, but it seems I'm doing a lot of new things since she came into my life.

"Bobby." Melissa's hand moves down to cover mine. "Take a breath. It's fine. *I'm* fine. I wouldn't have agreed to come otherwise. I appreciate you looking out for me, but it's not a hardship for me to spend uninterrupted time with you, and it's also not a hardship for me to meet and socialize with a bunch of professional athletes. I love sports, remember? And I work for a baseball team, so I'm used to being around a bunch of overpaid jocks, some of whose best behavior leaves much to be desired."

I flip my hand over and thread our fingers together. "I want this weekend to be good for you."

"And I want it to be good for you, which it won't be if you keep worrying about me. Please trust me when I say I'm fine. And if at some point I'm not, I'll tell you. Now for your 'truth.' Tell me how you're feeling about it for *you*, not for me."

I stroke her hand with my thumb as I summon up the courage to be honest with her. I'm known for my candor, but for once in my life I truly care about what someone else thinks of me. I can't look her in the eye when I say, "I can't stop imagining that you're going to get tired of me or decide my family or career demands are too much to deal with, and you'll want to leave me but be too kind to say so."

Melissa releases my hand and cups my cheek as she forces me

to look her in the eye. "It's not too much. And that's not the way this is going to go. There will be no playing of games between you and me, all right? We'll always tell each other how we feel and what we're thinking. That's the only way this can work."

My chest feels tight. "I want this to work so badly, but it's hard to believe it will."

"It's not going to work if that's your mindset. You can't be waiting for us to fail. Do you go into your business deals thinking they're going to fail?"

I shake my head. "Never."

"Then don't do that with us. Think of this as the biggest deal of your life. Are you going to let it fall apart because you're scared?"

I shake my head again. I can't let it fall apart. My heart is already too invested.

She gives me a soft smile as she moves her hand down to my chest. "I kind of like this insecure side of you. It shows me you're not perfect. But I like the usual confident, take-charge side of you, too. Let's try to go with that one most of the time, OK?"

"Deal." Then I seal that deal with a kiss that elicits a whoop from Estella when she brings our drinks.

"What did I tell you?" she asks Melissa. "Charmer!"

We both chuckle at her declaration, and we chat with her for a few minutes before she moves on to the next table.

"Is there anything you want to do here in Miami before we head to the condo?" I ask Melissa. "Have you been here before?"

"I've been to the Keys a few times," she says, "but I haven't spent any time here in the city. Maybe we can drive around a little before heading to the condo? And I'd love to go dancing somewhere tonight—not like a usual club, but a place with salsa dancing and that kind of thing. You up for that?"

"Up for spending a couple of hours with you in my arms?" I smirk at her. "I think I can handle it."

Melissa's cheeks flush when she asks, "Have you thought more about whether you'd like to spend all night with me in your arms?"

My hand makes its way to her thigh. "I have." It's a big step for us—for me, in particular—but I've decided I don't want to keep holding off if she doesn't want to. "And I would like to. With our long-distance situation, I'm not afraid the physical stuff will take over our relationship and keep us from also truly getting to know each other. We've already spent a lot of time talking, and we'll keep doing that over the phone. But with the limited time we get to spend together, I'd like to explore the physical side of our relationship." I squeeze her leg. "But only if we're on the same page. If you're not ready, then we'll wait."

Melissa cups my cheek in her hand. "I'm ready."

thirty-seven

. . .

Melissa

The dancing and our overnight activities were nothing short of magical. I'll spare the details, but it's clear neither of us regret our decision. To me, it reveals Bobby decided to go all in on us. He's not holding back any part of himself, and I'm glad for that. I know he's nervous things won't work out—not just for our sake but also for Kelli. But like I told him yesterday, it's not going to work if he thinks it won't.

"You ready?" he asks as we pause for a moment outside the luxury suite he and Diego rented at the football stadium. I can't begin to imagine how much it cost.

I squeeze his hand. "Bring it on, B.S."

"In the spirit of full disclosure," he says, "my middle name actually is Sebastian."

The laugh that spills out of me is more of a snorting fit. "You're kidding."

"Nope. Fitting that my initials really are B.S., right?"

I tilt my head up and kiss his cheek. "You're not full of it, Bobby Joe ... I mean Bobby Seb. Everyone knows you're a straight shooter."

"As straight as they come," replies a wry voice from behind us. I don't need to turn around to know it's Jimmie Zane, but I turn anyway.

Jimmie takes my hand and presses his lips to my knuckles. "Melissa, it's an absolute pleasure to see you again."

"Knock it off," Bobby says with a roll of his eyes.

"Dude, I can't win with you," Jimmie complains. "If I'm rude, I'm wrong. If I'm polite, I'm wrong. What do you expect me to do?"

"He makes a great point, Bobby." I shrug. "Maybe cut him a little slack."

"Fine." Bobby huffs. "Polite is the way to go."

"Thank you," Jimmie says with only a trace of sarcasm in his tone. "I appreciate your opinion on the matter."

"Sure you do," Bobby bites out as he shows the stadium worker our tickets and leads us into the suite.

Jimmie wastes no time heading to the in-suite bar and ordering a beer.

"Little punk kid," Bobby mutters. "I don't know why I put up with him."

I spin him to face me. "He just needs some guidance." I smooth down his tie. Leave it to Bobby Jacobs to wear a suit to a football game. "It seems like he hasn't had much of that in his life. I'm glad he has you to help him."

Bobby's face softens. "Yeah?"

"Uh-huh. He's just a kid, Bobby—barely old enough to legally drink but not old enough to make wise decisions without some good people helping him. Just pretend you're his dad or his coach and think about what kind of support he'd need from you in that role." I pat his chest. "Now, let's get some food. I'm starving."

"How are you starving? We just ate lunch two hours ago!"

"Yeah, but it was the first meal of our day, so it was actually breakfast." I shimmy my shoulders to remind him why we didn't eat breakfast at a normal time.

His cheeks pink, which I absolutely love. Not much flusters this man, but somehow I've managed to mess with his equilibrium.

"*This* is lunch," I declare. "Bring on the hotdogs and nachos!"

"You are good for Bobby."

"Yeah?" I say to Carmela, one of the foundation employees, as my eyes search out my boyfriend, who's chatting with one of his baseball clients. "What makes you say that?"

"He smiles every time he looks at you, which is every ten seconds. I don't know that I have ever seen him smile. Not that I've spent a lot of time with him, but when he has been in the office with Diego or Ash, he is all business all the time."

I nod, knowing exactly what she means, because he's the same when he's in my office.

Carmela fans her face. "But that dimple ..." She blows out a breath. "Good for you. Keep hold of him. He is not only handsome but a good man. I have always known this because Diego wouldn't have anything to do with him otherwise. Even though he can be frowny for no apparent reason, he is always kind to everyone in our office. And you cannot tell him I told you this, but when Isaac's dad passed last month," she surreptitiously points toward her co-worker Isaac across the room, "Bobby paid for his funeral and for Isaac and his family to fly home to Mexico for it. They wouldn't have been able to go otherwise. Well, I think Diego would have covered it, but Bobby jumped in first."

Tears fill my eyes at her words. "That's really sweet, but I didn't have anything to do with that. We didn't get together until a few weeks ago."

"I know. I was just making sure you know the kind of man Bobby is, though I think you already knew that. But the other reason I know you're good for Bobby is he has been patient with that young hockey player throughout this game, even though the kid has been obnoxious and over the top about ... well, everything. I overheard you talking to Bobby about him when you walked in. Bobby does not realize how much people look up to him and the positive impact he has on them without realizing it, and I'm glad you are helping him see that."

"What are you two ladies talking about?" Diego asks as he saunters up to us with a souvenir cup of beer in one hand and a soft pretzel in the other. I tear off a piece of the pretzel and pop it into my mouth.

"Bobby's dimple," Carmela replies without hesitation.

I choke on my pretzel, and she pats me on the back while Diego laughs.

"It is a work of art, is it not?" Diego asks. "Too bad not many people get to see it. But it's been out and about all day today." He nudges me with an elbow, since his hands are full. "And I think we all know why."

"I don't want you to go." Bobby's arms are looped around my back as we say goodbye at the bottom of the stairs outside the plane a few hours later.

"And I don't want to leave you. But I have to be at work in the morning, and you need to catch the red-eye back to L.A. in a few hours to get back for Nanette's follow-up appointment tomorrow, so we don't have a choice." I give him a quick kiss. "We'll see each other in a few weeks, though. And in the meantime, we'll be burning up the phone line."

"Wrap it up, lovebirds!" Diego calls from the top of the stairs. "It's almost our turn to take off."

Bobby kisses me soundly and then reluctantly lets me go. I wave at him from the top of the stairs before ducking inside so the stewardess can close the door.

"You're over here by me," Diego calls out and pats the empty spot next to him.

I settle into the cushy leather seat and buckle myself in. "Let me guess, I'm sitting by you so we can talk about Bobby."

"My favorite topic of conversation."

I chuckle. "I doubt that, but I'll let it slide."

"Good. Now, I don't need to know about what goes on behind closed doors …" He cocks an eyebrow. "Unless you want to tell me?"

I narrow my eyes at him. "Absolutely not."

"Eh, I had to try. I have to live vicariously through somebody these days. I never dreamed it would be Bobby Jacobs, but here we are."

"You're not dating anyone?"

"No, I am not dating anyone, and I won't be until my divorce is final. I do not believe it's right to do otherwise. Which is a shame, because Lola is dragging things out and demanding many, many things I have no intention of giving her, considering she slept with one of my former teammates. If she wants fifteen million dollars and a vacation home in Belize, she should ask *him* for it, not me."

"Makes sense to me."

Diego spreads his hands wide. "Of course it does. But we're not here to talk about me and my troubles. We are here to talk about you and my boy Bobby. How was your weekend with him?" He rubs his hands together. "Are you ready to tie the knot yet? I need to be a best man, Melissa. It's my turn. I have been in two weddings in three months, and I was runner-up in both. But since Bobby has no brothers, I will be in like Flynn."

"You ever wonder who Flynn is?"

"All the time. I figure he must be some strange little Irish man. But you are changing the subject. Answer my questions, *por favor.*"

"The weekend was great." I sigh and nestle my head into the leather headrest that seems to be formed perfectly for me. I hope Diego doesn't want to chat the entire ride, because I could easily fall asleep in this seat, and let me tell you, I need the sleep. "I couldn't have imagined it any better than the reality."

"That is what I love to hear."

When Diego is silent for a few seconds, I turn my head toward him, because I can't imagine he's done talking about Bobby and me. He looks like he's debating whether or not to say what he's thinking.

"Spit it out," I order him. "You know you're going to say it, so don't keep me waiting. As much as I enjoy talking to you, I also enjoy sleeping, and I intend to do some of that on this flight."

"Ooo, didn't get much sleep last night?" He waggles his eyebrows.

I poke his leg. "Stop it. Now you're the one changing the subject."

"Would you really move to L.A. for Bobby? If you fall in love, I mean."

I nod. "I would. I don't want to leave my parents and my friends in Chicago, but I'm a fully healthy adult who can fairly easily adapt to living somewhere else if it means I can be with the man I love. Bobby doesn't have that luxury."

Diego purses his lips. "What if he did?"

My eyebrows draw together. "What do you mean?"

"Bobby has spent the last thirteen years of his life sacrificing for Kelli and Nanette, and rightfully so. He also doesn't regret a minute or penny of it. But what he forgets is those two love him as much as he loves them. I think they would happily make sacrifices for him to help him get the happiness he deserves, if he'd only give them the chance."

My eyes widen. "You're saying you think they'd be willing to move to Chicago with him?"

"I do."

"Have you mentioned this to him?"

"No."

"Why not?"

"Bobby is a proud man. He sees himself as their protector—their provider. Disrupting their lives is not something he would easily consider. This isn't a conversation to have lightly with him. And I'm not a good person to initiate it."

I press my hand against my chest. "Well, I don't think I'm a good choice for that conversation, either."

"No, no," he pats my knee. "I'm not saying that. I think the idea needs to come from Kelli. He'll initially shut her down, but she's a lot like him. If she doesn't get what she wants, she will keep going after it. And usually, if he knows something will make her happy and won't hurt her or turn her into a spoiled brat, he'll end up giving it to her."

"But how do we ..." I shake my head. "You know what? I don't need to have a part in this. I don't want Bobby to ever feel like I've manipulated anything to get him to move. In fact, I'm not sure that them moving to Chicago is the best idea anyway. Kelli has her friends and school and her soccer team. Nanette has her

… well, I'm not sure what she has, but her medical team is there, and I'm assuming she has friends and maybe family. I don't really know. But none of what they decide to do is up to me. I need to stay out of it. I appreciate your thoughts on it, but I'm not going to ask you to do or say anything one way or another. However, I do want to know why you think he won't want to hear it from you. He loves you like a brother. You know that."

"I do know that. And that's part of why he won't listen. Him moving to Chicago will benefit me greatly, because I love him and want to see him more often. I have a … what's the word … some kind of interest?"

"A vested interest."

Diego snaps his fingers. "Yes, I have a vested interest in him moving to Chicago. He'll think I'm trying to get him to move just to be near me, which I know won't work, because I've always tried to get him to live where I live. Yet he still lives in California, much to my dismay."

I settle my head back against my seat. "Well, you do what you gotta do, but leave me out of it from here on out. I don't even want to know if you talk to Kelli or she talks to him about it. I only want to hear about it from Bobby himself."

"Aye-aye, *senorita.*"

thirty-eight

...

Bobby

I need to play another game of "Truth or More Truth" with Melissa—with me being the truth teller. I haven't lied to her, but there are things she needs to know about my childhood. I doubt what I need to tell her will scare her off if nothing else has up to this point, but I don't feel like she can fully know me until she knows everything. And the longer I put off telling her, the more upset she'll be that I didn't tell her earlier. I should've told her a few weeks ago in Miami, but I didn't want anything to ruin our time together. And now I keep putting it off.

I also need to tell her my plans for my career and how it'll be changing over the coming months.

"Dad, can I talk to you?"

The sight of my daughter standing in the doorway to my office makes me smile. She's in her pajamas—light pink with bunnies tonight—and looks more like a little girl than she usually does. She also should've been asleep an hour ago, but here she is.

"You can always talk to me, baby."

Kelli glares at me and crosses her arms over her chest as she enters the room and curls up in her green chair. "How many times do I have to tell you not to call me baby?"

I hold my hands up in surrender. "Sorry. Old habits die hard."

"Well, you need to assassinate and bury that one."

"Got it. What do you want to talk to me about?"

"Remember when I said you should kinda retire?"

"I do." I haven't been able to think about much else than that prospect and Melissa for weeks. I'm about to tell Kelli some of what I'm thinking when she continues speaking.

"I've changed my mind."

My eyebrows shoot up. "You have?"

"Well, a little bit." She holds her thumb and pointer finger a half-inch apart.

"What's the little bit?"

"I still think you need to not work as much and to send some of your clients packing. But I think you should keep all the ones in Chicago."

I give her an assessing look. "Even Jimmie Zane?" If this is because she has a crush on him, I'm dropping him tomorrow.

She takes a deep breath. "Especially Jimmie Zane. He needs you, Dad. I read this article about him in *Hockey Digest* — "

I hold up my hand to stop her. "Hang on. You read *Hockey Digest?*" Sure, I subscribe, but I didn't think my daughter read the host of sports magazines I typically leave scattered about the house. "Since when?"

"Since I decided to investigate Jimmie Zane."

"And why are you investigating Jimmie Zane?" I grit my teeth, hoping she's not about to tell me it's because she thinks he's cute or some other such nonsense.

"To try to figure out why he's always making dumb decisions. I thought it might have something to do with his family, and I think I'm right."

My jaw relaxes at her comment. "What's your assessment, then?" This should be interesting.

"Did you know he had a sister who died when she was twelve and he was sixteen?"

"Yes, I know that." I knew it even before the article she's referring to. "You think that has something to do with why he is the way he is?"

"I do. Mom thinks so, too."

I tilt my head to the side as I assess her. "You talked to your mom about Jimmie?"

"I did. She's really smart, you know."

"I do know. You often tell me that's where you get your brains from." I move my hand in a rolling motion. "Go on. Tell me more about Jimmie."

"Well, I know his sister died in a freak accident, though I don't know what kind of accident, and I also know his parents don't go to any of his games."

"How do you know that?" She's right, but it's strange she knows it. There was nothing about his parents in the article.

She shrugs. "I have my sources."

"Oh, really?"

"Mmhm. Confidential ones. Anyway, he says he plays in memory of his sister. But I think maybe his parents blamed him for her death, and that's why he's so messed up."

Her words slam into me like a freight train. How did I not see this before? I mean, I knew his parents aren't an active presence in his life, and he considers his current and former coaches and teammates to be his family, though that's not uncommon in the hockey world, where kids often leave home at an early age to play competitively. But of all people, I should've been able to put two and two together.

Kelli folds her hands together on her lap and sits up straight. "In conclusion, I believe Jimmie needs you because you kinda know how that feels. You can help him learn to be a good person, because your parents were terrible to you, but *you're* a good person."

My throat closes so I'm barely able to choke out the words, "I'm a good person because of you, kiddo. I wasn't very good before you came along, but then I decided I had to be."

"Well, maybe you're the person for Jimmie that I was for you. He can be a good person because you came along for him."

After I hug Kelli good night and send her back to her room, I spend some time thinking about everything she said. I'm more certain than ever that I need to tell Melissa about my childhood.

But I'm not as certain about where I want my career to go, because I can't drop Jimmie now. Even if Kelli is wrong—and I don't think she is—if she thinks Jimmie needs me, I can't let her down.

As I consider what that means for my plans to cut back, I realize I don't have to make this decision alone. While I had planned to tell Melissa what I was going to do, if I want her to be a permanent part of my life, I need to let her be part of my decision-making process.

Even though it's well past midnight in Chicago, I pick up the phone. I told her I'd call tonight, and although I've been delayed by Kelli's bombshell, I can't go back on my word, even if it means waking Melissa up.

"Hey," Melissa says sleepily into the phone. "I thought you'd forgotten about me."

"Never." I kick back in my chair and prop my feet on the desk. "Kelli came in to talk, and then I needed some time to think before calling you."

"Yeah?" She yawns. "What were you thinking about?"

"About you … me … us … my career."

"Your career?" I hear sheets rustling on her end, like she's adjusting her position in bed. "What about your career?"

"Over the past several weeks, I've been thinking about the possibility of cutting back on work to spend more time with the people I care about." I was going to say "love," but I'm not ready to use that word yet with her, even though I'm certain it's accurate. I love Melissa with all of my being, and it scares the heck out of me but also makes me feel a sense of stability and support I didn't know I needed.

"And who are these people you care about? Do they include me?"

"Of course. And also Kelli, Diego, Nanette, Ash, Randall, and their wives." I tick them all off on my fingers as I name them, surprised by the amount of people I genuinely want to spend time with these days outside of work. "I don't have enough free time to give those relationships and friendships the attention they deserve, and that needs to change."

"Wow, this is big, Bobby Seb."

I smile at the new nickname, though I'll admit I miss "Bobby Joe" a little. "Yeah. It's huge for me. I'm trying to figure out what it'll all look like, and I'm trying to anticipate how people will respond."

"And by 'people' you mean …?"

"My clients, their teams, other agents, the sporting world in general," I explain.

"And you care how they'll respond?"

My inclination is to give a blanket no in response, but I take a minute to truly think about it before giving an answer. "I don't care how most of them will react to the news, and I'll need to deal with some fallout for sure. But I care about how my clients will respond—the ones I might need to let go through no fault of their own."

"You don't care about what your peers will think at all?" Melissa asks.

"No." I bob my head back and forth. "Well, maybe a little bit. I can't say it won't sting when some of them inevitably say I couldn't hack it. But I'll know the truth about why I'm cutting back."

"All right. So what does cutting back look like?"

"That's what I want to get your thoughts on because I'm not sure. Kelli suggested I keep the guys who play in Chicago and let everyone else go. That way I only have one city I need to travel to on a consistent basis. I currently have four guys there, which is a manageable amount and the most I've ever had in one city. But what happens when one of them gets traded? Diego's the only one with a no-trade clause, and he intends to play in Chicago until he retires."

"Kelli's been talking to you about this?"

I shrug. "It was her idea to begin with, back when you and I first got together. And Diego has mentioned the same thing, although he wants to be my *only* client."

Melissa chuckles. "Of course he does."

"The problem with that is he has at most five or six years left in him. What would I do when he retires? I can't do nothing. It's not in my nature."

"No, it's not. I think it makes sense to keep the Chicago guys. And if any of them get traded or leave during free agency, you can cross that bridge when you come to it. It may be years before that happens, and by then, maybe you'll be in a position where you can travel to wherever they end up. But I'd like to point out that if you keep all your Chicago guys, that includes Jimmie Zane. You'd be OK with keeping him?"

"That leads to the other thing I wanted to talk to you about." I tell her what Kelli said about Jimmie.

"Her hypothesis makes sense to me. Do you ..." She hesitates before finishing her question.

"Do I want to tell you about my childhood and what Kelli meant when she said my parents were terrible to me? If that's where you're going, the answer is yes. I'd already planned on telling you about that tonight, and I wish I'd told you sooner, but I didn't. I don't like to talk about it. In fact, I haven't ever talked about the details to anyone other than Nanette, Diego, and Kelli. I didn't want to tell Kelli, but Nanette thought she deserved to know, so after she turned thirteen, I gave her a semi-sanitized version. I've told Ash and Randall a little bit, but they don't know everything."

"It's OK, Bobby. You know I'm fine with you telling me things at your own pace."

"I do. Thank you." I take a deep breath. "My dad was a violent man. He didn't often lay a hand on me or my older sister, but he hit my mom on the regular. One night when I was fourteen, it got so bad I called the police. I was afraid he would kill Mom if I didn't do something, but I wasn't big enough yet to try to stop him. Plus, I didn't want to fight—I didn't want to be like him." I close my eyes as I remember that night.

"That was a brave choice for a teenage boy," she says. "What happened when the police showed up?"

"They took one look at my mom's bloody face and bruises and hauled my dad off to jail. Mom was so mad at me, but I didn't regret it. The problem was, she wouldn't press charges against him. And back then, a lot of people didn't care if a man was beating his wife. They thought it was his right. So the police had no grounds to keep him, and he came home."

Melissa sucks in a breath. "And then what?"

"I thought he'd beat me, but he didn't. He simply pretended I didn't exist. He didn't look at me, didn't speak to me, didn't acknowledge my presence in any way. But he kept hitting Mom. My sister turned eighteen not too long after that and moved out to get away from our parents, so it was just me and them at home. And once again, one night it got so bad I thought he'd kill her, so I called the police again. I snuck out the back door so I wouldn't be home when they arrived. When I went back later that night, Dad was gone, and Mom was irate with me again. She said it was my fault he hit her in the first place, because he was so mad about me calling the cops before."

"Oh, Bobby," Melissa whispers, and I can hear the tears in her voice. "You know it wasn't your fault, right?"

I nod as I wait for the lump in my throat to subside. "I do now. Even back then I didn't fully believe it was true, but I was just a kid. I didn't know. But that's not all. The police kept him overnight, and he had the bright idea to try to take a cop's gun away. In the resulting chaos, he was shot and killed."

Melissa audibly gasps. "Oh, no."

"Yeah. And guess who Mom blamed for that, too? So then *she* refused to acknowledge my existence. She didn't cook for me, didn't clean my room, do my laundry, anything. I finally summoned up the nerve to talk to my school counselor about it. He's the one who helped me get emancipated and into college early. I've had no contact with my mom since. And I've not seen or heard from my sister since she moved out—not even when Dad died."

"I'm so sorry, honey," Melissa says through her sniffles. "I wish none of that had happened to you. But believe me when I say it's nothing short of a miracle that you turned into such a stable, caring man after all that. I'm so proud of you for not letting that bring you down, for being strong and making something of your life, for being an amazing dad to Kelli and friend to Nanette and Diego and Ash and Randall, for going above and beyond for your clients even when they do dumb things. You are an absolute wonder."

By the time she's done, tears are flowing freely down my face, which is not a common event for me. I wasn't sure how Melissa was going to respond to my story, but that wasn't it.

"I wish I was there to hug you," she says.

"I wish you were here, too," I choke out.

"I want you to have some support right now—someone who's there with you. Would Nanette be mad if you woke her up?"

"No," I shake my head, "but I doubt she's asleep yet anyway. She's a night owl." I swivel my chair so I can see her house. "Her bedroom light is still on."

"Then go over there. Please promise me you will."

Who is this woman who cares enough about me and trusts me enough that she'd send me to my ex for comfort?

"Promise me, Bobby Joe."

I smile as I wipe my face. "I promise. Melissa, I ... thank you for listening, for understanding." Can I tell her I love her, or is it too soon? "I ... I care about you an awful lot." Apparently I can't tell her.

"I care about you an awful lot, too, Bobby," she says softly. "I hope you're able to get some rest tonight. Call me tomorrow."

thirty-nine

. . .

Melissa

"I'm doing it—I'm releasing all my clients except the four in Chicago," Bobby says over the phone the night after we talked about the possibility.

"Really?" I sit up straight on the couch, where I've been lying down watching Johnny Carson on TV. "You're sure this is what you want?"

"I'm positive this is what I want, and it's what's best for me and my family and friendships and my relationship with you."

The two of us haven't talked frankly about our finances, but I feel like I need to bring it up now. "I don't need to know your full financial situation, but will your new income be enough?"

He chuckles. "Thanks for worrying about me, but yes, it will. My house and cars are paid off, and I've made some great investments. To be completely open about this, I can survive comfortably for the rest of my life without any more income at all."

I shouldn't be surprised by his admission, as I have many friends who make enormous amounts of money. But some of them still somehow live paycheck to paycheck. I was hoping that wasn't the case with Bobby, but knowing he's debt-free and set for life is a little unexpected. I sometimes forget he's quite a bit older than me, though. Not many people my age would be in his position without having a trust fund, which Bobby most certainly doesn't have.

Bobby continues, "But I can't just sit around and do nothing. I need to work."

"I get that." I kick my socked feet up onto my glass-topped coffee table. "So how do you go about releasing your clients? Do you find them a new agent or leave that up to them?"

"I can't control who they go to next, but there are a handful of agents I trust and will recommend to them. I'll also talk to those agents once I let my clients know and fill them in on the situation. I'm not worried about any of my guys not being taken care of. While there are some bad apples in this profession, as well as a lot of mediocre agents, there are also a few I'd trust with my own career if I were a professional athlete. I'll do my best to make sure my clients get the best new agent for their needs."

"Of course you will. What's next, then, now that you've decided? You call your guys and let them know?" I get up to make some hot chocolate. We've been dealing with frigid temperatures for days, and my radiator is having trouble keeping up.

"It's not something that can be done overnight. Each league has rules about how players can change agents. I'll be required to give written notice to each of them, but I also plan to meet with them in person." He then explains how everything works with terminating contracts and such. "It could be months—potentially even years—before I can get out of some of the contracts if a player doesn't want to break ties with me. I'm just hoping they'll be understanding about it."

"I know the baseball players are starting to report to spring training. So that means you'll be heading back down to Florida and to Arizona?" I take a sip of my freshly made drink and my body relaxes as the warmth makes its way down my throat.

"I will. You think you can convince your boss to let you go to Arizona for a few days while I'm there? Maybe meet with the customer relations team at the stadium to swap ideas or something?"

"Let me know the dates, and I'll see what I can do." Some of the front office staff go to Arizona for a couple months during spring training, but my position isn't one that's needed down there. "If they say no, maybe I could take a quick weekend trip. Some sunshine and warm weather would be nice."

"As well as the company of your favorite guy?"

"Oh, yeah, Diego will be there, won't he?" I tease.

His responding growl makes me giggle.

I add, "He really is the most attentive man."

I shiver against the cold as I trudge the few blocks home from my office to my apartment after working a few hours later than usual to make up for being out of the office on Thursday and Friday. I resorted to wearing ski pants last week before I left for Arizona, as I couldn't take the cold on my legs anymore, even with the thickest pantyhose I could find. My skirt is tucked into a tote bag slung on my shoulder, along with my heels, since I'd look pretty ridiculous wearing heels with these pants. They also do absolutely nothing to keep my feet warm.

The four days I just spent in Arizona spoiled me with the warm weather. My boss agreed to send me down to spring training for two days, after I explained I wouldn't need housing, a rental car, or a food stipend, so the costs would be limited to my plane ticket. Rumors have been flying around the office about Bobby and me, so I think my boss knows the primary reason I wanted to go down there and why almost everything was paid for, but he didn't say anything to that effect.

Since I was working Thursday and Friday, I stayed in Arizona for the weekend to spend even more time with my boyfriend. We hadn't seen each other in more than a month, so our time together was long overdue.

It's also been more than a month since Diego talked to me about how Bobby might have the freedom to move to Chicago, but Bobby hasn't mentioned anything along those lines. I wonder if that's because Diego didn't talk to Kelli, or Kelli or Nanette don't want to move, or Kelli didn't talk to her dad, or—worst of all—because Bobby outright vetoed the idea. I know I said I didn't want to get involved, but I'd really like to know where that issue stands. I almost brought it up in Arizona, but I want him to take the initiative on it.

While I'm still open to moving to California if this relationship continues to progress, I'd like to at least be able to have a conversation with my boyfriend about the possibility of him moving to Chicago. I know it would be a complicated move, but since he's already made the decision to limit his clients to the ones who currently play in Chicago, it makes more sense for him and his family to move here than for me to go there. And frankly, it makes sense even if you take me out of the equation. I don't like the idea of him not even considering it, so I hope that's not the case.

He also hasn't explicitly invited me to go to California to meet Kelli and Nanette, which is frustrating. I know Kelli is dying to meet me, because I've heard her wheedling him in the background of a few of our calls. I'm also excited to meet Kelli, because I'm certain I will absolutely love her. And I'm also anxious to meet Nanette and assess how she interacts with Bobby. If everything seems as platonic as Bobby claims it to be, then from what I've heard about her from both Bobby and Diego, I think we could become friends.

My phone is ringing as I unlock my apartment door, and I dash across the living room to answer it.

"Hello?"

"Is this Melissa?" a young woman's voice asks. It sounds suspiciously like what I remember Kelli's voice sounding like.

"It is. Can I help you?"

"Yeah, this is Kelli—Kelli Jacobs."

Nausea builds in my throat. "Is your dad OK? Your mom? What's wrong?"

She huffs out a laugh. "No, sorry, nothing's wrong. Well, not the kind of wrong you're thinking. Dad and Mom are both OK."

I close my eyes and let out a slow breath as I drop onto the couch, still bundled up in my winter gear. "Good. That's good." But why is she calling? "Does your dad know you're calling me?"

"Um, no? But please don't hang up! I really need to talk to you. Promise you won't hang up?"

I sigh. I don't think Bobby will love that I talked to his

daughter without talking to him about it first, but I can't just hang up on her. She sounds desperate. "OK, you can talk to me. But you have to tell your dad you called me. You don't have to tell him everything we talk about, as long as you're not planning to tell me you're doing something illegal or harmful, which I don't think you are, but you need to tell him we talked. That's the promise I need from you."

I'm starting to sweat under all my layers, so I unzip my coat and ski pants and do my best to take them off while holding the phone to my ear.

"I promise," Kelli says, "even though he's not going to like it. But I can deal with him. And it's not about anything bad. It's ... maybe it's good? I think so, at least."

"What's on your mind?"

"I want us to move to Chicago, but my dad won't listen to me."

I freeze with my pants halfway to the floor and my coat dangling off one arm. "What?"

"I want us to move to Chicago," Kelli repeats, "because that's where Uncle Diego and you and Randall and Ash are, and it's where all Dad's clients are gonna be, and I think it's where he really wants to be. But he thinks we need to stay here for me and Mom, and we don't agree. Sure, I'll miss Whitley and my other friends and my team, but I'll make new friends. Plus, Whitley's parents are loaded so she can come visit. And if Dad's around all the time, he can even coach my new soccer team. Mom says she can find new doctors, and I told her she can be friends with you and Wendy and Leslie, and she can make more friends. My dad needs this. He's never had friends before, except for Uncle Diego, and he's never ever had a girlfriend. And *all* of you are in Chicago. You gotta help me convince him, Melissa. You just *have* to!"

I fall back down onto the couch and yank off my pants but leave the coat halfway on. "You're really sure you'd want to move?" What teenage girl actually wants to move to a new state? Usually they resist moves with the force of a freight train. They think leaving their friends will be the end of the world.

"Yes. Would I randomly choose to move to Chicago? No. It gets totally frigid there. It bet it's like zero degrees right now. But I can deal with that if living there makes my dad happy. And I think it will."

"But he doesn't agree?" I finally pull my coat the rest of the way off.

"He just shuts me down when I try to talk to him about it. He won't listen to me or to Mom. But I think maybe he'll listen to you."

Somehow I doubt that. There's a reason Bobby won't consider moving and hasn't talked to me about it. And I'm not sure I want to know that reason, because I'm pretty sure I won't like it. But I need to know.

"Kelli, your dad and I have only been dating for a couple months." And I thought we cared enough about each other to talk about stuff like this, but apparently not. "I don't know that we're at the point where I can ask him to consider moving his family to Chicago for me."

"But he asked if you'd be willing to move to California before you even started dating! It's not fair that he thinks you should move, but he won't do it, even though Mom and I are fine with it. And it's not just for you—it's for everybody. No offense."

As much as I want to keep asking Kelli questions, I know I shouldn't. I need to end this conversation and then decide what I want to do about it.

"None taken. I appreciate you telling me all this. I'll think about what I want to do, but you and I don't need to talk about this again, all right? I don't want your dad to think we're conspiring behind his back. And as much as I want to talk to you more and get to know you, we can't talk again unless your dad says it's OK."

Kelli sighs. "I hate this. I hate that he doesn't want us to talk or to meet yet. And I hate that he won't listen to me about moving. He's so stubborn!"

She's not wrong, but it's probably best that I don't say it.

"Stubborn or not, he's your dad, and even if you don't agree with him on this, I hope you don't let that change anything about your relationship. He's a great dad, and I don't want you to forget that."

"I won't," she says softly. "OK, bye, Melissa. Thanks for listening to me."

"You're welcome, honey. Have a good night."

"You, too."

I hang up with a sigh, pull an afghan over me, and curl up on my side.

Why didn't Bobby talk to me about this? And if he's not willing to even consider the possibility of moving, then is he as invested in this relationship as I am? I love him. I haven't said it yet, but I've been feeling it for awhile. I'm just not sure his feelings are as strong as mine are. He has been more open with me about his feelings than I thought he might be, but I can tell he's still holding back.

I've been willing to sacrifice being close to my friends and family in order to be with him. But if he's not willing to sacrifice … I don't even know what he'd be sacrificing, actually, if he moved here. He'd be bringing his daughter and her mother with him, and he'd be in the same city as everyone else he cares about as well as all his clients. I don't see the problem with that. I need to talk to him, though I wish we could have this conversation in person. But I'm not waiting until I can see him again, because who knows when that will be? This long-distance thing is much harder than I thought it would be.

forty

. . .

Bobby

"You did *what?*" I practically shout at my daughter over the phone.

"Don't yell at me." Kelli's voice is trembling, and I immediately regret my tone. "And you heard me. I called Melissa. I know you said I couldn't call her until you gave me permission, but I did it anyway, and I'm not sorry. Not one bit. And there's *nothing* you can do about it from Arizona."

Oh, boy. Here we go with the teenage attitude.

She's not done. "If you don't want me to break your rules, then you shouldn't make stupid ones. And do you want to know why I called Melissa? Because you refuse to see how dumb you're being about us moving to Chicago—or *not* moving, since you're so dang stubborn. And why haven't you talked to her about it? You just spent four days with her. She's your *girlfriend.* You *love* her. You want to *marry* her. And don't even try to convince me you don't, because that would be a lie, and *you don't tolerate liars.*"

She's on a roll, and I don't say anything for a few seconds to make sure she's finished. In the meantime, my stomach clenches, because deep down, I know she's right—about all of it. But there's one key piece she's missing. I'm terrified we'll move to Chicago, and Melissa and I will break up, and then where will we be? I'll be left with no girlfriend and no friends, because let's face it, they'll all choose her over me. Well, maybe not Diego, but the rest of them will. And I will have uprooted my daughter and her mother and moved them halfway across the country for no reason whatsoever.

"Don't you have anything to say?" she demands with a sniffle.

I close my eyes and shake my head as I lie back on my hotel room bed. "Kelli, I love you, and I always will. But right now you're trying my patience more than you've done since you were a toddler."

"I don't care." I imagine her stomping her foot, just like she did when she was three and didn't get her way. "Why won't you move to Chicago? What's stopping you? Because it's not me or Mom. She wants a fresh start, and you know me, I can make friends anywhere. It's one of the maaaaany things you love about me. And it's something I did *not* inherit from you. You don't make friends, like, ever because you're too busy working and flying all over the country and being a giant old grumpy pants. But somehow, miraculously, you've made friends in Chicago and you have a totally amazing girlfriend there. So that's where you need to be. It's where we *all* need to be."

I can hear her begin to sob, and my chest aches from not being able to wrap my arms around her right now. "Kell, baby, there's things you don't understand—reasons why moving to Chicago isn't the best thing for us."

"Then explain it to me! Tell me why you won't do this!"

"I … I …," I rub my chest. "I can't. I'm sorry, but this conversation is over. I love you so much, Kelli, but this isn't going to happen. I need you to accept that."

"Well, I won't. Because your reason is dumb. I don't even know what it is, but I know it's dumb. And we'll end up staying in California, and you won't be happy, so then I won't be happy, which means Mom won't be happy, and we'll all just be stuck here together in an empty pit of despair. And now I'm going to get off the phone before I say something I might regret. I love you, but I don't like you right now."

My heart feels like it's being stabbed with an ice pick. "I love you, too, baby."

"Don't call me baby! Good-*bye.*"

The dial tone sounds in my ear, and I drop the phone back into the cradle. Within seconds, my fingers begin to tingle, and sweat forms on my forehead while my breathing grows shallow. Knowing I only have limited time before I feel unable to move, I force myself off the bed and into the bathroom to splash water on my face while attempting to take deep breaths. I slump down onto the floor and don't know how long I sit there gasping for breath with my head between my knees before the phone starts to ring. I don't make any attempt to answer it and hope it won't ring too many times before the hotel's system cuts it off. After five rings, it blessedly stops. In less than a minute, it rings again. Again, I don't answer. I don't have the energy to leave this cool, tiled floor. In fact, there's a towel within reach, so I may just use it as a pillow and sleep here tonight, regardless of the fact that my thirty-six-year-old bones won't be happy with that choice.

I force myself to think of anything but the conversation I just had with my daughter. Or more accurately, the conversation she had with me, since I didn't contribute much. I count backward from two hundred. Next, I list off the entire 1963 Dodgers roster—the year they swept the Yankees to win the World Series. Then I go through that year's Yankees roster.

The phone rings yet again while I remain on the bathroom floor, and I'm halfway through trying to remember all the James Bond movies in order when there's pounding at my door. I tense at the sound but don't get up. A few seconds later, the pounding starts again.

"Bobby, open the door!" Diego's voice filters to me in Spanish. After a few seconds, he adds, "If you don't come to this door, I'm getting the manager to open it up. And you know they won't hesitate to let the great Diego Sanchez into your room."

He's not wrong. The staff at this hotel think he hung the moon. I think he tips them more than they make in their actual paychecks.

"Fine, I'm coming," I say loudly enough he should be able to hear me. "Keep your shirt on."

As I pull myself up and stumble to the door, I hear him ask, "Why would I take it off?"

When I finally get the door open, Diego takes one look at me and lets out a string of Spanish curses. Then he takes me by the shoulders, turns me around, and keeps ahold of me until I'm sitting on the edge of the bed.

He squats down in front of me with his elbows resting on his knees. "What's going on, brother?"

"Why are you here?"

"Nanette called me. She said Kelli was upset after talking to you, and once Nanette got the details of your conversation out of her, she tried calling but you didn't answer. So she called and asked me to check on you. I know you probably don't want to talk about it, but I'm not leaving until you do."

I don't doubt that. "Did she tell you what Kelli and I talked about?"

He sighs and drops down onto his knees. "Yes, and I have an admission that may make you angry. But you must promise to forgive me." He arches an eyebrow. "Promise?"

I let out a long breath. "I don't know yet. Why don't you just tell me what it is, and then we'll see how forgiving I feel?"

"I'm the one who gave Kelli the idea of moving to Chicago." He winces as he anticipates my reaction.

I can't decide if this feeling rolling through me is anger, frustration, defeat, or all three rolled into one. "Somehow that doesn't surprise me."

His forehead wrinkles. "Really?"

"You already successfully convinced me to give up most of my other clients. Why not try to get me to move to Chicago, too? I just wish you would've talked to me about it instead of sending my daughter to do your dirty work."

He snorts. "Would you have listened to me? No. If you won't listen to the people who will be most affected by the move, why would you want to hear it from your future best man? Why can't you just let yourself be happy for once and do something for *you* instead of for Kelli and Nanette—especially since they're willing to give up a lot in order for you to do it?"

I look down at my hands, which are clasped tightly in front of me to try to keep them from tingling again. "It's not that I don't want to be happy. And I'm working on being OK with the idea of letting the girls sacrifice for me for once."

He reaches out and clasps my joined hands. "Then what is it? What's the real problem?"

I've not said these words out loud since I called the police on my dad the second time, so it takes me a second to force them out. "I'm scared."

Diego releases my hands and flings his arms out. "My friend, of course you're scared. You're in love for the first time in your life. Fear comes with the territory. But think about what you'll lose if you let fear win. Do you want to lose Melissa?"

My gaze snaps to his. "No." That's why I don't want to move.

"Well, you're going to if you won't consider moving. She now knows you're not willing to do what you demanded *she* be willing to do before you would date her. She's already been hurt by one man who didn't love her the way he should have. She's not going to put up with that again."

My eyes widen. "She told you about Jeremy?"

He shrugs. "We had a lot of time to swap stories on the drive from Arkansas to Chicago. We bonded over our cheating exes. Anyway, I'm not saying you have to actually move. That decision is one you and Melissa will have to make together. But if you're not willing to consider it and discuss it with her, she is going to walk away, and I would fully support her decision."

My stomach drops at the thought. I can't let that happen. I can't lose the only woman I've ever truly loved—the only woman I ever want to love. The irony is that while I'm afraid I'll lose her if I move to Chicago, I'll definitely lose her if I don't move. I'm usually a logical man, but the logic of this situation has eluded me for weeks.

I look my friend in the eyes. "I need to call her."

"Yes, you do. Are you ready to do that now?"

"Not really, but I can't leave her wondering any longer. I need to fix this."

Diego finally stands, and he pats me on the head. "That's a good boy."

forty-one

. . .

Melissa

Bobby didn't answer when I tried calling his hotel room an hour ago, and I'm tempted to believe that means he doesn't want to talk to me. But there's no way for him to know who's calling him, and he might not even be in his room. It's dinner time in Arizona, so he's likely out with Diego, because his afternoon game would be long over.

Since I haven't been able to talk to Bobby, I've spent the last hour in a spiral of anger and hurt. It would help if I called one of my friends to talk this out with them, but I don't, because it's late and I don't want to bother either set of newlyweds.

When the phone rings, I try to rein in my emotions in case it's not him. Nobody else needs me growling at them right now. But considering the time, it's almost certainly him.

I reach over the arm of the couch and pick up the receiver. "Hello?"

"Hey, Pookie."

I will not smile at the nickname. *I will not smile.*

I smile. *Ugh.*

Then I sigh before wiping the smile back off my face. "Hi, B.S." I don't say anything else, because I want to see if he'll bring up the elephant in the phone line.

"I hear my daughter called you tonight."

"Indeed, she did. And she had some very interesting things to say."

"Yeah. I'm sorry I haven't talked to you about it."

I shake my head. "The problem isn't just that you haven't talked to me about it. It's that you don't seem to be considering it, which makes me think you really don't care about me as much as you claim to."

"I do care about you, Melissa, so much. In fact, I should have told you this before, but I've fallen—"

"No!" I slice a hand through the air. "If you're about to say you love me, don't. This isn't the time. If we make it past this conversation, you will choose a romantic time to say that to me, not when I'm angry and hurt."

He's silent for a few seconds. "OK. I understand. But please give me a chance to explain."

"I'm listening, but I can't imagine that what you're about to tell me will be an acceptable excuse for not considering moving or talking to me about it."

Again, I'm greeted with several moments of silence. Then he says, "Remember when you said you like my insecure side?"

I massage my aching chest as everything starts to make sense. "Yeah, I remember."

"Well, I hope you still like it, because ... I'm scared. I know we talked about this before—that I shouldn't let my fear get in the way of us, but that's what happened when I thought about moving. It's not that I don't want to live in Chicago, or even that Kelli or Nanette don't want to move. It's that I'm afraid I'll rip them from their lives in California and then I'll end up messing things up with you. And then we'd be all alone in a new city. I'll have moved them there for nothing."

"Bobby," I breathe out. "You wouldn't be alone if we broke up. Not that I think we will," I clarify, "but Diego and Ash and Randall love you for you. You were friends with them before we got together. Randall and Ash asked you to be in their weddings after only knowing you for a few months, for goodness sake. Yes, I've known them my whole life, but on the minuscule chance we'd break up, they're not the type of men who would choose sides and cut you out."

He doesn't respond, but I can hear him breathing.

I continue, "I think I know where this is coming from, though. You need to remember that those guys are not your parents or sister. They won't shut you out or pretend you don't exist if you do something they don't like. They won't disappear from your life. And neither will I. Your parents were terrible examples of the way people should treat the ones they love. Although, considering the way they treated you, I don't think they actually loved you. And that hurts my heart for you, Bobby. But you now have people who love you unconditionally. You already know what that means, because I'm sure you've done things to make Kelli or Nanette or Diego angry with you, but they still love you and care about you and want to be in your life."

Bobby clears his throat. "Kelli just told me she doesn't like me."

His voice cracks at the end, and it kills me to hear it.

"She's an emotional teenager, Bobby. And honestly, with the way you've been acting about moving, she has a right to not like the way you've been acting, which she's gotten confused with thinking she doesn't like *you*. But she does like you. She loves you. I know she does. You know she does. She's just angry right now, and rightfully so."

"Yeah," he says in a hopeful voice. "She did say she loves me."

"There you go. She's not going to give up on you even when she's angry. And neither am I. But you have some apologizing and thinking to do. You need to talk to Kelli and Nanette—really talk. Tell them how you're feeling, and have a serious conversation about what the three of you moving would look like for all of you. And if it'll help, go ahead and call some Realtors and some schools and some doctors, so you'll have an idea of some of the logistics. Think through what it would take to move your office and assistant to Chicago, too. But also talk about what it might look like for the three of you if I move there, because both options need to still be on the table.

"You'll be home on Wednesday, and then I'm going to fly out

there for a quick trip this weekend so I can meet your daughter and ex-wife. It should've happened before now, and I was being patient with you, but that time is over. We need to spend some time together to make sure we all click. I have no doubt we will, but I think you need to see it for yourself to believe it. And then the four of us will talk about the possibilities of who might move where, since it affects all of us."

"OK," he says in a much stronger voice than before. "That sounds like a great plan. But I'm paying you back for your plane ticket."

"You'd better," I tease, trying to lighten the mood. But then I realize there's one more serious topic I need to bring up with him. "Now, I know I told you not to say the l-word to me yet, and I'm sticking to that, but I think you need to hear this from me right now. I love you, Robert Sebastian Jacobs, more than you could possibly know. And I don't plan to leave you. So let's get this all figured out so we can be together and be happy."

"You are the best thing that has ever happened to my Bobby," Diego says on the phone the next evening.

Though that makes me smile, I say, "I think Kelli is the best thing that ever happened to him, and you come in a close second, but I appreciate the sentiment."

"Hard to argue with that. How about we agree that we're the three best things?"

I chuckle as I stir the marinara sauce bubbling on my stove. "I can agree to that."

"Good. Now, I need your opinion on something."

"Let me hear it."

"Bobby does not love it when I stick my nose into his business without him asking, but I am going to do it again. I would like to offer Nanette a part-time job if she moves to Chicago."

I suck in a breath. "At your foundation?"

Bobby told me Nanette's maternal grandmother immigrated to California from Mexico as a teenager, and she taught her granddaughter Spanish, so she's fluent, as is Kelli. Nanette also used to teach in an inner-city L.A. school where the majority of students were from families who came to the US from Mexico and Central America. She would likely understand the complexities of immigration, which is what Diego's foundation focuses on.

"*Sí*. She would be perfect. I don't know why I did not think of this sooner."

"So what do you need my opinion on?" I dip a spoon into the sauce to taste it.

"Do I call Bobby and tell him this before he and his girls discuss the move? Or do I call Nanette? Or would it be best for you to bring it up when you're there this weekend?"

Of course Diego knows about our plan for the week. It's understandable that Bobby often knows Diego's plans, since he's Diego's agent. But it usually doesn't work the other way around with an agent and client. The friendship between these two men astounds me. They truly are like brothers.

"The respectful thing to do is call Nanette," I explain. "She's the one you're offering the job to. Also, think about whether this particular job—or a different one—is something she could do from California if they don't move. From what Bobby has said, it frustrates Nanette that she's not able to work a consistent job any more. She wants to be able to contribute to her own finances and not feel so reliant on Bobby's generosity. So if there's something she can do from there, even for only a few hours a week, that would be great. In fact, even if she ends up living here in Chicago, she might not always feel physically well enough to go into the office, so some flexibility would be nice even here."

"I knew you would tell it to me straight. You are a smart biscuit, Melissa."

"I think the term is 'smart cookie.'"

"Not when you learned English from an British lady. Anyway, thank you for the advice. I will think about what you said about her working from home and see what Ash, Carmela, and I can come up with before I call her. But I *will* call her tomorrow."

forty-two

. . .

Bobby

I make it home from Arizona in time to pick Kelli up from school on Wednesday afternoon. She squeals when she opens the door and throws herself over the console to hug my neck.

"I love you, Daddy. I love you so much! I know I already told you this, but I'm so sorry I said I didn't like you. That was mean, and it wasn't true. I didn't like what you were doing, but I'll always like *you*. I promise."

I pat her back. "I know, baby ... Kelli. I'll always like you, too."

She lets go of me, settles into her seat, and buckles up.

"I'll also always love you." As I pull out of the school's drive, I think about what I said to Emily at Ash and Leslie's wedding. "Speaking of love, you were right. I do love Melissa, but I want you to know I'll never love her more than I love you. I love her differently than I love you, but I love you both equally, OK?"

She sighs, but it's a good sigh. "Yeah, it's OK to love her as much as me, though sometimes it might be hard, because I'm pretty awesome."

She giggles, and I poke her leg.

"By the way," I say, "I haven't told her I love her yet," though I did try, but she was right to stop me, "so don't let it slip this weekend when you see her."

She gasps. "I'm going to finally meet her? Are we going to Chicago?"

While I called Kelli yesterday and told her we'd discuss a possible move when I got home, I decided to tell her about Melissa's visit in person, so I could witness her reaction. It was worth it.

"No, she's coming here."

"Ohmygosh, ohmygosh, ohmygosh!" She stomps her feet on the floorboard and squeals again. "I finally get to meet my new best friend."

I can't help but smile at her excitement.

"I'll stay in my room at Mom's house when she's here, though," she declares.

"Why?" I figured she'd want to spend as much time with Melissa as possible.

When I glance over at her, she waggles her eyebrows. "You know why."

I groan. "We've talked about this, Kell. The two of us," I motion between us, "will not be discussing my sex life, and I'd appreciate if you'd not even mention that it exists."

She snorts. "I didn't technically mention anything this time. You're the one who made it weird."

"What did I do to deserve this?" I mutter. "You're supposed to be grossed out by the idea of me having sex, not being my wingwoman."

She holds both palms face up. "What can I say? I'm a modern woman. I mean, I don't want to think about the details, because that's totally icky, but as a concept, it's cool."

For the rest of the ride, she chatters about school and her friends. I never have to worry about awkward silences with my daughter. She's always happy to talk enough for five people.

When I follow her into the house, Nanette is sitting at the kitchen table with a dazed look on her face, and my heart leaps into my throat. She's been doing so well the past few weeks that Opal moved back home and only spends a couple hours a day with Nanette when I'm out of town. While I've told Nanette she's welcome in my house anytime, she never comes over here on her own without a direct invitation, so I'm concerned something bad has happened.

"What's up, Nan?" I ask carefully. "Everything OK?"

"Yeah, Mom, why are you over here? I was gonna come see you in a minute."

The haze finally clears from Nanette's eyes, and her gaze zeroes in on me. "Diego offered me a job."

I freeze. "What?" My sneaky little friend mentioned nothing about this to me.

"He called and offered me a job with the foundation. It's part-time, and while it would work best if I'm in the office in Chicago, I could do a modified version of the job from home." She presses two trembling fingers to her mouth as tears fill her eyes. "I didn't know if I'd ever be able to have a real job again."

Leave it to my friend to make Nanette's dream come true. I'm not sure why neither of us thought of this option before.

Kelli races to her mom and throws her arms around her neck from behind, almost choking her. "Mom, this is perfect! You said yes, right? You told him you'd do it?"

"Not yet," Nanette says as she removes Kelli's arms from her neck and turns sideways in her chair so she can look at our daughter, who drops into the seat beside her. "I told him I'd need to talk about it with you two first."

"But we want you to take the job!" Kelli gives me a beseeching look. "Right, Dad?"

"We want you to be happy, Nan," I say as I take a seat across from them. "If this job will accomplish that, I'll support you all the way. You know that."

"And it means we have to move to Chicago!" Kelli exclaims.

"No, honey, it doesn't. I can work from here if needed." Nanette looks at me. "You ready to have this conversation, or do you want to wait?"

"Let's do it now!" Kelli says as she bounces in her chair.

"Why don't you fix us all a snack first?" I say to my daughter. She usually eats something as soon as she gets home from school because she's starving. "That way none of us will get worked up simply because we're hungry."

Kelli rolls her eyes. "I know 'we' means me. But I am hungry, so OK."

She heads into the pantry and soon brings a few bags of chips to the table. "Pick what you want," she orders us before heading to the kitchen to pour three glasses of lemonade.

"All right, I'm ready." Kelli pops a Cool Ranch Dorito into her mouth after she takes her seat.

"First," I say, "let's talk about what it would look like if Melissa moves here." I hold up my hand when Kelli starts to protest. "I'm not saying that's what's going to happen. We're going to talk about both options, and we'll start with that one. Let's discuss it on its own merits as if it's the only option. Don't compare it to moving to Chicago."

Kelli shrugs. "I don't think much would change for Mom and me." Her eyes go wide. "Wait. You're not going to kick us out if Melissa moves here, are you?"

"Kelli Marina Jacobs!" Nanette's teacher voice is making an appearance. "Of course your father isn't going to kick you out. Why would you think that?"

She looks back and forth between her mom and me. "I don't think he'd kick *me* out of *this* house, but it might be a little weird to have an ex-wife in the backyard if the new wife is living here."

I sigh. "Kelli, you and your mom aren't going anywhere if Melissa moves here. Your mom will still live in the guest house, and you'll have a room in both houses."

Kelli's nose scrunches. "Melissa would be OK with that?"

I realize in this moment that I haven't specifically asked Melissa about this, which is an obvious oversight on my part. I think she'd be fine with it, but I can't answer for her. I can't very well ask her in front of Kelli and Nanette this weekend, though, so we'll need to discuss it before she gets to the house. But how do I answer my daughter's question now?

"Melissa is a very understanding and caring woman," I hedge, hoping that will be a good enough answer for Kelli. "And she knows how much I want to keep both of you close."

Nanette narrows her eyes at me, knowing I didn't answer the question, but Kelli nods.

"Well then," Kelli says, "I don't think my life would change that much if she moved here. I'd have somebody else who's there for me," she holds up a finger, "and an extra person to drive me around."

"Melissa is not going to be your chauffeur," Nanette chastises. "That will not be her job." She then looks at me. "What about her job, though? If she moves here, she'll have to find a new one."

"Yes, she will," I reply. "That is, if she wants a job. If we get married, she won't need to work if she doesn't want to."

Nanette shakes her head. "Don't you assume that's what she'll want. In fact, I can't really see you being interested in a woman who wants to just stay home and be a lady of leisure."

"You're right. I think she'll want to work." She maybe won't want to work full-time once kids come along, but I don't say that because Kelli will have another squealing fit at the thought of a baby. "She has an Ivy League education as well as experience on Wall Street and with a professional sports team, so she shouldn't have trouble landing something new here."

Kelli says, "But it would be silly for her to move here and find a new job, only for you to be going to her old city all the time for *your* job and spending time with *her* friends." She gives me a pointed look. "I know those friends are your friends, too, but that doesn't seem fair."

"Great point, kiddo." Nanette pats Kelli arm.

"I know." Kelli smirks at me.

She's right about all of that, but I need to get us back on track. "Let's take the focus back to the two of you and not think about Melissa or me for a minute. Pretend we don't matter. Is there anything negative for either of you personally if Melissa moves here but nothing else changes about our living arrangements? Will your lives be upset in any way?"

Kelli and Nanette look at each other, their profiles nearly identical. They hold a silent conversation and then turn to me as one.

"No."

Kelli adds, "But that doesn't mean it's the best option, because you and Melissa *do* matter. We care about your happiness a lot. So now let's talk about moving to Chicago."

I lean my elbows on the table and look Nanette in the eye. "You stand to lose the most if we move. You'd have to find new doctors, and you'd be far from your brother and cousins." Her parents and grandparents have all passed away, but she's close to some members of her extended family.

"They have busy lives," she says. "I rarely see them now when I only live an hour away from them. It's not worth us all staying here for the handful of days a year I see them. I'd actually spend more cumulative hours with them if I move away but come back specifically to visit them once or twice a year."

I nod. "Makes sense."

"And I've already called all my doctors and asked for referrals in Chicago. None of them seemed concerned about the possibility of me moving. It's a big city, and there are good hospitals there. It's not like we'd be moving to the middle of nowhere."

I settle back against my chair. "When did you call your doctors?"

"A few weeks ago."

"We kept hoping you'd come around," Kelli says around a mouthful of chips. Thankfully she swallows before continuing, "And Whitley has some cousins in Chicago who go to a school a lot like ours. She said she could have her mom get us the school's name and phone number."

I take a sip of lemonade as I look back and forth between the two of them. "You've already planned this all out without me, haven't you?"

Kelli nods. "Pretty much. Moving there makes so much more sense than Melissa moving here. And it'll make you happy, which will make both of us happy. Is moving going to be easy? Nope. It's gonna be a lot of work. I mean, on top of doctors and schools, we gotta find a place to live. And it needs to be close to your friends and have a place for Mom to live on the property." She smacks her hand on the table and shoots me a stern look. "Because one thing I *won't* agree to is moving there and having Mom not live by us."

I give her a soft smile. "That's not going to happen. We'll find a place that's perfect for all of us."

Kelli grins. "All *four* of us, you mean?"

forty-three

. . .

Melissa

My plane is touching down at LAX, so the countdown to seeing Bobby again has almost ended. While I thought I'd be anxious about the conversations to come and about how all three of them are feeling, I'm oddly calm. Now that we're all being open and honest about our feelings and our fears, I know we'll figure out what's going to be best for all of us.

The only slight anxiety I'm feeling is about meeting Nanette. I've chosen to trust Bobby when he says there's nothing romantic between the two of them, regardless of the fact that she lives in his backyard. But what if I get a different vibe from her? What if she's secretly pining for him, and he has no clue? And what if she and I don't get along? Will she be jealous of me or resentful that I've taken her place in Bobby's life? For that matter, will Kelli end up feeling jealous or resentful? There are so many unknowns in this situation that it's impossible not to feel a little bit of stress.

When I step off the jetway into the gate area, the first face I see is Bobby's. Even though it's only been five days since I last saw him, I've missed him terribly, and putting eyes on him is like coming home. Which is ironic, since our future home is what we'll be discussing. But I've just now realized that wherever he is will be home for me from now on, no matter the location.

I drop my bag and jump into his open arms, and he swings me

out of the way of the passengers behind me so he can kiss me soundly.

"I've missed you," he whispers when we come up for air.

"It's only been five days since you saw me and four since you talked to me." I smile up at him.

"Feels like a lifetime."

"Agreed. Let's not go that long without talking ever again."

He lifts an eyebrow. "It was your idea!"

"I know, and it was a smart one, but not necessarily an easy one."

"True. Now, I have something I need to tell you."

My stomach drops at his serious tone. Is he about to tell me there's no way they can move to Chicago? If that's what they decided, that's fine. I can move here. But I really, really want us all to live in Chicago.

"O–OK," I stutter.

He takes my face in his hands and swipes one thumb over the corner of my mouth, making me tremble. "I love you, Melissa Imogene Teague."

I don't know whether to cry with happiness or laugh at his guess at my middle name. So I do both as I squeeze him tightly. "I love you, too, Bobby Joe."

"Does my declaration of love earn me the right to finally know your middle name?"

I've been holding out on him because it drives him crazy, but he's right. It's time to give in. "It's Helen. That was my grand-mother's name. She died just before I was born."

He gives me a sad smile. "I'm sorry you never got to know her."

"Me, too, but let's not dwell on that." I do a silly little dance in his arms. "Because you love me!"

He laughs and pulls me in for another kiss. Then he slings my duffel bag over his shoulder and clasps my hand in his as we make our way through the concourse.

"Did you check a bag?"

I laugh. "Oh, you're funny. Of course I did!"

"You'll only be here for thirty-six hours! How could you need more than what will fit in this bag?" He jerks his head toward the decent-sized duffel hanging off his shoulder.

I shake my head at him. "It's like you've never met a woman before."

He shrugs. "Nanette never liked to travel much, and whenever I take Kelli somewhere, it's usually for a week or two, so multiple bags are warranted."

"You're such a man."

"I sure am." He squeezes my hand. "And don't you forget it."

"Not likely to happen."

"Almost there," Bobby says nearly an hour later as my eyes are starting to droop. It's past 11:00 California time, which means my body thinks it's after one in the morning.

I rub my eyes. "Good. I'm ready to sit somewhere that's not moving."

He chuckles. "Before we get to the house, I have a question to ask you. I know we said we wouldn't talk about moving at all until we were at the house with Kelli and Nanette, but I need your answer on something first. Please don't get mad at me for asking, because I think I know the answer, but Kelli asked me this question that's actually meant for you, and I've never asked you since I assumed, but you know what can happen when you assume, so now I'm asking."

I blink a few times. "That was very convoluted, but I think I get what you're saying. Go ahead and ask."

"If you were to move here, or even if we move to Chicago and get a similar setup, would you be OK with Nanette continuing to live in the backyard and Kelli splitting her time between the two houses?"

I smack his arm with the back of my hand. "Of course I'm OK with that! What kind of person do you think I am?"

It's obviously not ideal to have his ex living on the property, but it's a unique situation and is what's best for both Kelli and Nanette. It would be petty and cruel of me to object to those living arrangements, and I'm neither of those things. Now, if I determine that Nanette still has feelings for Bobby, we'll need to revisit this conversation. But I don't think that's going to be necessary.

"Ouch!" He rubs his arm. "I told you not to get mad and that I already knew the answer. But I had to officially ask you so if Kelli asks again, I can give her your answer instead of either answering for you or giving a non-answer, which I did the other day."

"Ah, the ol' non-answer lawyer trick. You've tried using it on me a time or two." I smirk in the darkness.

"Didn't work, did it?"

"Nope. Because, as Diego says, I'm a smart biscuit."

Bobby barks out a laugh. "He's a pretty smart biscuit himself."

He turns onto a street that winds up and to the left. Over the past few minutes, the houses have consistently gotten larger, and now we can't even see the homes. They're hidden behind thick hedges and gates, with only a few lights twinkling through. Bobby turns into one of the drives and pulls up to a keypad mounted on a terracotta pillar. He punches in a code, and wrought iron gates swing open.

My mouth gapes a few seconds later when we follow a curve in the driveway and the Mediterranean-style home comes into view. The white exterior appears to be glowing due to the uplighting spaced around the perimeter.

I knew Bobby had money, but I didn't realize he had *this* kind of money. Coming from a wealthy family, I've been in plenty of homes like this, but I doubt many are fully paid off, like Bobby said his home is. The place is both massive and gorgeous, and I'm sure we're only seeing a portion of it from this angle. He presses the button on his garage door opener as we circle around the side of the house to the four-car garage.

As we pull inside, the door into the house flings open, revealing a pretty teenager with French-braided dark-brown hair. The smile on her face could not be any bigger, and I think I spy a dimple in her left cheek. She rushes to the car and opens my door before I can reach for it.

"Hi, Melissa! I'm soooo glad I finally get to meet you!" Kelli leans in and flings her arms around my neck. Her exuberance is as heartwarming as it is surprising. Bobby told me her personality is nothing like his, but I wasn't sure what to expect.

"Kelli, give her some space, will you? You don't even know if she's a hugger," her dad chastises as he climbs out of the car.

As Kelli lets go of me, I assure her, "I'm a hugger. You can hug me anytime you want. Let me get out of the car, and we can do it properly."

After another hug, we make our way into the house, which is even more stunning than the outside. I'm surprised by the amount of color, but I expect most of the bright, colorful touches are due to Kelli, who's wearing a color-blocked shirt that's undoubtedly from United Colors of Benetton.

Kelli claps her hands together and asks, "Are you ready for the grand tour? Wanna see my room first?"

"Baby," Bobby says, but then pauses when Kelli glares at him. "Sorry. *Kelli*, it's late, and Melissa's internal clock is on Central Time, which is even later. You can give her the tour in the morning. We all need to get to bed, so we'll be rested and ready to talk tomorrow."

Kelli pouts and tries to argue, but Bobby holds a hand up, and she presses her lips closed. It seems they've had this conversation more than once already. She gives us both a tight hug, tells us good night, and then heads to an outside door off the kitchen, which surprises me.

With a grin, she says, "Sleep tight, don't let the bedbugs bite, and make sure to do a few things I'm not old enough to do!" And then she's out the door, slamming it behind her.

I turn to Bobby with a questioning look. "What was that about?"

"She informed me she'd be sleeping at her mom's while you're here so you and I can have some *privacy.*"

My cheeks heat. "You're kidding."

He presses a kiss to my forehead. "Nope. She's incorrigible, that one."

"I guess so. But I'll admit I'm not opposed to doing a few things she's not old enough to do."

Bobby chuckles as he grabs my bags and tilts his head toward the stairs visible through the entryway into the living room. "I'm opposed to *not* doing those things. Up the stairs with you, Pookie. No dawdling."

forty-four

. . .

Bobby

I told Kelli not to come over to the house before nine in the morning in order to give us plenty of time to sleep. But since I'm used to getting up at five, and Melissa's body is on Chicago time, we wake up with hours to spare. That doesn't mean we have to actually get up and start getting ready for the day, though.

"Can we take a nap today?" Melissa murmurs against my chest. I woke up to her curled around my side, much like the morning in the trucker motel in Illinois, but with fewer clothes.

I tap my temple. "I'm putting it on my agenda right now."

"You think Kelli is going to abide by your agenda?" she asks.

"I have every reason to believe she will not."

Melissa laughs, lightly ruffling my chest hair. "I like her. Granted, I only spent a couple minutes in her presence last night, but she seems like a great kid."

"A little overenthusiastic, maybe, but yeah, she's the best."

She raises her head to look me in the eye. "I love how much you love her."

I stroke my hand down her hair. "She's easy to love."

"I'm pretty sure you'd love her just as much if she was hard to love."

I smile at her. "I think you're right. There was a time when I didn't believe I was capable of loving someone as much as I love my little girl, but I've proved myself wrong."

"Yeah," she lays her head back down, "you're just a big softie, remember, B.S.?"

"I do." I think that's the nickname I love the most, because it's a side of myself I don't let many people see.

"And you love me, too." I feel her smile against my skin.

"I do." I love her so much it both makes my chest ache and makes me feel like I'm floating, which is a strange combination, but it's the only way to describe it. I want to go ahead and tell her we've all agreed to move to Chicago as long as she's on board with that, but I promised Kelli I wouldn't say anything without her being there, and I promised Melissa I would let her be part of the decision-making process.

There is one thing I think I can safely talk about, though, without bringing my daughter's wrath down upon me. "Diego offered Nanette a job, no matter where we live."

"I know."

"You do?" I crane my neck so I can see her face, and she tilts her head to look at me.

"Yeah, he called me to ask for advice."

"On whether or not to offer my ex-wife a job?" I'm not sure how I feel about that.

"No, he already had his mind made up on that. He wanted to know if he should have you or me tell Nanette, or if he should contact her directly."

"Ah." I nod. "You made the right decision."

"Of course I did."

I tickle her side, and she squeals and swats me away before lifting up onto her elbow to look down on me.

"I love you so much, Bobby Joe."

A cheeky grin takes over his face, and he glances over at the alarm clock. "We have plenty of time for you to prove that to me once again before my daughter comes knocking."

When we finally roll out of bed, it's still not nine o'clock, and Melissa asks if my pool is heated. When I answer in the affirmative, she cheers and digs a bikini out of her suitcase. She holds it up like a trophy.

"To the pool!"

"Just a warning," I say wryly, "the second Kelli spots you out there, she'll be joining you. And I can almost guarantee she's currently either already outside or camped out by a window watching for any sign of you."

"Sounds good to me. Swimming is no fun alone." She waltzes into the bathroom with her swimsuit in hand.

While I'd love to join her in the pool, I decide to let the two of them spend some time getting to know each other without my presence. So I head to the kitchen and start prepping for breakfast, which is when we'll be talking about the move. That way we'll get it out of the way and can move on with enjoying the rest of the weekend.

Several kitchen windows, as well as the glass door, face the pool, and I watch Kelli race out of her mom's house in her pink-and-white striped swimsuit within minutes of Melissa heading outside. Every time I glance out, they're laughing and splashing or playing some kind of game. Twenty minutes later, Nanette joins them. I watch as they interact, and I'm smiling like a fool, but I don't care. I want the three most important women in my life to love each other as much as I love all of them, and it appears that's exactly what's beginning to happen in my pool.

I give them fifteen more minutes before wandering outside, and I drop down to the edge of the pool to let my legs dangle in the water. Kelli immediately splashes me, which makes Melissa dissolve into giggles.

"Pull him in! Pull him in!" my girlfriend begins chanting, as she wades toward me.

The other two join in, and I don't put up much resistance as the three of them each grab a limb to pull me into the pool. Expecting something of this sort to happen, I had donned a pair of swim trunks and a thin t-shirt instead of regular clothes when I dressed earlier. Kelli latches onto my back like a monkey and tries to dunk my head under. After resisting her efforts for a few seconds, I let her push me under, but then I twirl around under the water, grab her waist, and launch her up and out toward the deep end. She resurfaces with a splutter and gives me the evil eye while trying not to smile.

"Sharks and Minnows!" Kelli yells. "Dad, you're the shark!"

Melissa screeches as I lunge toward her, and she glides away. "Hey, you gotta stay in the middle of the pool, Mister Jaws!"

We play a few rounds of the game before I declare it breakfast time. I head inside to change out of my wet clothes, and the women are still drying off and goofing around poolside as I bring the food and drinks out to the large outdoor table. I crank open the red-and-yellow umbrella to give us some shade while they don colorful robes Nanette brought out for the three of them.

"Melissa," Kelli says around a mouthful of fresh fruit, "do you really want to—"

"Kell, don't talk with your mouth full," her mother cuts in.

Our daughter holds her hand over her mouth while she finishes chewing. "Sorry. Anyway, do you really want to talk through both options, or is it OK for me to just tell you we're moving to Chicago?"

"Kelli!" We talked about this, but I should've known she wouldn't follow the plan. At least she gave Melissa some time to get to know her before declaring we'll all three be descending upon her city in a few months.

Kelli huffs and crosses her arms over her chest. "There's no reason to waste time talking about something we're not going to do, Dad."

All eyes turn to Melissa, and she looks at me for a few seconds before looking first Kelli and then Nanette in the eye. "I am perfectly willing to move to California if that's what's best for all of you. Why upset three lives instead of just one, right? But I would definitely not complain about you three moving Chicago, if none of you are opposed to it. Then I'd have everyone I love in the same city."

Kelli throws her hands up in victory, and Melissa smiles at her before turning to me with love in her eyes.

I reach over and grasp my girlfriend's hand. "I'll have everyone I love in the same city, too." It stings a little that Nanette will have to leave her extended family behind in order for me to have my dream, but like she said, she rarely sees them anyway. That's not a compelling reason for us all to stay here.

"Awww, look at you two," Nanette says, and she's not being sarcastic. Believe me, she can be, but this is not one of those times. "I can't tell you how happy this makes me for both of you—for all of us, actually. I think this move will be great for everyone. Kelli will be able to spend more time with her dad, and I'll be able to go to back to work."

I need to have a private conversation with Melissa, so I look at her and nod toward the house. "Help me bring out breakfast dessert?"

"Breakfast dessert? What's that?" Kelli asks. "And why don't we have it every day?"

"It's only for special occasions," I tell her as Melissa and I head to the house.

When we get inside, I pull her to where the others can't see us, and I kiss her deeply.

"I love you so much," I say as I cradle her face in my hands, "and I love that you seem to have bonded with Kelli and Nanette already. Am I right about that, though? I need you to be honest with me if not. That doesn't mean the end of this, but we might need to slow things down if there's any tension between you and either of them. I can understand if you need more time to get to know either of them before making a big life decision that will involve them."

"No," she shakes her head, "no tension. I'll admit I was a little worried that Nanette might still be in love with you and you're too close to the situation to see it. But she seems genuinely excited for you and me, like a friend or sister would be. I don't get the feeling that she has any sort of romantic interest in you." She goes up onto her tiptoes and kisses me on the nose. "Is it weird that I may someday live next door to your ex-wife? Yeah. And the three of us will need to sit down and hash out what that looks like and what rules we'll all need to put in place to make us all comfortable." She shrugs. "But we'll work it out."

I give her a soft smile. "I'm so relieved and happy that

you're so accepting of our weird little family. I honestly never thought I'd find that, and I was OK with it, but now I can't imagine you not being part of my life—of our lives. I can't wait to be able to see you every day and kiss you every day." I press a quick kiss to her lips. "I don't want you to feel pressured time-wise, though. I don't expect you to move in with me as soon as we get to Chicago, whenever that may be. It'll take a few months to get everything arranged, and we want Kelli to finish the school year here. Unfortunately, you and I might see each other less during that time, but our days of being apart are numbered."

"I'm excited to eventually be with you every day, too." She pats my chest. "And I don't feel pressured. Once you're getting close to moving in, we can talk about where I'm going to live. I'll be in the middle of my lease, but I can always look into subleasing if needed. Now, let's grab this breakfast dessert and get back out to Kelli. I'm sure she's dying to talk details."

"You know her so well already."

I give Melissa another quick kiss before directing her to the plates already loaded with generous pieces of Kelli's favorite cinnamon-roll coffee cake.

"Did you make this?" She sounds like she's joking, and for good reason. I don't seem like the baking type.

"I sure did."

She almost drops the two plates she's carrying. "What? Seriously?"

I shrug as I open the door. "I love to bake." I add in a low voice, "Don't tell anyone."

Melissa laughs. "Oh, I'm telling everyone. And I'm going to make you bake for me on a weekly basis."

"Done." I would bake for her every day if it would make her happy.

"Is that your world-famous cinnamon-roll coffee cake?" Kelli snatches a plate out of my hand when she sees what's on it.

"Manners, my child. And that's exactly what it is, though I'm not sure world-famous is the way to describe it since only a few people have ever eaten it."

"It *would be* world-famous if you weren't so worried about people knowing you love to bake."

"She's not wrong," Nanette says. "Now, I'd like to hear if Melissa has any suggestions on where we should look at homes in Chicago."

My girlfriend looks at me. "Did you talk to a Realtor this week?"

"I talked to one here about listing this house, but I wanted to wait to talk to someone in Chicago until you could be part of the conversation. Hopefully someday my house will be your house, too, so I want to make sure it's in the location you'd like to settle down in, because the neighborhood doesn't really matter to any of us, as long as we're close to Kelli's school. I also want you to like the actual house." I chuckle and look at each of the women in turn. "It might be difficult finding a property all three of you women will like, but I think we can ultimately make it happen."

"I'm not picky," Nanette says, and she's right. Sometimes I wished she voiced her opinion on tangible things more than she does. She's not shy about giving her full thoughts on everything else, though.

"I'm sure we can work things out." Melissa bites her lip. "Before coming here, I wasn't sure which areas and neighbor-hoods would be appropriate to recommend, but now that I've seen all this," she sweeps her arm around, encompassing my entire property, "it doesn't seem like price is going to be an issue." She raises an eyebrow at me.

"I think anything you suggest is going to be in my price range," I say in a wry tone. I don't like to discuss my wealth, but if Melissa might someday be my wife, she needs to know what she's dealing with financially. "So lay it on us."

"Well," she takes a deep breath. "I'd like you to consider my childhood home in Evanston."

I'm surprised by this revelation, but it's a good sort of surprise.

Melissa continues, "My parents have been talking about downsizing to a property that's smaller and all one level, so it's easier for my dad to get around." She looks at Kelli and Nanette.

"He had a stroke a couple years ago. He's mostly recovered, but stairs are difficult for him, and the master suite is on the second floor of the main home. They've been making do with the rooms on the ground level, but the bedrooms and one full bath on that floor aren't large, which also makes getting around a bit difficult for him."

My daughter and ex-wife express their concern for her dad.

"You're sure they really want to move?" I place a hand on Melissa's thigh. "This isn't just something they talk about but will never actually do?"

"I talked to my mom about it this week," she explains. "I didn't tell her about the possibility of you moving there, because I didn't want to get her excited only to later disappoint her, but I did say I knew someone who might be interested in an off-market sale. She said they truly want to move but need a kick in the pants, because it'll be hard to leave their long-time home, but they know it's past time to do it. So this could be the perfect solution for everyone, if you three like the place. If not, we'll figure something else out for both your house and for my parents."

"That all makes sense," I say. "Tell us more about the property."

"The main house is a mock Tudor style and is similar in size to this one—maybe a little smaller. Kelli could have my old set of rooms, which includes a large bedroom, full bath, and an attached playroom—or whatever you'd want it to be since you probably don't play with toys anymore." She thoughtfully directs that part at my daughter. "Maybe an art room, or even a bunk room for when you have sleepovers?"

Kelli swallows a bite of coffee cake and nods excitedly. "Both of those would be cool! You think we could do a combo?"

"There might be room for that," Melissa replies with a smile. "Those rooms are upstairs, along with the master suite." She doesn't give details on that area, but I'll ask about it later. "Then there are two smaller bedrooms downstairs with an adjoining bath between them, an office, a breakfast room, a formal dining room, and two living areas. In the backyard, there's a two-bedroom guest house—one bedroom is upstairs in the eaves, so that one could be Kelli's—and there's also a space downstairs that could be used as a home office, along with a full kitchen and a living room. There's also room to add onto it if necessary. The property has a pool and a putting green as well. It's a few blocks from the lake and about a mile away from the Hamiltons. The school I attended along with the Hamilton boys is just a few miles away, if you'd want to look into it as an option for Kelli."

"That all sounds almost too good to be true," Nanette says to Melissa and then looks at me. "Can we work it out to go visit in the next few weeks? I'd like to see the houses and visit a few schools while they're still in session so I can get a good feel of them for Kelli. And I want to visit the foundation's offices and meet everyone before giving Diego a final answer on the job."

"I'll make sure a trip happens," I tell her as I stack my empty plates on top of Melissa's. "Let me look at my schedule, and I'll give you the dates so you can start setting up school visits."

"Great." She stands and pats our daughter on the shoulder. "Kell, why don't we clean up the dishes, since your dad fixed it all for us?"

"But I want to keep talking to Melissa," Kelli whines.

"And you can do that again in ten minutes," her mother says. "But right now, you're helping clean up."

Kelli pouts, but she stands and grabs some plates. "Fine."

Once they've cleared everything but our drinks and are inside the house for at least a few minutes, I pull Melissa out of her seat and onto my lap, making my chair's aluminum frame creak under our combined weight.

She giggles and wraps her arms around my neck. "What are you doing?"

"Keeping you close while I can. These next few months are going to be hard."

"The concrete below us is going to be hard when this chair collapses and we land on it."

"We'll be fine." She shifts, and the chair creaks again. "Or maybe not. Hop up for a sec." She does, and then I scoop her up in a fireman's carry and run for the pool.

"Noooooo!"

"Oh, yes!" I shout as I cannonball us both into the deep end of the pool.

After we surface and she splashes me in retaliation a few times, I pull her to my chest so she can wrap herself around me while I tread water.

"Your parents' home sounds like the perfect place for us."

"I really think it will be, as long as all of you like it."

I give her a quick kiss before paddling us toward more shallow water where I can touch the bottom. I'm in good shape, but there's no reason to wear myself out when I can move a few feet and stand. We kiss again but keep it fairly chaste, since my daughter is likely watching us through the kitchen window.

"Tell me about the master suite," I say after helping Melissa peel the wet robe off and flinging it to the pool deck.

"The bedroom is huge—plenty big enough for your California king with lots of room to spare. There's also an attached living area and a breakfast nook with a mini kitchen. It has two walk-in closets, and the bathroom is enormous. The tub is my favorite part."

"Oh, yeah? Why?"

She smirks. "Because it's big enough for two." Then her smile drops and she covers her mouth with a hand. "Oh, gross. That's my parents' bathroom. I don't want to think about them having a tub big enough for two!"

The laugh that erupts out of me can only be described as a cackle. "It's funny how you're grossed out by that kind of thing, but Kelli isn't."

"I guess she's more mature than I am." She shrugs.

"We can renovate the bathroom if that'll help. Anything for you, my Pookie."

"Right back at you, B.S."

epilogue

· · ·

Melissa

August 1989
Evanston, Illinois

"**K**elli, come on! We gotta go!" I yell.

I'm waiting for her in the kitchen of our new home. Well, it's her new home, but my old home. We've been here for almost two months now, and while it's sometimes strange to be living here without my parents, it's also the fulfillment of a dream I didn't know I had six months ago. I had assumed I'd inherit the home when my parents passed away, but I hoped that would still be a decade or three down the road. I also hadn't been sure I'd be able to afford to keep it, so I didn't allow myself to think about potentially living here ever again.

My future step-daughter finally careens into the room carrying a gift wrapped in light yellow paper and skids to a stop next to me.

"I hope it's a girl! I really, really, *really* hope it's a girl!" She flings her empty arm around me and squeezes tightly.

I extricate myself from her grip and usher her out into the garage. "I know you do, but please don't be visibly upset if it's a boy."

"I won't. I'm just so excited for Aunt Wendy and Uncle Randall!" she gushes as we load into the car, where Nanette is already waiting for us. "Are Aunt Andrea and Emily on their way?"

I start the car and back out of the garage. "Their flight from Little Rock will arrive in a couple hours. Your dad is going to pick them up from the airport and bring them straight to the hospital."

As soon as Kelli met Wendy and Leslie, she started calling them her aunts. And she decided that since Andrea is Wendy's sister, she's also an aunt. The kid now has more aunts and uncles than she knows what to do with, and they all spoil her rotten. Bobby and I are hoping that with the arrival of this new baby, the focus on Kelli will die down a bit, since it's starting to go to her head. We want her to love her new "family," and we're glad they immediately accepted her as one of their own, but we need some normalcy around here, and the extravagant gift giving really needs to stop. The kid has more than she'll ever need already. But it's really hard to complain about how happy she is to be here and how seamlessly she and Nanette have both fit into everyone's lives.

While we make the short drive to the hospital, Kelli keeps up a monologue from the backseat about all the things she's going to do with and for the baby, as she has declared herself the official babysitter of Baby Hamilton.

Nanette and I smile at each other, happy at how excited she is. I thought Nanette and I would get along and probably be friends, but it turns out we're kindred spirits, as Anne Shirley would say. We share a lot of the same interests, we have a similar sense of humor, and she's been a great resource for me when trying to figure out how to deal with all of Bobby's various moods. Instead of us being rivals, she's more of a mentor to me in that area. It's a strange friendship, but it works for us.

"I feel bad for Tonya and Sonya," Kelli says with a sigh. "They both have to leave for college next week, so they won't get to spend much time with their new niece or nephew. Of course, I start school the week after that, but at least I'll still get to see the baby every day."

Though Tonya and Sonya are the sisters of Kelli's new "uncles," she doesn't call them her aunts, as they're not much older than she is. They've also adopted her and have spent more time with her than I would imagine most older teen girls would.

"Kelli," her mom says, "you're not going to see the baby every day."

"But why not? I already love her ... or him ...," she reluctantly amends, "so much! I won't be in the way, I promise. I can help change diapers and give bottles and—"

"You're going to be a great help," Nanette cuts in. "But not every day. They'll want time together as a new family of three, and Wendy and Randall will need time to bond with their baby without other people running in and out all day every day. You'll get plenty of time with them and the baby, though. Don't worry."

When we arrive at the hospital waiting room, the place is in a state of minor chaos. Wendy's parents are here, along with Ruth and her new boyfriend, Tonya and Sonya, Ash, Diego, and now the three of us. Randall and Leslie are both in the delivery room with Wendy. She asked if I'd like to be there, too, but I declined because she doesn't need the room cluttered with onlookers. I'm hoping Leslie isn't having to spend more time keeping Randall calm than supporting Wendy, but I think that might be too much to hope for.

Diego is pacing and muttering about how Wendy needs to push this baby out before he has to head to the stadium. I'm thinking he should just be glad today's game is at home and is a rare night game, so he can be here now, but I'm not about to state my opinion on that. Nanette is trying her best to calm him down, but she's only mildly successful.

Wendy's younger brothers soon arrive from Milwaukee and add to the noise in the room. I feel bad for the other family that's quietly awaiting the arrival of their baby, though I'm also amused by their awestruck expressions at being in the presence of the highly agitated Diego Sanchez.

We're still waiting when Bobby arrives with Andrea and Emily a few hours later. It's past time for Diego to leave for his game, but none of us have been able to convince him to go. Nanette maybe could've, but she and Ruth's boyfriend headed out twenty minutes ago to grab some food for everyone, since it's now the middle of the afternoon and nobody has eaten lunch. I'm hoping my fiancé will have better luck than the rest of us with getting Diego to head to the stadium.

At first, Bobby doesn't notice Diego, since he zeroed in on me the moment he stepped into the room and came directly over to kiss me hello. But it doesn't take long for him to spot his friend—and more importantly at the moment, his client—and read him the riot act about being late to batting practice and setting a bad example for his teammates. Diego crosses his arms and acts as if he's not going anywhere for all of about twenty seconds before he gives in to Bobby's stare and begins saying goodbye to everyone, including the other waiting family, who finally got up the nerve to introduce themselves to him an hour ago. They're now fast friends and Diego promised them tickets to a future game along with signed jerseys for everyone, including the baby.

Bobby makes his way back over to me, tugs me down next to him onto a hard, vinyl-covered couch, and slips his arm around me. "You doing OK?"

I give him a soft smile. "Yeah. I'm so excited for them. I just hope everything goes smoothly in there and the baby is fine."

"Hopefully we'll know soon." He murmurs in my ear, "They could all be waiting on us in this same room in a year or so."

Tingles race through my body at the thought. Last month, Bobby asked me to marry him when we were at Diego's resort in the Dominican for a few days. Kelli wasn't happy she wasn't there to witness it, but we let her announce the news to everyone else, which mollified her quite a bit. We're getting married in October, since Bobby turns thirty-seven next month, and we'd like to start adding to the family sooner rather than later.

"I hope they are." I give him a quick kiss. "You know Kelli is going to want to be in the delivery room, right?"

"Not gonna happen." His head gives a decisive shake. "I love that kid more than life itself, but I can't let my little girl see me pass out when it's crunch time. She needs to keep thinking I'm invincible."

I laugh. "Leave it to you to call giving birth 'crunch time.' And you'd better not pass out on me. I don't want you to miss a second of experiencing your next child coming into the world."

"I'll do my best to stay on both feet the entire time."

"What are you two talking about?"

Neither of us noticed Kelli approaching, and I hope she didn't hear what we were discussing or we'll never hear the end of it.

"How much we love you," her dad says, which is partially true.

She narrows her eyes at us. "Somehow I doubt that."

I shrug. "Your dad said, and I quote, 'I love that kid more than life itself.'"

Kelli inspects our expressions for a few more seconds. "Yeah, I could see that." She nods. "I'm pretty lovable."

She shrieks when Bobby grabs her waist and pulls her down onto his lap.

"You're a mess," he says to her, "but you're *my* mess."

"Our mess," I correct with a smile as I squeeze Kelli's arm.

At that moment, Randall bursts through the waiting room door with his hair disheveled and a giant grin on his face. "It's a girl!"

IF YOU ENJOYED THIS BOOK, JOIN AUTHOR DANA WILKERSON'S ROMANCE MAILING LIST!

When you join the list, you receive bonus scenes and stories, writing updates, sneak peeks of upcoming books, book recommendations, and much more. Come join the fun!

To join, go to danawilkerson.com and click "Sign Up."

There's a new sports romance series featuring the kids of the Throwback RomComs characters!

Read *Blocking the Chaos*, the first book in the new KC Crew Sports Romance series starring Amber Hamilton (Ash and Leslie's daughter) and Austin Jacobs (Bobby and Melissa's son).

Find it now on Amazon!

TOTALLY 80S MYSTERIES
by D.A. Wilkerson

Available on Amazon

About the Author

Dana Wilkerson is the author of the Throwback RomComs and KC Crew Sports Romance series. She has been a professional writer and editor for two decades and was the collaborative writer of two non-fiction *New York Times* best sellers: *The Vow: The True Events That Inspired the Movie* (Kim and Krickitt Carpenter) and *Balancing It All* (Candace Cameron Bure).

She is also the author of the Totally 80s Mysteries cozy mystery series as D.A. Wilkerson.

Dana lives in Oklahoma and enjoys traveling, reading, being an aunt, binge-watching crime shows, and attending Oklahoma City Thunder basketball games.

Find Dana Online

Pinterest, Facebook, and Instagram: @danawilkersonbooks

Website: danawilkerson.com